How to Marry a Princess

How to Marry a Princess

Shivkumar Wayal

Notion Press

Old No. 38, New No. 6
McNichols Road, Chetpet
Chennai - 600 031

First Published by Notion Press 2016
Copyright © Shivkumar Wayal 2016
All Rights Reserved.

ISBN 978-1-946515-63-6

To those who love,

To those who are loved and

To humor, which apparently loves

bringing them together

Preface

This feels like such a long time coming, but finally it's ready for you. After numerous attempts to make it humorous, and countless edits by myself and by editors, I believe the book is finally in its finest form.

I am overwhelmed and grateful to be able to put a book out, and put it out the way I want. To say writing this book was more than fun would be an understatement. I have enjoyed each and every moment of this journey.

I hope you would like the book and write back to me and that you would have as much fun reading it as I had writing it.

In the end, it was all worth it.

Seattle, October, 2016.

Acknowledgement

You are about to begin reading a novel that took me many months. I am exceedingly thankful and indebted to following people in my life who supported me and contributed to bringing this book to you.

My wife Trupti and my daughter Ruhi, without you this book would not have been possible. I am incredibly indebted to both of you for being so supportive, for holding on to your anger while sacrificing family time and for encouraging me without knowing if I would ever publish my book.

My parents, who always believed in me and who still think that there is nothing that I can't do. You are the wind beneath my wings.

My in-laws, for being so proud of me and indirectly setting high standards for me to live up to.

My friends, for being so supportive while patiently waiting for my book, although with suspicion. Also, for not hating me for being absolute best in everything I do and for getting used to my sarcasm.

Mridula Vinayak, project manager at Notion press for being so supportive and accommodating. The whole team at Notion press, you people are awesome.

All the other publishers, without whom this book would have been in your hands two years earlier.

As much as I want to resist the urge to write this, but I finally give million thanks to the authors whose work made me believe I can do better and inspired me to write.

Lastly, now that the book is out of my hands, it belongs to you, the readers. I thank to all you readers who kept inspiring me and made me take this exhilarating journey.

Chapter 1

A bashful smile lingered on Satvik's face. He had just talked at length over the phone with Shubhangi, his bride-to-be. There was still a night ahead to endure alone before their wedding day.

It was in that jubilant moment, Satvik heard a hasty knock, thrice repeated, at the door. He opened the door with an expectation to see his three best friends returning to the bachelor party. Instead, he saw two odd men standing outside, one of them pointing a gun at him.

"Hands up!" the man with the gun shouted.

Bewildered by this sudden intrusion, Satvik raised his hands in response to the gun pointed at him. He stepped back as the two men walked inside.

"Hello," Satvik said with a curious smile not knowing how else he could have loosened the tension in that strange situation.

"Hello," the man said pointing the gun at Satvik's face. He must have realized it wasn't the kindest gesture. He extended his right hand to Satvik while still holding the gun in his left hand.

"I am sub-inspector Chagan. And this is constable Popat," he said without softening his hard stare.

"I am Satvik."

"We know that," constable Popat said in a stern voice.

Chagan waved the gun at all the corners of the house while Popat kept strict watch on Satvik. Satvik did not understand what was happening and looked at constable Popat baffled.

"What's going on?" he asked.

Popat kept quiet with his tightly folded hands resting on his potbelly.

"Where is she?" Chagan asked.

"She? Who?" Satvik replied with a question.

"You know who I am talking about."

"No, I really don't."

Constable Popat noticed empty glasses and bottles of alcohol on the table. He guessed there were more men having a party a while ago.

"Where are your gang members?" Popat asked.

"What?"

"Where are the other members of your gang?" Popat said pointing fingers at empty glasses and bottles.

"What gang? What members? I don't understand what is going on," Satvik said.

"Where is the girl you kidnapped?" Chagan asked as he flashed a photograph.

It was Shubhangi, as beautiful as ever. Her enchanting smile made Satvik forget he was being held at gunpoint.

Her thought brought a smile on his face even in that tense moment.

"That's Shubhangi. My bride. We are getting married tomorrow," he said.

"You are not getting married to anybody anytime soon. You are going to jail for the rest of your life," Chagan said.

"I don't understand. I haven't done anything wrong."

"You kidnapped her."

"No, wait. There is some kind of confusion. Shubhangi is not kidnapped."

"Don't try to fool us. Her father told us everything about you. How you tortured his family and kidnapped his daughter," Popat said.

"That's not true. Her father is a liar."

"Where is she then?"

"If you allow me to make one phone call, you will understand. You can talk to her yourself," Satvik said.

"I don't trust him," Popat said looking at Chagan through the corner of his eyes.

"You think we believe you. You want to make a call so members of your gang know about us?" Chagan asked.

Popat pulled Inspector Chagan aside.

"What do we do now?" Popat asked.

"We take him with us," Chagan said.

"But we don't have the girl," Popat raised a valid question.

"Remember Mr. Mooni filed the complaint against him? Now we have him, he will tell us about the girl," Chagan said.

"You mean we torture him?" Popat asked.

"If it comes to that."

"What if other gang members killed the girl because we caught their leader?" Popat asked.

That made Chagan think. Popat attempted to appear busy pondering on the 'operation black cat,' the name Chagan had given to the rescue operation.

"We have their gang leader. Others will fall in the trap. Worst case, we could negotiate to exchange their leader with the girl," Chagan said.

Clearly, not the best idea, Popat thought.

"But don't we want the kidnappers?" Popat asked. His unending questions irked sub-inspector Chagan.

"It's too late in the night. Let's take him to the police station and then decide what to do next," Chagan said.

They mutually agreed that a dangerous kidnapper like Satvik needed to be behind bars as soon as possible.

"You are under arrest for kidnapping a girl. We will find her. And, we will find your gang members too," Chagan said with a stern face.

"You know that keeping an innocent in jail is a crime? You don't have any proof I kidnapped anybody. You could be in a serious trouble for this. And, why should I believe you are the police? You are not even in uniform," Satvik warned.

"Are you trying to threaten us? Don'
know it very well," Popat said and flasl

For the first time in his life, Satv
was taken to the police station in the

He knew it would just be a matte.
would be freed. His friends Sindbad, Amit and Gopa₁ ..
soon come to home and find him missing. They would get
him out before morning. Then everything would be all right.
He would be married to Shubhangi the next day.

Sadly, he was expecting too much from his drunk friends
who had gone out to bring more alcohol in the middle of
the bachelor party that night. No one returned home to find
Satvik missing until next morning.

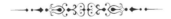

Sindbad was a colorful butterfly in a beautiful garden. He
kept flitting around flowers for many hours until his wings
felt tired and his head heavy.

Finally, he couldn't balance himself anymore and
spiraled towards the ground. He flapped his wings frantically
to save himself from the free fall. With a loud thud, his head
smashed on the ground and shattered into pieces. Then
everything went dark. He knew he was dead.

He cried for hours.

He was not certain what happens after death. He waited.
He could still smell the captivating fragrance of the garden.

e first time, he experienced how it is to be dead, to be ss, free from gravity. His soul lingered in the garden, a ghost, for a long time. He couldn't really say how long for how many hours or for how many years. It must be like that when one is dead, he thought, time becomes meaningless.

Then a bright light filled his eyes. He saw white clouds floating around big golden gates. He knew it was heaven. It had to be, for hell could only be dark.

He was no longer a butterfly but his head still felt heavy and his neck stiff. His eyes were still adjusting to the brightness. When he managed to open his eyes, they met the rotating blades of a gyrating ceiling fan above his head. He felt if he did not move, the squeaky fan would fall on his head and smash it again.

After debating with himself for a long time, he concluded he was indeed a human who dreamt of being a butterfly.

Alcohol is a bad thing. He murmured. It wasn't his first hangover. But this one made it difficult to make sense of his position in the space and time continuum.

That's exactly what his friends and he wanted, to lose themselves, when they started partying last night. They wanted an unforgettable bachelor party a night before their best friend Satvik's wedding.

He turned his head slowly and could not believe what he saw next. A massacre of women, their bodies spread on the floor everywhere.

"What the hell!" he screamed, as he made sure he was not mistaken.

Sudden shock shook the hangover off his delirious mind as he stood up. Before he could come to terms with reality, his wide eyes handed him a bigger surprise. It wasn't a massacre of women. They were men draped in fancy feminine clothes sleeping on the floor.

All signs of his hangover died down quicker than he imagined. He had never seen such a sight.

"Good Morning, Sindbad!"

He was startled and looked in the direction of the voice. It was a man in a mini skirt.

"Who are you? How do you know my name?" he asked.

"I am Rajat. Here, have some coffee," he said as he came near and offered Sindbad a cup of coffee.

Sindbad hesitated for a moment but he knew caffeine would help ease the hangover.

"Thank you. Now, why am I here with you?" Sindbad asked.

"Don't you remember anything?"

"I don't. Who are you people? And where are my friends?" Sindbad asked as he sipped coffee.

"Okay. First of all, these people you mentioned are my friends and whatever you may be thinking about us, we are not eunuchs, and not gay," he said.

Sindbad looked at him in disbelief. That is exactly what he had thought about them.

"We are cross-dressers. We do it for money. We earn money at traffic signals and in weddings. Business, you know?" Rajat said.

"I know," said Sindbad trying not to offend him.

As caffeine made its way to his still intoxicated brain, he felt better. Rajat walked towards him and sat next to him.

"How do you know my name?" Sindbad asked.

"You told me. Remember? We partied and danced together last night. Near the railway station, on the road," he said as he smiled at Sindbad.

Sindbad tried to remember partying on the road with him, but in vain.

"I must be really hammered?" Sindbad said.

"You were. That's why you are here. You passed out on the road. We brought you with us."

Sindbad kept staring in the blank trying to remember if that ever happened.

"You really don't remember anything, do you?"

Sindbad shook his head in denial.

"Do you at least remember the fight you had with the police constable? You and your friends beat a cop. He had to run away," Rajat said.

That can't be good, Sindbad thought.

"What happened exactly?" he asked.

"You came on a scooter with your friends to buy booze near the railway station. A police constable stopped you and demanded money," Rajat said.

"And that's why I beat him up?"

"Well, he took the money but refused the challan. So you pushed him. He punched you and that's how it started. People cheered for you. You beat him till he ran away," Rajat said laughing at him.

Sindbad vaguely remembered having a scuffle with a police constable for the challan. It's not a crime, arguing with a cop. But beating him up certainly is. Sindbad tried but could not justify his beating a cop to himself.

"Then what happened?" Sindbad asked.

"Once the cop ran away, you and your friends bought us drinks. It was a party on the road. We all drank and danced well past midnight. In fact, we drank until most of us passed out, including you," Rajat revealed.

Sindbad could not believe all that had happened through Satvik's bachelor party. No wonder he was a butterfly for most part of the night.

"Where are Amit and Gopal?" Sindbad asked.

"Who?"

"My friends? The two men who came on the scooter with me?" Sindbad asked.

"They went into the railway station."

"What?"

"I mean, I saw them going toward the railway station during the party," he said.

"But why would they go to the station?"

"No idea, I wouldn't know why. One of your friends was totally wasted. He was acting crazy and running everywhere," Rajat said.

"Must be Gopal. The one with a beard? "Sindbad asked.

"No, the other one."

"What? Amit? He never drinks alcohol. No. You got him drunk?"

"Don't blame me," Rajat said as he shrugged his shoulder.

This had to end badly. Amit never drank alcohol. He was no less than a drunk was, when he really wasn't. If he was drunk, chaos must have ensued.

"He ran towards the railway station and your other friend followed him. You were too drunk to understand anything that was happening around you. My guess, your friends must be home waiting for you," Rajat said.

"Let's hope so."

Sindbad felt better after drinking coffee. He was thinking straight. He looked at the clock on the wall. He couldn't believe, it was 9 AM.

It was an important day. It was his best friend Satvik's wedding day. He had many things to take care, many arrangements before the wedding in the evening.

He checked his phone. No calls. Strange, he thought. He was gone for long and no one cared. Neither Satvik nor Amit nor Gopal called him to check if he was fine.

Something was amiss.

"I should go," Sindbad said.

"Your scooter is outside. We came on your scooter," Rajat said.

Sindbad was delighted to know he had scooter for a ride home.

"Thank you for the coffee and everything else. I must go now," Sindbad said getting up hurriedly.

He shook hands with Rajat and rushed outside. There, on the front porch, stood Amit's hideous green scooter in all its majesty. He was never so happy to ride that scooter as he was that morning.

—•⇢•⟨⦇⦈⟩•⟵•—

Amit was about to visit *Hyderabad* for the first time in his life. He always wanted to, but never so unwillingly.

He had just survived the most horrible night of his life. As the train entered *Hyderabad* station, Amit felt another urge to throw up. He had lost count of his visits to the toilet in the moving train. After vomiting all night, there was nothing left in his stomach. That did not help with his urge to throw up.

Amit never drank alcohol, at least until the extended bachelor party last night. A prankster in the partying crowd handed him whiskey mixed in cola when he refused to drink alcohol. His body had never experienced such an abundance of alcohol. It did everything to get rid of it.

If it wasn't for the alcohol, he wouldn't have followed the beautiful girl he thought he saw entering the railway station.

She looked so irresistible he couldn't help but run after her. As she boarded the train, he jumped on to it too.

But before Amit could catch the girl of his first ever drunken fantasy, the train chugged on slowly. It shook and stirred the alcohol in his stomach. As the train left *Pune* station, with it started Amit's unending quest to empty his stomach. It lasted until the train reached *Hyderabad.*

Gopal always behaved like an obedient friend whenever he was drunk. He just followed Amit into the train and could not get him off it in time. Soon, he managed to squeeze himself between two berths and succumbed to deep slumber.

In the morning, Gopal woke up and looked at Amit's drained face. It was evident that he had had a rough night.

As the train pulled into *Hyderabad* station, they came to terms with reality. They ended up in *Hyderabad* when they were supposed to be in *Pune,* preparing for their best friend's wedding.

As they got down at *Hyderabad* railway station and walked as if they never did before, they attracted the attention of one of the ticket collectors with a ripened handlebar moustache, who had developed a keen sense of judgment detecting passengers travelling without tickets. With just once glance at them he knew they were ticketless. He dragged them to a corner and asked them to hand over every penny they had in their pockets. Not having any option but to pay for breaking the law by travelling without tickets, they paid the bribe to the ticket collector.

They walked out of the busy *Hyderabad* railway station when Amit received a call from Sindbad. He knew it was going to be difficult to explain the situation to him.

"Hey, Good morning," Amit answered.

"Where are you? Why is no one home?" Sindbad asked.

"We, umm, we are in *Hyderabad*," he said.

"Hyderabad?"

"Yes, *Hyderabad*. Gopal and I just reached at *Hyderabad* railway station," Amit said.

"Are you kidding me? What are you doing in *Hyderabad*? And where is Satvik?" Sindbad asked.

"It's a long story. Somebody got me drunk. We boarded the train and could not get off in time. We just reached *Hyderabad*," Amit said.

"What do you mean you could not get off a train? Why would you even board a train? I can't believe it. How can this possibly happen when two of you are together?"

"You won't understand what it is to be drunk for the first time in life," Amit said and tried to explain what happened with him through the night.

Sindbad couldn't blame Amit and Gopal. He too woke up with strangers and did not remember a thing about it.

"Well, obviously the bachelor party has gone all wrong. I just came home and Satvik is not home. He is missing. He left his phone at home. And now you guys are in *Hyderabad*," Sindbad said annoyed by the situation.

"Have you checked at Chhaya Sadan?" Amit asked.

"No, I haven't. He may be there. I wanted to check with you first. It's strange he would go out without letting any of us know about it," Sindbad said.

"I am sure he is at Chhaya Sadan," Amit said.

"What about you? Only a few hours are left to the wedding. It's not over yet. You should be here, not in *Hyderabad*. I just hope you make it to *Pune* before the wedding."

"We'll make it. We'll catch the first flight we get and we'll be there before you know it."

"You better."

———•—•—•◦⊙◦∘∻∘◦⊙◦•—•—•———

The morning of his wedding day should have been the happiest morning of Satvik's life. He did not wake up to a beautiful morning. He had experienced the worst night in the police station.

Satvik was kept in one of the two cells in the station. Chagan and Popat were surprisingly nice to him and treated him well.

They left soon after putting him behind bars. There was no one but a junior constable who, they said, slept in the front room. Satvik never saw him but believed them. Besides, he wasn't the only person locked up. There was a man who slept in the adjacent cell and kept Satvik awake through the night with his loud snores.

Satvik couldn't sleep. The worrying part was that nobody including his three best men knew he was in jail. He knew if his friends could not find him in time, the wedding might never happen. Shubhangi would not be part of his life.

Life without Shubhangi was unimaginable. She was the best thing that ever happened to him. Through the night, he kept remembering every moment he had spent with Shubhangi.

It was all like a dream. He could never forget the day when he first saw her. It was the day that changed his life forever.

Chapter 2

It was a typical warm summer evening of *Pune* when Satvik met Shubhangi. Satvik and his twelve children eagerly sat in the auditorium for the annual award ceremony. They all were confident about Leela winning the coveted 'Chakrapani award.'

Satvik loved all his children equally, but Leela was his pride. All her siblings loved their elder sister dearly. She was bright, always topped her class and won awards. The children eagerly waited to hear her name announced.

"And now, it's time for the final and the most prestigious 'Chakrapani award' for citywide excellence. This award is given by the royal family of Chakrapani *of Palam*. To present this award, may I call upon the granddaughter of King Yashvardhan Chakrapani, her royal highness, Princess Shubhangi," announcer said.

An exceedingly gorgeous girl in an equally beautiful gown walked up to the stage. As she walked, the frills of her gown swirled excitedly. She waved her hand while a warm smile adorned her face. Her vivacious smile lit up the entire auditorium. All the men gazed at her curiously. Women looked at her with envy.

Satvik waited for her to announce the winner. The 'Chakrapani award' was the most prestigious award in *Pune* for high school students. Leela always wanted to win it.

In her sweet voice, the princess announced the name they all wanted to hear, "Leela Bharat."

The auditorium resounded with applause. Satvik and his children were proud of Leela.

As Leela walked up to the stage, Satvik realized how fast she had grown. She was thirteen. It had been five years since she first became family.

The princess was amazed at Leela's brilliance. She talked briefly with her before handing her the winning trophy. Leela turned towards the audience in that small auditorium. It was full of children her age and their parents. Her eyes searched for her family, her brothers and sisters, and her Satvikpa. Tears gathered in her eyes as she smiled and waved at them.

"Thank you for the award. This is for you Satvikpa and for my little brothers and sisters," she said waving at them.

She signaled her siblings to join her on the stage.

One by one, all of them ran on-stage before Satvik could stop them. Vijay, two years younger than Leela, guided the rest of them on to the stage. In the end, it was three-year-old Nafeesa, youngest of Satvik's twelve children and the newest addition to their family, who walked merrily with her teddy bear squeezed in her hands.

They all clung to Leela. For them, she was the best sister in the world. The auditorium burst in loud applause again.

The Princess, who still stood by Leela, was amused by little Nafeesa. She carried Nafeesa down the stage. In return, Nafeesa hugged her and kissed her on her cheeks.

A high tea party followed the award ceremony. Many students and their parents left. Few lingered talking among themselves.

"I am so proud of you," Satvik said looking at the trophy Leela handed him.

"I know Satvikpa. You would be proud of me even if I hadn't won," she said.

"Can I hold it?" Nafeesa asked.

"Sure you can," Satvik said carefully handing the trophy to Nafeesa.

All his children were happy. They munched on snacks as they mingled with their friends from school.

"Congratulations!"

Satvik turned towards the enchanting voice. It was the princess.

That was the moment when their eyes first met. Her gray eyes felt like a deep ocean. Her lips shined like pink pearls. She had the most beautiful smile. He had never seen someone so beautiful.

The princess smiled gently and said "Hi. I am Shubhangi."

He remained spellbound by her royal charm.

He managed to say, "I… I am Satvik, how are you?" he replied with a voice that did not sound familiar to him.

He felt an imaginary glob in his throat rising, ready to choke him. He tried to swallow it immediately but his attempt failed miserably.

"I am fine, thank you," she spoke gently with a smile on her face.

He wondered if it was appropriate to shake hands with a princess. Before he could decide, his hand had extended itself and stopped midway.

Shubhangi sensed his awkwardness. She shook his hand gently. The soft touch of her hand made him skip a heartbeat. He smelled the sweet fragrance emanating from her body. He fought hard to take his eyes off her unblemished face.

"You must be so proud," she said.

"Yes, I really am."

"Are they all your children?"

"Yes, twelve to be exact."

"Well, you definitely look young to have so many children?"

"I am young. I mean I am not that old. I am not married," he said and realized how clumsy he sounded. It wasn't the answer she was looking for.

"I am not their biological father," Satvik explained.

She knew he couldn't have been their father.

"So, you run an orphanage?" she asked politely.

Satvik was taken aback by this impoliteness. It wasn't the question he expected.

"No, I don't," he said curtly.

She was puzzled by his curtness. She saw expressions on Satvik's face changed quickly.

"They are not orphans. I am their guardian and not their father, but they are my children. If that's what you were asking," he said.

He was obviously hurt by her remark.

"I am sorry. I did not mean that," she said apologetically. That's when Leela joined them.

"Thank you for this," she said to Shubhangi raising the trophy in her hand.

"You earned it," Shubhangi said.

"Can I tell you something?"

Shubhangi nodded her head.

"You are very beautiful," Leela said.

"Thank you," Shubhangi said bashfully.

Shubhangi and Leela kept talking while Satvik stood by them. Shubhangi wanted to know more about Leela and her brothers and sisters. She was also curious about the man who was their father but not their father.

Satvik kept stealing glances at the princess. Her ethereal beauty mesmerized him. He came to his senses when Shubhangi turned and started to walk away.

With her tall and slender frame, she walked with the grace of a true princess.

Leela's success made everyone happy. The children sang and danced in their van as Satvik drove them to their home, Chhaya Sadan.

Satvik had purchased the cream-colored Volkswagen van for them two years ago from an old Parsi doctor who had a big family. Satvik loved the van the instant he saw it. It was old. Nevertheless, it was big, like a minibus, and could carry all his children.

Children loved the van. They cleaned and repainted it themselves. They had their spots fixed in the van. The van was a big part of their lives. It helped them to school, to the doctor, to the playground and everywhere else.

Satvik drove it occasionally. It was Badrinath, the caretaker at Chhaya Sadan, who usually drove the children around. Badri uncle, as they fondly called Badrinath, never allowed them to sing and dance in the van. That's why children loved it when Satvik drove them. He played their favorite songs and allowed them to sing and dance.

As they entered the gates of Chhaya Sadan, they saw Jeejeebhoy eagerly waiting in the front lawns. Leela ran towards him with the winning trophy in her hands. A smile spread across Jeejee's old face.

Jeejee, even in his seventies, took great care of Satvik's children. They were Jeejee's children too. If it wasn't for Jeejee, there would not have been a Chhaya Sadan.

After spending a cheerful afternoon at Chhaya Sadan celebrating Leela's success, Satvik left for his home. He did not live at Chhaya Sadan with the children but frequented

Chhaya Sadan on weekdays and spent his weekends with his children.

Satvik stayed with his best friend Sindbad in an apartment near their office. Satvik and Sindbad had known each other for many years and worked at the same software company. Their best friends Amit and Gopal lived nearby.

Satvik, Sindbad, Amit and Gopal partied over most weekends.

It was a special day. Leela had won the Chakrapani award. Satvik arranged a party that night to celebrate Leela's success.

A thought of Leela's award reminded Satvik of princess Shubhangi. Her beautiful smile still lingered in his mind. He pondered over those moments again, remembering how she spoke with warmth in her voice, how she smiled, how the flutter of her eyelashes revealed her deep gray eyes.

Satvik didn't like it when Shubhangi referred to Chhaya Sadan as an orphanage. He hated when people thought of Chhaya Sadan as an orphanage. All his life he grew with that label. He was an orphan.

He was not sure if it was the love she showered on his children or the way she carried Nafeesa in her arms, Satvik somehow knew Princess Shubhangi wasn't insensitive.

Out of his uncontrollably growing curiosity, he searched internet for princess Shubhangi. It returned many news results with her pictures. Shubhangi, the young princess of Chakrapani, was part of many charitable causes. As he read about her social work and her participation in social activities, he was fascinated.

Looking at her smile in the pictures, his heart raced.

Satvik and his friends celebrated Leela's success with a party. Partying mostly involved excess booze, except for Amit who was a teetotaler when it came to drinking alcohol.

Loosened by alcohol, Satvik brought up the Princess he had been thinking about the whole day.

"You are not going to believe this. I met a real life princess today," he said.

"What princess?" Sindbad asked.

"She was the one who presented the award to Leela." Satvik said.

"How do you know she was a princess? Was she wearing a tiara?" Amit asked trying to poke fun at him.

"The award was sponsored by her family, the Chakrapani Award. They addressed her as a princess. She was gorgeous. I have never seen anyone so beautiful," Satvik said.

"Maybe you haven't seen enough," Gopal said sparking laughter.

"I am serious, I looked her up on the internet, and she really is a princess," Satvik said.

"Are you serious? You searched her on the internet?" Sindbad asked.

"I did, but only because I didn't believe it, like you guys. I was curious."

"Is it because she is hot?" Amit asked.

"That too," Satvik said as they all laughed.

"So?" Sindbad asked.

"So what?" Satvik answered.

"That's it? Do you have her number? You obviously like her."

"No. I don't. I am just intrigued by the fact that we have princesses even in this modern age," Satvik said.

"That can't be all. There has to be more to that story," Sindbad said.

"As she happens to be the most beautiful woman you ever saw in your life," Amit added.

"And you stalked her on the internet and did a background check,'" Gopal quickly added.

"So, since you obviously like her so much, you should get her number and ask her out," Sindbad said.

They all made fun of Satvik through the rest of the evening.

Helping those in need was in Shubhangi's nature. Not because she could afford helping others and people appreciated it, but she genuinely loved it. Her father, King Nandivardhan, did not approve of her ways of spending money on the undeserving. But, being a princess and an only child, she could do what she wanted.

Shubhangi was rarely impressed. That was part of being a princess. She was impressed with award winner Leela's brilliance. When she realized that Leela was an orphan, she instantly became her fan.

When Shubhangi talked with Leela during the award ceremony, she told Shubhangi about Chhaya Sadan, their home. Looking at Shubhangi's curiosity to know more about Chhaya Sadan, Leela invited her for the lunch over the weekend.

Satvik, the father of the twelve orphans, also intrigued her. All those children were so happy and in love with each other. She knew they were a family and not part of any orphanage.

She felt guilty for asking Satvik if he managed an orphanage. She knew he took it to heart and looked miffed about it. He was different from the men she usually met.

As weekend arrived, Shubhangi was eager to visit Chaaya Sadan.

On Sunday afternoon, Shubhangi went to Chhaya Sadan in her chauffeur driven car. It was located at a peaceful location. It was seemingly an old bungalow, but was big and nicely built. She did not expect it to be such a big house.

As she entered through the front gate of the house, she saw children playing on well-maintained lush green lawns.

They ran towards her and dragged her inside holding her by her hand.

They took her to their rooms. They had three big rooms to themselves. Their rooms were very well kept and were decorated with their paintings. With bunk beds, they had lots of space to study and to play inside.

Leela introduced Shubhangi to Amma and Sakhubai, women who took care of the children and managed the kitchen. *Madrasi* Amma, looked strict. Leela told her she was the loving one. She had two children of her own but they died in a car accident. She never went back to *Madras* and stayed at Chhaya Sadan to take care of them. Sakhubai was gentle and if the children wanted to eat something special, they made their request to Sakhubai who listened to their demands. Amma and Sakhubai were like mothers to them.

In the end, Leela took Shubhangi to Jeejeebhoy, an old man in his seventies. He was kindhearted. He talked with Shubhangi for a long time.

When Shubhangi asked, he told her about how Chhaya Sadan came to exist.

"Four years ago, I wanted to sell this house and go to my village to spend the rest of my life. When Satvik first came to me, he said, Jeejeebhoy, I want to buy this house for my children. At the time, he was guardian to eight children. He didn't have enough money. He had just started working and there was no way he could take a loan and pay that kind of money," Jeejee said with a smile remembering the past.

"There was something about him that moved me. I don't have children of my own. My wife died a few years ago. I wanted to retire. So, I gave him Chhaya Sadan. I asked him if I could stay with his children. I remember, he cried like a child.

These were his children. Now, they are mine too. He knows the pain of being an orphan. He was an orphan. He had not seen much affection growing up. He doesn't want anyone to be an orphan," Jeejee said.

Shubhangi understood why Satvik was upset when she asked if Chhaya Sadan was an orphanage.

"Where is Satvik?" she asked.

"He doesn't stay at Chhaya Sadan. He stays in an apartment near his office. He visits frequently."

"I can't imagine how you manage to take care of all these children, you do it so well," Shubhangi said.

"Well, they are our children. Amma, Sakhubai, Badri, we all enjoy taking care of them. After my wife's death, I wondered how I could live all alone. In a way, Satvik and his children gave me a second life," Jeejee said.

"It's amazing how they get along with each other, like brothers and sisters. Do they fight like brother and sisters? Do they demand things?" Shubhangi asked curiously.

"Sometimes. But mostly they don't. They love each other. They play with each other but hardly fight. Hardly demand," Jeejee said.

"Really? That's nice."

"Deep down, they know the truth. Satvik and I don't show them sympathy. That'd sadden them. We are a family. This is the only family they have."

"I don't know how to say this, but, is there a way I can help? I want to help," Shubhangi asked.

"Satvik doesn't like to take help. It's not an orphanage. He works hard to earn for these children."

"I understand." Shubhangi said.

Satvik had gained a respect in her mind. He was indeed a different man, a noble one, she thought.

Shubhangi joined the children for lunch at a big table. She felt at home, at peace with the children. Jeejeebhoy, Amma, Sakhubai all were happy to be part of their lives.

When Shubhangi was about to leave, Nafeesa clung to her.

"Can you make me a princess too?" She asked making everyone laugh.

"You are already a princess," Shubhangi said.

Shubhangi felt overwhelmed by the love Chhaya Sadan extended to her. She felt she knew all of them, as if she was a part of their family. She wanted to help but she knew they did not need her help. They had it all.

Chapter 3

As the days went by, other priorities of their lives took precedence. Satvik was busy with his job, while Shubhangi was busy being a princess and devoting time to social work. They had forgotten about their meeting.

It was after more than a month, they ran in to each other. It was an encounter Satvik would have liked to forget.

It was Sunday evening. Satvik took his children to 'Sambhaji Park,' a serene place where grandmothers helped their aged husbands with walkers and mid-aged couples jogged in similar outfits. With high palm trees, green lawns and jogging tracks, it was a good park for everyone.

As the children played and ran around in the park, they noticed princess Shubhangi.

"Princess," Leela pointed in her direction.

Before Satvik could turn and look at Shubhangi, the children started running in her direction. Shubhangi was busy reading a book seating under a tree. In a flowery sleeveless grown, she sat as the frills of her gown beautifully folded on the ground. the evening breeze played with her wavy hair. When Shubhangi noticed the children running towards her, she got up and greeted them.

She looked at Satvik and smiled.

"Hi, how are you?" She asked.

"Good, Thank you. How are you?" Satvik replied.

"I am fine, thank you."

"Sorry, they disturbed you," Satvik said.

"No, it's perfectly alright. They made my day," She said as she brushed Nafeesa's nose with her fingers.

It was a site to look at. Satvik had forgotten how beautiful the princess looked. Looking at her, he realized why he had thought about her so much.

"It's good to see you again," Satvik said.

"Grrrr… bhow!" he heard a bark.

Scared, he turned in the direction of the growl. As if ready to pounce on him, a shining white Pomeranian dog stood staring angrily at him.

Satvik hated dogs. Dogs didn't like him either. As a child, he was bitten by dogs. Twice. Each time he had to get fourteen injections around his belly button. Since then he strived hard to stay away from dogs, at least until that day.

The thought of unpleasant shots in his belly scared him. The hairy white lump of growls turned in to a big monster, ready to tear him in pieces.

"Lemony!" Shubhangi said looking at dog.

So it was Shubhangi's dog. That didn't make it any less dreadful. Sure, it was a Pomeranian and looked cute, but it wasn't entirely adorable. And what kind of name is Lemony? It must be the thing about royal dogs, that they are over-pampered. Satvik's head filled with random thoughts as he tried to retain his calm around Lemony.

"Lemony!" Shubhangi said pointing a finger and admonishing the dog.

Lemony didn't budge a bit. Satvik could see hatred in Lemony's eyes growing with her growling. Satvik and Lemony locked their eyes on each other as if playing 'who blinks first?' His eyes begged to spare his life. Lemony's eyes changed, as if remembering an enmity from a past life.

"Does she bite?" Satvik asked.

"Bhow!" the dog barked before Shubhangi could answer his question.

Satvik jumped and broke the eye contact. He ran in the opposite direction, slowly at first. When he noticed Lemony started chasing him, he ran for his life.

Satvik heard the dog running with an atrocious bark. It awakened a roadrunner in him. He was running as fast as he could. Joggers felt he was a first time jogging enthusiast and ignored his completely outrunning them.

Satvik ran in the front closely followed by Lemony. The children and Shubhangi ran behind them. Shubhangi Kept asking Lemony to stop but she was beyond listening. Lemony was faster and louder in her intentions.

Satvik kept looking back at the dog while he ran ahead. As he looked back, he stumbled on the curb. Before he could balance himself, he fell on his back and hit his head hard on the curb.

"Lemony… lemony … bad dog!" he heard Shubhangi's voice coming closer. The Princess running to save him from the dog was not nearly romantic but it felt better in that adverse situation.

He slowly opened his eyes only to meet Lemony's eyes. The dog stood on his chest with its eyes eagerly waiting for his eyes to open. He felt the dog looked at him, smiling villainously and showing all its drool drenched razor sharp teeth, ready to pierce his flesh.

"Lemony, Statue!" Shubhangi shouted as she came near. It must have worked. Lemony did not move.

"Get off!" Shubhangi said pinching dog's ear.

Satvik saw Lemony stepping off his chest smirking at him as if he was a defeated soldier. That was the last thing he could remember before the darkness spread in front of his eyes.

———◆•◆•✦✧❁✧✦•◆•◆———

Satvik woke up to medicinal smell in a hospital room. As he opened his eyes, he saw Shubhangi seating next to him and children standing in circle around his bed. Leela quickly went out to inform the doctor.

His head felt heavy. He touched it to find it wrapped in a bandage.

"How do you feel?" Shubhangi asked.

"Better," he said nodding his head with a reassuring smile.

"I am so sorry. I never expected Lemony to behave like that. She never chased anyone in the park," Shubhangi said leaning towards his face.

Satvik looked at Shubhangi trying to remember if the dog had bitten him.

"Am I bitten?" he asked.

"No, Lemony will never do that. She is a good dog. Sometime she chases strangers but she never bites."

That's when doctor entered the room.

"How do you feel now?" Doctor asked the same question.

"I feel better. What happened to me?"

"Your head was hit hard. You blacked out with head trauma. There is a little swelling and concussion. You need a good sleep and you will be good to go tomorrow morning."

"What do you mean tomorrow morning?"

"You are staying here tonight."

"No, I am not. I feel better. I can come tomorrow for checkup."

"Your head is wrapped in the bandage. You need to be monitored for swelling through the night."

"Please stay for tonight," Shubhangi said pressing his hand with her soft hands.

Satvik agreed without really agreeing to the doctor. He had no choice when Shubhangi insisted. He thought that's the problem with hospitals. They have turned hospitals into hotels. Why should he be in the hospital if there was nothing wrong with him and pay exorbitant fees?

When doctor left after checking him, Shubhangi told him how they got him there.

"After you blacked out, we rushed you to the hospital. My chauffeur drove your van and brought all of us here." Shubhangi said.

That's when Sindbad, Amit and Gopal dashed inside. Badri followed them. They looked at Satvik and his bandage wrapped head in astonishment. He was lying on the bed and a beautiful girl sat next to him.

"Look at that and we thought you needed us," Sindbad said.

"I informed Jeejee and Sindbad uncle on the way to hospital," Leela explained Satvik.

Shubhangi got up from the bed and gave his friends a space. They came close and surrounded him. Satvik introduced them to Shubhangi.

"So you are the princess," Amit said.

Shubhangi shook her head in agreement and smiled.

"Satvik talks about you a lot," Amit continued.

She glanced at Satvik but he avoided her glance. Satvik felt embarrassed. He had never mentioned her to them except for once.

"Shall I take kids home?" Badri asked.

Satvik nodded. Children went with Badri, one by one, waving hands at Satvik and Shubhangi.

"I should probably go too," Shubhangi said.

Satvik didn't want her to go. Not without getting her phone number. But he hesitated to ask her in front of his friends. His friends had already embarrassed him. She sensed his hesitation.

"I will come by tomorrow morning," She said.

"You will?" Satvik asked.

"I will," she added.

"I will wait for you. Thank you, for everything," he said.

She smiled and left.

As Shubhangi walked out of the door, his friends jumped on him.

"She is absolutely gorgeous," Sindbad said.

"What did I tell you?" Satvik said.

"How did you get in to hospital and that too with her? We need to know this story. I am hungry. Are you hungry? Let me get something to eat before you start," Sindbad said and dashed out.

When he was back, Satvik narrated to them the story how they met in the park and how her dog chased him and put him in the hospital. As they munched on the snack, Satvik's friend teased him.

"Dude, she is into you, I can tell. She looked worried about you," Sindbad said.

"And she was seating so close, only a girlfriend would do that," Gopal Added.

"May be because it was her dog that put him here," Amit said.

"Amit has a point," Satvik said laughing for the first time.

Satvik felt better among his friends. As they munched on snacks, they talked about his fear of dogs.

"You would imagine her dog as a cute looking puppy but she was a full grown ugly lunatic bitch," Satvik said in anger.

"Say that to her and you will never see her again," Sindbad dared him.

"Pomeranian dogs are supposed to be cute and friendly but this one neither looked cute nor was it friendly," Satvik vented in frustration.

"You know dogs are said to have a great sense. They can detect the intentions of a man. They always protect the daughter of their owners from men who are trying to beguile her. I guess that dog must be skilled," Sindbad quipped.

"But don't get scared yet, the dog is just the first of her family members and probably one with a kind heart," Sindbad added with obvious sarcasm in his tone.

Shubhangi felt bad about Satvik spending the night in the hospital. She felt responsible for the accident. But she knew Lemony would never have bitten Satvik.

It was almost two years ago Shubhangi first brought a little Pomeranian puppy. It was then just a cute little ball of white fur. She named her 'Lemony' not just for a streak of lemon colored hair patch on her wonky tail, but also for her bitter-sweet nature.

King Nandi, Shubhangi's father, did not approve of Lemony roaming freely in his palace, Pushkar Mahal. He thought, for a dog to have Lemon colored hair was not normal. Besides, he believed, if anything that Pomeranian dog could never have, it was royal demeanor.

Lemony was a smart dog. She was always around Nandi seeking his attention in numerous possible ways. His dislike didn't last long. He slowly grew fond of her. Lemony did things he thought a dog should do, bark at strangers, stay at the entrance and most importantly give him the respect he deserved as a king. Soon he started treating Lemony like his other daughter.

Shubhangi knew Lemony just wanted to scare Satvik. But she couldn't resist believing that he was in hospital because of her. She felt guilty.

Next morning, she packed breakfast and went to the hospital to visit Satvik.

Satvik had already gotten ready. The doctor had cleared him to go home. He waited for Shubhangi. He knew she would come.

As Shubhangi entered his room, the fragrance of her freshly washed hair swept across the room. She looked exquisite in an embroidered *Kameez*, which complemented her fair skin. Her eyes sparkled and a smile spread across her face as she greeted Satvik, "Good morning."

"Good Morning," Satvik replied.

"How do you feel?"

"Never felt better."

"I've brought breakfast for you," she said.

Satvik hesitated at first but when she insisted, he agreed. They sat next to each other. She opened the basket and spread the elaborate breakfast that would put to shame a sumptuous lunch.

He was enchanted by her presence. She apologized for what Lemony did. He tried to pretend as if it didn't matter.

"Do you hate dogs?" She asked.

What? No! I don't hate them. I love to hate them, every one of them- he wanted to say.

"No, I don't hate them. I just don't like to be near them. I was bitten by dogs when I was a kid," is all that came out of his mouth.

"Once Lemony knows you, she would be sweet. You would love her," Shubhangi explained.

"I am sure she meant no harm," he said.

They laughed together as she told him stories about Lemony scaring many royal guests. Shubhangi talked with enthusiasm. But he could hardly pay attention. He was lost in her charm.

"Do you know I once visited Chhaya Sadan?" she asked changing the topic.

"Jeejee told me about it."

"Leela invited me to Chhaya Sadan, I couldn't resist."

"How did you like it?"

"I can't tell you how amazed I am. It's such a noble cause. What you are doing for those children, it's not something anyone can do. It takes someone with a big heart," she said.

Her words rang like music in his heart. He was humbled by her words, and embarrassed by her praise.

"I don't know about that. But thank you, it is very generous of you to think so," he said.

"I know it's your family. I wanted to apologies for calling it an orphanage when we first met. I am sorry," she said.

"You don't have to be. You wouldn't have known. But enough about me. I know about your work too. How you like to help people. And you are part of so many social organizations," he said.

"How do you know so much about me?" she asked.

He felt embarrassed again. He had no answer for her question.

"Who doesn't know about you?" He said.

She kept looking at him. He knew she was not convinced.

"Okay, I searched you on the internet. I wanted to know more about you," he said.

Shubhangi smiled. She didn't know how to react to his admission that he was curious about her. She smiled bashfully. She couldn't help blushing and was thankful the nurse showed up at the door.

"Sir, you asked for discharge? Could you please sign?"

"Yes, sure," he said as he got up and went to her.

Shubhangi packed the tiffin boxes. Satvik glanced at her while he signed the documents. Her slender fingers moved with elegance. Her wavy hair kept falling on her face. Part of him wanted to stay there with her and spend more time.

As they walked outside the hospital, he felt they would never meet again. He wasn't sure how he could ask her for her phone number.

"The children really like you. They think you are part of some kind of a fairytale, the most beautiful princess ever," he said.

"It must be true then, children speak the truth," she said looking at him with a smile.

He gathered courage and said, "It's true, you are the most beautiful princess."

She laughed bashfully at his suggestion.

They came out of the hospital compound walking as slowly as they could.

"So, here we part again," Satvik said.

"Yes, we do," She said.

"Thank you, Princess Shubhangi, for everything you have done for me."

"Call me Shubhi, will you? Shubhangi is too formal," she said.

"Shubhi?" he said looking at her. Shubhi, ah, it sounds lovely. He thought.

"Yes, Shu-bhi' she said

"Okay. Shubhi," he said.

She smiled, "See, it feels so friendly."

Friendly? Did she say friendly? An alarm rang in his head. Was he heading to become merely a friend? He consoled himself. After all, it always starts with a friendship. He smiled at his shameless imagination.

"Yes it does," he said.

Then there was an awkward silence as if both of them wanted to say something. Satvik knew it was his only chance. He had to say something before it was too late and they never see each other again.

"Shubhi, can I ask you something?" he said with hesitation.

"Sure."

"Would you like to go out with me sometime?" Satvik asked. He had never asked any girl out in his life.

"You are asking me out on a date?" she asked with her eyebrows raised.

"Maybe, I don't know. I don't want to run in to you after months like I did yesterday," he said.

She laughed.

"Okay. Here, it has my number on it," she said handing him her card.

Before entering her car, she came close and hugged him. It was a partial hug but that made his day brighter. He stood frozen, waving at her for a long time.

As he returned home, he was lost in her thoughts. Even after his ghastly experience with Lemony, he was happy. He hated Lemony, but the dog had brought them closer. Close enough to call her Shubhi and score a date.

Satvik felt as he had never felt before. Her thoughts filled his mind with an inexplicable gush of joy, with unlimited possibilities. As if, she held the key to his happiness. He was not sure if that was a good thing.

With her phone number, Satvik could not resist for long and sent Shubhangi a message. Soon they started exchanging messages. Within a day, they planned their date, a museum visit followed by lunch.

He eagerly waited for the weekend.

When they met for their date, he was surprised to see her. She wore denims and a t-shirt and came on a scooterette. She being a princess, he never imagined her driving a scooter in a casual attire. Despite her girl-next-door appearance, she looked gorgeous. He felt more comfortable talking to her.

They started for the museum on her scooter. Sitting behind her, he inhaled the fragrance of her freshly washed hair. Her wavy hair, riding in the wind, felt smooth when they touched his face. Her shoulders, her waist, her hourglass figure in western clothes felt delicate and inviting at the same time. He wanted to hug her nubile body and hold her close to him.

They spent the afternoon in the museum. She could talk about everything. He could listen to her every word. It wasn't just her beauty; he felt her knowledge too was intimidating.

When they finished the museum tour, it was time for lunch.

"Where do you want to go for lunch?" Satvik asked.

"I have a surprise for you," she said.

"Surprise? What is it?"

"Now, would it be a surprise if I told you?"

Satvik smiled hesitantly. He feared she would select one of those restaurants that served no good food but emptied his pockets.

"All right! I will tell you. There is this Kerala restaurant called 'Kairali.' They serve this amazing fried fish, it's one of my favorites. You would love it," she said smacking her lips.

Did she say fish? His senses were alarmed. He didn't like fish. He never ate fish and never wanted to.

He loved fish, their beautiful colors, amazing shapes and the way they looked so vulnerable. They never failed to amaze him in tabletop aquariums or on television channels solely devoted to them. But, that didn't make them edible, he thought.

His mind filled with fearful anticipation. He thought he should let her know he doesn't like to eat fish. One doesn't really have a choice when a princess insists and drags you holding your hand.

Shubhangi, without looking at the menu, ordered her favorite fried fish, brown rice and Kerala curries. A cheerful smile spread across her face.

She was a foodie and liked all kinds of food. While they waited, she talked about the fried fish and Kerala food with enthusiasm. It did not occur to her to ask if Satvik ate fish.

For a moment, he thought he should let her know. She would understand. After all, humans and fishes cannot exist together, that's why they live separately on land and in water. His mind tried to justify his anxiety towards fish consumption in numerous ways.

All the justifications his mind came up with were too lame and too late. The waiter arrived with large service tray in hand. He swung around and neatly spread the dishes on the table.

"Wow! This looks amazing! Shall we?" Shubhangi cheered him prompting to start feasting on the fish.

"Yes," he sheepishly smiled back at her.

His eyes popped in astonishment looking at the fish that looked almost alive, as if ready to jump on him. Its eyes, fins, skin, everything was undisturbed even after frying. Its mouth was agape as if gasping for air and its eyes were wide-open, eagerly seeking an escape.

With a knife and fork in his hands, he looked at it only to realize it was staring at him, as if asking 'you too, Brutus?'

Satvik almost said 'sorry.'

"What are you waiting for?" Shubhangi asked inquisitively.

"I am thinking where to start, it looks so delicious," he said and smiled at her.

He must be imagining things as he thought the fish blinked at him. He braced himself and avoided looking at its wide eyes. Love tests one in more ways than one can imagine, he thought.

A fish without water is a terrible thing. That must be true when you are eating it too. He was just about managing to swallow it with water. It was difficult to drink fish down and keep a delighted expression on the face at the same time.

Shubhangi was enjoying her favorite dish. Her eyes sparkled with delight, which helped him forget his misery for a bit. She was half done with her fish while he had just started.

"Hmm… It's delicious!" he kept saying after every bite he swallowed.

Shubhangi excitedly asked, "Shall we repeat the order?"

"No, no, I am full," he insisted using frantic gestures to emphasize it.

It was in her presence, looking at her mesmerising smile, he could finish the fish. By the time the waiter arrived to clear the dishes he couldn't help but stare at the leftover bones that reminded him of the fishbone diagram he studied in school.

He was eager to get out of the restaurant and as far away from the fish as he could.

Chapter 4

Thereafter, Satvik and Shubhangi met every weekend. Satvik's initial inhibitions were gone. He learnt to control his unruly heart and to manage the sudden uncontrollable outburst of feelings when confronted by the flutter of her eyes, or turn of her lips that formed one of her beautiful smiles.

Shubhangi, too, looked forward to spending time with Satvik. She was besotted by his selfless nature. He was unlike other men who constantly sought her attention.

On one Saturday evening, they were meeting after six long days. Satvik drove her scooter while Shubhangi sat behind.

She kept her hands lightly on his shoulder. Her touch drove a sweet wave of goose bumps through his body. She felt the shudder of his shoulder. She pressed her hand and smiled in his ears as if reassuring him. If she sat behind, he could drive her around forever, he thought.

When she noticed a *Chaat* stall, she asked him to stop. Satvik almost laughed when she said she wanted to eat *pani-puri*. But she was excited at the thought of *pani-puri* and dragged him to it.

"I can't imagine a princess like you would have a taste for *pani-puri*," he said.

"Not just the taste, I love *pani-puri*. Don't you love it?"

"I don't remember the last time I had it."

"Well, you are going to have it today."

"Sure, I think I will," he said.

"You will, and you will be surprised."

She closed her eyes as her lips pouted after having a *pani-puri*. She moaned a little. His heart raced and mind wandered shamelessly looking at her ecstatic state. She wouldn't let him just steal the glances at her. She insisted that he try it. He couldn't gather much resistance against her and ate his first *pani-puri* with enthusiasm.

It was a ball of fury. It burst into a plethora of hot spices with tangy water in his mouth, sending a wide and previously unknown sensation to his brain, to his eyes and to his nose through some interconnected passage. Water found a way through his nose and through his eyes, sending him coughing uncontrollably. She laughed aloud until she saw tears in his eyes and his futile attempt to hide them.

"I am so very sorry," she said holding his hands and squeezing it hard.

Her closeness made his mind forget the effect of the tangy water. The squeeze of her hand provided much needed warmth to unlimited possibilities his mind had been garnering.

"I am fine, thank you," he said, now in control of his senses.

"Did you like it?"

"Like it? I love it. It's great. I want more."

47

"Ah! It's like a firework of tastes. Did you feel the crunch of *puri* after drinking that water? Inexplicable feast," she spoke with enthusiasm.

She ate *pani-puri* to her heart's content while Satvik's adventure was limited to a few. Satvik couldn't believe he actually liked it so much.

They spent the rest of the evening together in a park talking. No amount of time spent together seemed enough.

"It's Sunday tomorrow. What are you up to?" she asked.

"Not much. What do you have on your mind?"

"Would you like to join me for hiking, and boating?"

"That sounds great, where?" Satvik asked, unable to imagine the princess hiking in wilderness.

"Do you know the *Durga* hill? It's in a small village along the expressway to *Mumbai*. The plan is to hike the hill. Then there is a *Launar* lake nearby which has boating. It will be fun. We will start in the morning?"

"Just the two of us?"

"Yes of course, unless you need more for company?"

"No, no, I was just curious if Lemony will be joining us?"

"Oh, I see. You still hate her. No, not lemony. We would be gone for a long time. Besides she can't walk up the hill," she said laughing.

"With or without Lemony, I am in," he said with enthusiasm.

Next morning, Satvik braced himself to impress Shubhangi. Sindbad suggested he might have overdressed for a hike. On his insistence, Satvik made changes to his wardrobe to make it more suitable for hiking.

It was obvious. Sindbad could feel Satvik was falling for the princess. Looking at his joyous mood that morning, he asked Satvik.

"Do you think you love her?"

"I like her. I think she likes me too. But love? That's far-fetched."

"But you would know if she loves you. I mean you should be reading signs."

"That's the thing. My mind stops working when I am with her."

"So you don't know if she loves you, but you are sure you don't love her, right?"

"I told you, I don't know," Satvik said with a smile.

"You sound stupid."

"No, I am serious. She could be just a good friend."

"It's obvious that you are head over heel in love with her. If she is not freaked by the way you look at her, she must love you. From what I can tell, you love each other. All you have to do is make a move."

"What do you mean a move?"

"Look in to her eyes when you talk to her. Hold her hands. Lean towards her. Put your head on her shoulder. And if she allows, steal the moment and kiss her."

"Kiss her?"

"Yes, kiss her."

"That's little too much."

"Then you should forget dreaming about her. Dude, she is a princess. You think she could care less about your hesitation."

"Maybe not, but such things can't be planned. I will know when the moment is right."

"Then at least keep your eyes open for the right moment. If you love her, you have to tell her."

Satvik knew Sindbad was right. He was falling in love with Shubhangi. He knew she liked him, but he wasn't sure if she loved him.

Shubhangi wore a pink top and denims that snuggly fit her form. Her hair was neatly pulled together and pinned. She looked young, energetic but nothing like a princess.

Chauffer drove them to the bottom of the *Durga* hill.

They started climbing up the hill with backpacks on their shoulders. Ascending the hill was not easy. They had to climb on unpaved terrain, avoiding small trees, shrubs and rocks. There were only a few climbing up the hill on that rocky side.

Shubhangi looked delicate but she was tough. For Satvik, climbing the hill was not easy but having her by his side kept

Shivkumar Wayal

his spirit high. They talked freely about the things they never talked before.

On their way, they met a troop of monkeys scouring along the route, jumping on branches of trees and chasing each other. A few young monkeys were playfully staring at the trekkers, trying to scare them but getting scared in turn. Few were brave enough to take food offered by trekkers.

By the time they reached the hilltop, it was noon. They were tired and hungry. The view from the top was extremely beautiful and made them forget their tired legs and rumbling stomach for a while.

The circular hilltop was bigger than Satvik imagined it to be. Trees lined on either sides of the path that led to the Goddess *Durga* temple. The temple walls were exquisitely carved with deities.

A beautifully sculptured idol of Goddess *Durga* with celestial weapons in her eight arms adorned the temple. Shubhangi folded her hands and closed her eyes while offering prayers. Satvik finished his prayer in a moment and admired the devout innocence on her face through the corner of his eyes.

Even with her eyes closed, she could feel him stealing glances at her. She knew he was falling for her. Most men did. But she didn't mind Satvik's feelings towards her.

After offering prayers, they had lunch in the garden while they talked. Shubhangi talked about her friends and her work.

"Most of my childhood friends have left *Pune*. Many are abroad for higher studies. Few have gone to good universities outside *Pune*. Anamika is the only best friend I have in *Pune* and she too is leaving for *Mumbai*," Shubhangi said.

"I joined an NGO after my graduation. We help kids with cancer and single mothers who need support to survive. I like helping people. I think it's my thing," she continued.

Listening to her, Satvik could feel the sincerity in her words. Satvik rarely opened up himself to others. On her insistence, he told her his story.

"I don't remember my parents. I was an orphan before I knew how to walk. All I remember is growing up in a group of children in an orphanage. I loved that place. It was home for me.

The man, who owned the orphanage, loved us all. He spent his money. He gave us names. He wasn't rich but took care of us and paid for our school. As the numbers grew, it became difficult for him.

Eventually, when he couldn't take care of all of us, the orphanage was taken over by the government. But I stayed with the old man." Satvik said.

Shubhangi listened to him carefully.

"He died when I was fifteen. He was a good man. He loved me like a son. He left me some money. I worked at small jobs and studied hard to become an engineer. If it wasn't for him, I wouldn't be here. I owe him my life. But there is nothing I could ever do for him. He would have wanted me to do what he did for me, to take care of children like me. Chhaya Sadan is my way of carrying forward his legacy. It's my family. The way I was his family," Satvik said.

Tears gathered in Shubhangi's eyes as he told her about his past.

After lunch, they started climbing down the hill. It was easier than climbing up. The time passed quicker than they imagined.

The chauffer drove them to the *Launar* lake close to *Durga* hill. It was almost evening when they reached the lake. Located in the picturesque setting, *Launar* lake was surrounded by lush green hills.

Instead of a fancy motorboat, they rented a swan shaped couple's pedal boat. Its top was covered to protect from the sun. Together, they enjoyed cool breeze in the warm, sunny evening as they paddled. Satvik was ecstatic to sit beside her in that romantic setting. He was amazed at the harmony with which they paddled.

Shubhangi told him about her royal family, her ancestry. About their kingdom *Palam* and how they moved to the city of *Pune*.

"It's still hard for me to believe there are still princesses in India," Satvik said.

"I don't believe it either. But, it's not my choice. I inherit it. Even if I don't want it, people treat me like a princess. That has always been my biggest fear. Do you think I behave like a princess?" she asked.

"No, your majesty, I don't think so. But I can tell you, it feels good to pedal a boat with the princess."

She laughed.

"But really, how is it to be a princess?" Satvik asked.

"Well, it can't be bad. But it's also not as interesting as it sounds. There are too many protocols, too many restrictions. Everything you do is scrutinized by people. You can only be seen with a particular part of society. Who you meet, who you talk to, everything matters. People judge you.

My Father works hard despite being King, to keep the prestige alive. My mother has few friends. Even I have few friends. On the other hand, your life is free from the public eye. You can do whatever you want. You are truly free.

When you are a royal and you have money, people around you are always ready to take your orders and serve you. It's kind of boring. Always makes me wonder, what would it be like to not be a princess?" she said lost in thoughts.

"I can imagine. Still better than being anybody else. You can't complain about anything really, can you?" he said trying to cheer her up.

"I am not going to lie. Being a princess, living a lavish life in Pushkar Mahal, is not something I don't love," she said.

"There you go!"

"You know what, why don't you come visit Pushkar Mahal? Let's plan something next weekend," she said excitedly.

"Okay, But…I… I don't know."

"I visited Chhaya Sadan, that too without your invitation."

"I never met a royal family before."

"Don't worry. I am not asking you to meet my family. They are attending a function next Sunday. They won't be home."

It relieved him. He wasn't ready to meet any of her family members yet. He couldn't say no if it was just her.

They planned his visit to Pushkar Mahal over the next weekend.

The sky filled with the striking shades of golden colors, exhaled from the eloping sun, splashed across the grand canvas. The radiant glow of the sun lent a soft silver lining to the clouds.

After boating, they walked on the shores of the *Launar* lake. She held his hands. They had come closer to each other than ever before.

"Beautiful, isn't it?" She asked looking at Satvik.

"Absolutely breath-taking. I don't know how I can thank you enough for bringing me here," he said.

"Pleasure was all mine," she said and smiled a beautiful smile at him.

'Pushkar Mahal' was written in big, glossy letters on the main gate of the palace. The palace stood on a highland in a rich community surrounded by big villas and huge gardens. It was guarded by a tall, thick fence wall.

As Shubhangi pulled her car in front of the main gate, guards ran around and opened the gates.

"Welcome to Pushkar Mahal," Shubhangi said to Satvik as she drove her Mercedes through the gate inside the palace. She took a roundabout and gently parked the car in front of the main porch. A driver came running and opened the doors of the car for them.

In the front of the house was a beautifully maintained garden with lush green lawn. The front garden had big trees near the fence wall casting their shadows on the lawn. It was the sculpture of a big lotus flower with sprinklers, built at the center of the roundabout, why palace was named Pushkar Mahal, a lotus palace.

Just by the main door, Satvik saw a big doghouse. He was scared a bit when he realized it was for Lemony.

"Don't worry, she is out with my parents," Shubhangi said.

He was relieved. Shubhangi and Satvik entered through the big doors of the palace. Servants walked around briskly. Satvik noticed that they avoided Shubhangi's gaze.

They entered a large hall adorned with royal furnishings. A big chandelier with numerous lights hung from the ceiling. A red carpet from the front door led to the stairs running to the top floor. There were many rooms surrounding the main hall on both floors.

On the right side of the hall, a big wall stood with rocks embedded in it. It was realistic enough to invite a rock climber with its lifelike rocky structure. A miniature waterfall dispersed water over the rocks in multiple rivulets, which finally united in a small pond at the bottom of the wall. A bonsai banyan tree with a wide girth and umbrella like crown made it picturesque.

Satvik walked up to the big fish tank encased in the rocky wall. He stood there looking at numerous wide-eyed fish, which completely ignored his presence.

He was in awe of the grandiose and majestic aura of Pushkar Mahal. After walking him through the hall and different chambers, Shubhangi held his hand and took him upstairs over the wide steps. The walls upstairs were adorned with paintings of the royal family members.

"This is my great grandfather, King Pruthviraj Chakrapani," she said pointing at the painting. A bulky man with a thick handlebar moustache sat on a decorated chair in kingly attire. He had numerous pearl necklaces around his neck and a long sword in his hands.

"This is my grandfather, Yashvardhan Chakrapani. He was the last official king of *Palam*. He was King until kingdoms were dissolved after India's independence.

This is my father King Nandivardhan Chakrapani and my mother Queen Devyani," she said pointing at the painting of the couple.

King Nandi, Shubhangi's father, was a fat man. He looked stern. For no obvious reasons, Satvik felt scared of him. Her mother looked like an elegant queen. Her mother sat on a throne while her father stood behind her.

"Now I know the secret to your beautiful smile," he said.

Shubhangi stood next to the painting and smiled at him allowing him to compare her smile with that of her mother's.

"Isn't hers better than mine?"

But Satvik was lost in her smile. He was enchanted by everything around him. The royal charm of Pushkar Mahal was intimidating for him.

"Where is your painting Shubhi?"

"I am just a princess. There is still time for me. My coronation is not done yet."

"What do you mean coronation? You will be coroneted?"

"Yes. Then I will be called the queen of *Palam*," she said and posed like a queen with her chin up.

They laughed together.

"You will make a great queen," he said.

"Thank you. I don't think that matters anyway. It's just a stupid tradition."

She took Satvik to her chamber. Her chambermaid waited outside. It was bigger than he had imagined. The flowery walls inside her chamber gave it the feel of a beautiful garden. Big mirrors with engraved golden borders adorned the walls. Long cascading curtains covered the door of the balcony of her chamber. The balcony faced the front garden and the neighboring villas.

It had everything one could ever imagine in a bedroom.

She pressed a button on a remote and music started playing. The ceiling suddenly changed colors and it appeared as if clouds have gathered. Stormy, thundering noises played in the background. Satvik felt as if he was standing in the middle of a storm.

She flicked the button again and ceiling changed into a starry night.

"Isn't it awesome?"

"I've no words. I have never seen anything like it."

Then she played soft romantic music. She came close to him and put her left hand on his shoulder. They performed a ball dance, she guiding him. They looked into each other's eyes as they danced. Her face radiated royal charm. He was in disbelief, unable to believe the closeness between them.

As music played, they danced in unison. She closed her eyes. Their lips came closer. She felt his breath on her soft lips. He wanted to kiss her soft, tender lips in a rapturous kiss. She decided not to resist him if he did.

Never once touching her lips, he remained in a near kiss for a very long time. She moved her face away when she heard a knock on the door.

"Come in," she said.

"Your highness, lunch is ready," chambermaid said.

"Shall we?" she asked.

"Yes, your highness," he said. She smiled at him.

"They don't have to always address me like that, but you are a guest and they are told to do so in front of the guests. That's protocol."

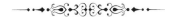

Those were the most beautiful days of their lives. They talked over the phone every night and met over weekends. With every passing day, he was more in love with her.

When Satvik was very certain, he decided to reveal it to Sindbad.

"I am in love," Satvik said.

Sindbad looked at him. He was serious.

"Finally," Sindbad said rolling his eyes.

"I think I am going to propose her," Satvik said.

"Are you serious?"

"Yes. I love her. And I think she loves me too."

"Congratulations. I am so happy for you," Sindbad said giving him a brotherly hug.

"But I need your help."

"Yes, you do. Why I am here? Don't you worry. Just tell me when. I would find just the perfect place," he said.

Satvik knew Sindbad had experience in such matters. His girlfriend Chahek would vouch for his smartness in the matters of love.

Satvik and his friends Sindbad, Amit and Gopal celebrated his acknowledgement of love with a party. His friends supported his decision to tell her how he felt.

After careful consideration, Satvik decided to reveal his love for Shubhangi by the weekend. Sindbad found a beautiful garden in The Blue Lagoon resort as a perfect place for their date.

Satvik arranged a date with Shubhangi on following Sunday.

Chapter 5

Satvik could not sleep thinking about Shubhangi's reaction the next day when he would open his heart to her. He was confused and unsure of her response. But he couldn't hold it anymore. He was ready to take his chance and tell her the truth.

He had a sneaking suspicion she knew how much he loved her. She would know what he was about to tell her. She would read him, his eyes, and his throbbing heart. She would run in to his arms.

In the limitless possibilities of her reaction, his heart sank every time it considered her denial.

The night behaved wickedly. It did not allow him a moment of sleep. His mind kept going over his date with Shubhangi the next day. He kept thinking about words he could use to express his feelings. He kept selecting them, rejecting them and forgetting them. It was as if words were not enough to express what he felt for her.

He couldn't imagine how many times he smiled in sleep until finally dawn broke. In the morning, his eyes beamed with the gratifying anticipation of meeting her.

—→·✦·❈·✧·❈·✦·←—

Built by a lake, The Blue Lagoon resort was known for its beauty. The huge garden in the middle of a picturesque lake made it the best place to wine and dine.

Satvik and Shubhangi sat outside in one of the small huts built for dining. The orange sky was unable to hide the moon that was already up. The moon, accompanied by a few bright stars, shined with potent intentions. The orange sheen of the sky made Shubhangi's face shine like that of a goddess.

After dinner, Satvik took her for a walk. They held hands as they walked on a narrow wooden bridge. They came to an island like garden in the middle of the lake and sat under a banyan tree.

Romantic retro songs played at a distance. Far away from the crowd, trees whispered to themselves. They had witnessed many expressions of love. They were about to witness it again.

The night fell swiftly. The silver white moon shined bright in the sky. The chilly breeze ruffled her curly hair and kept bringing it on her face. Her bangles tinkled as she attempted to sweep her hair back repeatedly, making the most pleasant sound. The air carried her sweet fragrance to him. It's her fragrance that he wanted to hold in his arms, sleep with it and live with it for the rest of his life.

He gently took her hands in his hands. She smiled at him. He could barely smile. Finally, the moment had arrived. He had been waiting for this moment much too long.

"Shubhi," he said softly.

She looked at him with her bright eyes.

"I feel as if we have known each other forever, like we would know each other forever. The thing that I love most in this world is your smile and the brightness in your eyes when you are happy. I want to keep you happy forever. I want to be with you forever. I can't imagine life without you," he said.

Her smile illuminated with every word he spoke.

"I never feel as complete as when I am with you and never feel as restless without you. You are my soul mate."

She kept looking at him. His eyes were filled with deep love.

"Life is strange. So is death. But love is delightful. Love is the meaning of life. For me, you are the meaning of my life," he said.

She looked at his face unblinkingly.

"I need you Shubhi, so much so that my happiness is dependent on you. My days would never be happy if I don't see you by my side every morning."

She smiled at him, her face brightened, her eyes shined.

"I was an atheist. I never believed in God. That's only till I met you. Now I want to believe in God, in Love. I may not be a prince, may not be rich, but I promise that there would be no one in this world who will love you as much as I do. I love you Shubhi," he said.

He saw tears gathering on the brink of her eyes. In that moment, with tears in her eyes, she smiled the most beautiful smile.

"I love you too," she whispered holding his hands tighter. Her whisper, clearly audible, carved every word on his heart.

He wanted to hold her tight in his arms but feared how he would hold someone so tender, so delicate and so dear to him. She bashfully ran in his arms and melted in his embrace. They embraced each other as if they have been waiting for that moment forever.

Her heart heaved tenderly in his embrace. His heart danced like a peacock. Their souls completed each other. Those moments changed their lives forever.

"Promise me, that you would always be by my side?" she asked with her eyes gazing in his soul.

"I promise," he said.

"I promise that I would always be with you. Till I die," she said and hugged him again as tears rolled on her cheeks.

He knew he was the luckiest man on earth. All the reasons that made him an atheist, ceased to exist that moment. He thanked God. He believed in luck, in the miracle and in the belief that sometimes God bestows you with something you do not deserve. All the scars on his orphan heart healed as he held her tightly close to his heart. Life was boring, long, but in those moments in her arms, it felt momentary.

Holding her face in his hands, he kissed her forehead, her eyes, her nose, her chin. Her lips parted, slightly pouted, provoking a kiss. Then she felt the reassuring warmth of his lips on her lips. Her lips felt soft and supple like a rose petal on a dewy morning. Their maiden kiss was tender, gentle, and full of love. They kissed for a long time.

The twilight hour was the finest hour of their lives. The resort, the lake and the young tree had become places to remember and to revisit. They had witnessed the most beautiful moments of their lives, moments they will cherish forever.

As they returned to the resort building, she walked with an exquisite grace befitting of a fine woman. He walked with her as if charmed. There was nothing left to say. Their hearts still talked to each other of the future, of the moments in the future when they would meet again.

She kept remembering his words like a romantic song. Every time she remembered them, she felt the same magic. Her eyes were brilliant. Her heart was filled with love. He felt he was still dreaming. As if it was a fairy tale, in which a beautiful princess found love in an orphan.

———•─•✦•◦❧⟊❦◦•✦•─•———

Satvik's friends were ecstatic to hear the news. It was a news that needed celebration. Satvik also wanted to introduce Shubhangi to all of his friends. He arranged for a party and invited them all.

It was after a long time all of Satvik's friends were together. That day, apart from Sindbad, Amit and Gopal, Gunjan and Chahek too joined the party. Chahek was Sindbad's girlfriend and a fashion designer by profession. Gunjan was Satvik's friend from his office.

Shubhangi brought her friend Anamika with her to the party. Satvik introduced Shubhangi to all his friends.

They all congratulated the couple.

On their friend's insistence, Satvik and Shubhangi retold the story of how they met, fell in love and finally revealed their love for each other.

"So, what made a princess fall in love?" Gunjan asked.

"His pure heart, he is a gentleman," Shubhangi said.

"And what did you find in her?" Gunjan asked looking at Satvik.

"I found my soul mate in her. And of course her beauty. And her eyes. And smile. Actually, everything about her," Satvik replied.

They all laughed at his reply. Through the party, their friends teased the couple.

"So finally you found your Greek Jesus," Anamika said to Shubhangi.

"Well, I got a better deal. And there really is a Greek Jesus in him, it's just not out yet," Shubhangi said.

No one understood what Shubhangi and Anamika meant by Greek Jesus.

"What's Greek Jesus?" Satvik asked.

"When we were in college together, Shubhangi was most sought-after. Boys fought to speak with her. Actually, most were scared of her. She had very high standards. While everyone dated, she was the one who found no one interesting. Once she told us, she would only date a man who is like a Greek Jesus.

We asked what it meant and she explained it to us. It would be a man with a body like a Greek God, but the heart

66

of Jesus. The man who has a serene face like Jesus," Anamika said.

"Really? Is that true?" Chahek asked Shubhangi while everybody else laughed.

"That's true but that was then. And I do find my Greek Jesus in him," Shubhangi said.

Sindbad, Amit and Gopal looked at Satvik. He looked neither Greek nor like Jesus. Satvik looked at Shubhangi puzzled.

"Well, you will do that for me, won't you?" Shubhangi asked.

"Do what?" Satvik asked.

"Be my Greek Jesus."

"I will do anything for you. But I really have no idea how to become a Greek Jesus," Satvik said.

"Leave that to me," Shubhangi said.

They all laughed at Satvik's dumbfounded face.

After the party, Satvik probed Shubhangi more about the Greek Jesus. She chuckled and said it was just a fantasy as a teenager. He knew if he could do anything for her, changing himself into Greek Jesus wasn't the hardest part of it.

To fulfill her fantasy, Satvik needed to build a body like that of a Greek God and perfect the divine look of Lord

Jesus. No matter how hard Satvik tried, he failed miserably imagining himself as a Greek Jesus.

Satvik never liked long hair and always kept his midnight black hair gentlemanly short. Looking like Jesus meant keeping long hair. She insisted he should grow them long enough. Growing hair was easy but building a body like Greek Gods was unimaginable. He never dreamt of joining a gym. He believed he was neither fat nor too skinny to fulfill the necessity of entering a gym. But he was in love and his love, apparently, demanded sacrifice.

"You think you will be a regular?" Sindbad asked when Satvik told him he was joining a gym.

"I don't. That's why I was wondering if you would join me," Satvik asked.

"No thanks, I am not stepping into a gym. Even if Chahek wanted it, I would not be able to do it. But good luck to you," Sindbad said patting his back.

After careful consideration, Satvik subscribed to a well-equipped gym with fancy machines. Negating his belief that he will only find people who are out of shape, the gym was full of muscular men sweating themselves relentlessly on fancy machines.

A group of bulky, muscular men were helping each other working out with heavy weights. They looked like they jumped straight out of a wrestling program on television. He could hear them grunting louder than the music played.

Satvik looked at himself in the mirrors on the wall and realized he wasn't fit after all. Some of them stared at him as if he was the last man on planet earth to join a gym.

"What's your goal?" the trainer asked.

It was difficult to explain the vision of Greek Jesus to him.

"I want to build muscles and have six pack abs," Satvik tried to put it in simple words. Trainer nodded with a contracted grin without looking at him.

"How long do you think it will take?" Satvik asked.

"It depends on how much efforts you put in. First, let's rip off the fat and then build some muscles, okay?"

"Okay," Satvik said. He did not understand what he really meant.

The trainer gave Satvik a tour of gym and finally asked him to run on a treadmill an hour a day for the next one week. Satvik was more interested in the fancy machines other people were using to pump up their muscles. He had no time to waste. But the trainer did not allow him to touch any of those machines.

"If you want to change yourself, all you have to do is listen to me and do what I say," the trainer said.

Satvik unwillingly decided to follow his instructions.

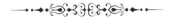

After confessing their love for each other, Satvik and Shubhangi could not bear the separation of a week. Despite

69

nightly phone calls, meeting on weekends seemed far too long a wait. They started meeting on weekdays whenever they could.

They visited Chhaya Sadan together on weekends. They took the children out on excursions whenever they could. The children loved Princess Shubhangi. They were always delighted to be with her and eagerly waited for her visits.

Despite Satvik's resistance, many times Shubhangi drove the van when they went out with the children. She always bought gifts for the children and played with them with a childlike enthusiasm. Spending time with Shubhangi and his children gave immense pleasure to Satvik.

Satvik felt his life couldn't be any better. Shubhangi had brought joy into his life. Everything was perfect. To his surprise, he was more regular to gym than he thought he would be. He was determined to be Shubhangi's Greek Jesus.

Chapter 6

Not before long, Satvik realized Shubhangi was a fashionista. She had a penchant for shopping and flair for fashion trends. Being a princess, she was skilled in the art of subtle differentiation, the art of minute detailing that made her stand out.

They spent weekends together, most of which was on shopping. In Satvik, Shubhangi found a companion for shopping. When they had no plans, shopping was the plan. She surprised Satvik with her ability to shop for hours together.

Shopping was not Satvik's favorite part of being with Shubhangi, but he had no choice. He was happy to spend as much time as possible with her.

Shubhangi was clear headed and had an unclouded sense of decision-making. That did not work when it came to shopping. She went clueless in trial rooms. More clothes she tried, more confused she got.

To Satvik, everything she tried looked good on her slender body, her fair skin. She made every new dress insignificant, making it a trivial part of her overall charm. He was mesmerized every time she twirled in front of him asking for his opinion.

"What do you think?" She would ask Satvik.

"Awesome, it looks really great on you!" he would reply with animated effects on his face.

She always sensed his diplomacy. Whenever he praised her and told her everything looks great on her, she ignored his advice.

"Really?" She would say rolling her deep gray eyes.

Sometimes that made him wonder about the importance she gave to his opinion. Over time, he learnt. When a woman wants an opinion from a man, all she wants him to do is to read her mind and tell her what she wants to hear. That's never easy.

He constantly observed her eyes for the brightness, which indicated her liking to the clothes she was trying. Her creamy face would turn crimson in anticipation of appreciation. All he had to do was to smile and to appreciate.

"Absolutely gorgeous!" he would say winking his eyes.

When no one was looking, he would secretly fly her a kiss. If she blushed, it worked. If she widened her eyes and stared in anger, he misjudged. It was a guessing game.

On one such Sunday morning, they had planned for shopping. Satvik woke up late. He missed his breakfast to be with Shubhangi on time.

Although there is nothing that could be remotely attributed to Mahatma Gandhi, but as it is in most cities, *Pune* has its Mahatma Gandhi road, called MG road.

MG road, an extremely up market road with shopping malls and restaurants, always buzzed with beautifully dressed young crowd. The girls wore tight jeans, high heels, evident mascara and walked hand in hand with their boyfriends. With their competition to look distinguished yet to belong to the same league, the street was usually full of latest fashions and accessories on their bodies. Many eyes met, hearts bonded and relationships ended on MG road.

When Satvik reached, Shubhangi was waiting for him. Her sunglasses pulled up her hair, the delicate strand of her necklace quietly shined on her slender neck. Her soft pink lips performed her pleasant smile. It made him forget his hunger for a moment.

She was in a good mood. That meant many hours of shopping.

For next two hours Shubhangi spent time looking at various designer clothes and trying them on. She kept trying and showing them to Satvik and kept looking more beautiful every time. All he did was to appreciate each one of them.

While she was busy trying, Satvik picked up a cherry red party gown. He was curious to see her in it.

"Are you sure? Don't you think it's little loud?" she tried to protest.

"No, it's not. Try it on for me, would you?" he insisted.

She came out of the trial room in that sleeveless red gown and twirled in front of him. The velvety gown tightly hugged her beautiful form. The red color of gown enhanced the color of her fair skin. He never imagined she would look so much of a temptress in that gown.

He felt a sense of pride.

"You look gorgeous," he said with his mouth agape.

She winked at him and quickly went inside. Her image still lingered in his mind. To his disappointment, she did not buy it.

"It's skimpy and tight. Besides, it's not my taste," she said.

"But you looked amazingly sexy," he said. She pinched him hard. He almost screamed.

Patience is a virtue put to test when you accompany a woman for shopping, especially when that woman is a princess. His enthusiasm died down by the time her shopping was half-done. He was hungry but could not elope from the scene. His stomach was screaming at him.

He felt dragged like a surrendered soldier whose hands were tied with bags full of shopping. He cursed shopping malls and their owners at once. Towards the end of her shopping, his legs ached with pain. He thought a glass of glucose would help regain vital energy to walk with her.

Finally, after what felt like many hours, she was done.

"That's enough for today. Let's go get some lunch. Are you hungry?" She asked giving him a cheerful smile.

He tried hard to put an appropriate smile hiding his happiness but failed miserably.

"I am dying of hunger, let's get out of here please," he pleaded.

"I guessed that looking at your face. Let's go to a 'Chettinad' restaurant, it's around the corner," she said.

———◆·◆·❦·✜❩❴❫·❦·◆·◆———

'Chettinad,' a south Indian restaurant famous for its authentic southern food, was a place for diners with exquisite taste. Despite its rustic charm, diners kept it crowded. They managed to get the table fairly quickly.

A man in a white shirt and even whiter *lungi* came running and suddenly stopped at their table. It startled Satvik. Then he realized the man in saintly white was a waiter. Ignoring Satvik's reaction, he spread two banana leaves on their table and vanished as quickly as he came.

Satvik raised his eyebrows suggesting his surprise to Shubhangi.

"Come on! You know food is served on banana leaves? It's a valued tradition in South-India," Shubhangi snubbed his surprise.

"I knew, but never ate on banana leaf," he said.

"Well, it's different. And yes, the food is yummy. You would love it," she said excitedly.

"Can't wait," he said.

First, it was rice. The waiter served a big pile of rice on his banana leaf. Satvik thought it was meant for both of them. Then he served same amount of rice to Shubhangi. Another waiter who looked like a sibling of earlier one came dashing. Satvik figured there was one waiter to serve one dish. They all come in sequence and same waiter never visited the table again.

In around ten bowls on banana leaves, ten different curries were served. Equal amounts of pickles and chutneys were served. He was hungry and relished everything.

Satvik felt the food was delicious and fulfilling. It titillated all his taste buds. When he was done, he was fully contented.

"The food is really good," he said in appreciation.

"What did I tell you?" she said.

Satvik was full and had no appetite for dessert. Shubhangi ordered *pista-kulfi*.

"Happy with the shopping?" he asked.

She blinked and smiled, "very."

"You should have bought that gown. I can't tell you how amazing you looked in it," he said.

"It was skimpy. I wouldn't be able to wear it for any occasion."

"You could have kept it just for me."

"If it's just you, do I have to wear anything?" she asked and blinked at him.

Satvik was taken aback trying to imagine what she had just suggested.

"Hold on to those dirty thoughts Mr. Satvik Bharat. There will be time for that, and now is not the one," she said laughing.

Shubhangi extended her *kulfi* to Satvik. While he relished on the *kulfi* from her hand, she held his other hand and kissed it ever so slightly. A smile spread across their faces as they lost in to each other.

"Shubhi!" a voice broke their trance.

Shubhangi looked in the direction and quickly pulled her hand while moving away from him. Satvik looked at her frightened face, which, a moment ago, beamed with happiness.

"What's wrong?" Satvik asked.

"Mooni uncle!" she said with a forced smile on her face.

Satvik looked in the direction. He came face to face with an old, bald man in Kurta and Pajama. His bulbous eyes held enormous anger making him look scary.

"Shubhi, what are you doing here?" he shouted as he came close to them.

Satvik tried to sideline himself from his line of vision. But the man stared at him in anger. Satvik inquisitively looked at Shubhangi.

His foremost thought was that they ran in Shubhangi's father, but she had called him 'Mooni uncle.' Besides, he had seen her father in the paintings and he wasn't the one.

"I came for shopping," Shubhangi said pointing at the bags as she got up from her seat.

Satvik stood up and tried to smile in an effort to loosen the tension. The bald man stared at him, steadily moving his gaze from top to toe. It was difficult but Satvik continued to spread as much smile as possible.

"With him? Who is this man?" He asked pointing his plump forefinger at Satvik.

This man, you are pointing at, is the man that woman loves, Satvik wanted to answer the bald uncle. By now, other diners noticed the commotion and curiously gazed at them.

"He is my friend Satvik," she said and continued to introduce them before they form opinion about each other.

"This is Mooni uncle," she said looking at Satvik.

"Hi," Satvik said and promptly extended his hand.

Mooni neglected his advance.

"Is he your boyfriend?"

"Why are you asking?'"

"It didn't look like you are just friends. Kissing hands and sharing food? All that with a stranger?"

"He is not a stranger uncle."

"Is he your boyfriend?"

Mooni asked a direct question. Shubhangi looked at Satvik. Her face became taut. He had caught them red handed. Satvik's throat dried gauging the seriousness of the situation.

"Yes, he is my boyfriend" she shook her head in agreement.

Satvik looked at her and then at her uncle. Mooni was in a shock. His eyes bulged out. He did not expect such a sudden disclosure of her relationship.

Mooni looked at Satvik with an obvious anger on his face. Shubhangi's words gave Satvik a courage he needed. He regained his posture and filed his chest with fresh air. It felt good.

"I am Satvik," he said extending his hand again.

Mooni ignored his gesture again. He saw through him.

"Come with me. I will take you home," he said looking at Shubhangi.

Shubhangi did not say a word. With a cautious fear, Satvik pointed at the bags to grab Mooni's attention. He intended Mooni to take those bags if he wanted to take Shubhangi home.

"What is your name again?" Mooni asked looking at Satvik.

"Satvik Bharat," he uttered those words with great difficulty. They came out like a whisper.

"Satvik?" he asked.

Satvik shook his head in agreement, his courage almost died down.

"Come here, I want to talk to you," Mooni said and dragged him aside away from Shubhangi.

"You stay there," he said to Shubhangi. Shubhangi stood there looking at them while Mooni dragged Satvik to the corner. Few of the waiters and diners inquisitively glanced at Mooni and Satvik.

"Do you know who she is?" Mooni asked

Satvik nodded. He was scared.

"She is the princess of *Palam*. If you don't want to get yourself killed, don't see her again," he said pointing finger at Satvik.

For the first time Satvik could see Mooni's face clearly. Bulbous eyes between his ancient baldhead and a pompous nose made him look scary. Satvik did not like Mooni threatening him. He was not good at handling threats. His face reddened with the rush of adrenalin.

"I love her," Satvik said gathering all the courage he could.

He felt the sense of freeing himself from all the restraints. As if, he had just declared his love to entire world. It was liberating.

Before Satvik could bask in the pride of the declaration of his love, Mooni pushed Satvik in anger. With an unexpected push, Satvik lost his balance and fell hard on the floor.

Shubhangi rushed to him and helped him get on his legs. Few of the waiters gathered around them ready to intervene in the flammable situation.

"What are you doing?" Shubhangi shouted at Mooni.

"This is your friend? He says he loves you," Mooni screamed at Shubhangi.

Satvik's elbow was bleeding from his free fall on the floor. When Shubhangi noticed his bleeding elbow, her anger rose. Her eyes filled with tears.

"Yes we do! I love him too and it's none of your business," Shubhangi spoke to Mooni in anger.

Mooni realized he might have gone a little too far with it. Hearing Shubhangi's words, Satvik forgot his pain.

"Princess, enough of this drama, please come with me," Mooni said mellowed.

Satvik looked at Shubhangi. She had regained her composure. She blinked her eyes as if assuring him everything will be all right.

"I will see you later, bye." She waived her hand before walking away with her uncle.

"Bye," Satvik whispered.

Mooni turned and gave Satvik an angry stare before taking the bags and walking away.

Shell shocked at what had transpired, Satvik stood there for a minute. He kept looking at them as they disappeared. A stream of blood trickled down his forearm.

He was the center of attention of the entire restaurant. People looked at him and whispered to fellow diners trying to make sense of what had happened. Satvik was least worried about them. He walked dragging his feet. Adrenalin rush masked the pain of his wounded elbow.

He was scared. Shubhangi never told him about Mooni. Mooni did not look like one that belonged to a royal family. But he happened to be close enough to Shubhangi to hurt him. There could be many Mooni's in the royal family. Satvik thought.

Chapter 7

It was hard to believe but Mooni Dixit was treasurer of the Chakrapani family. He was also an official advisor to King Nandi. Mooni took more pride in being the royal advisor more than a treasurer. Mooni was also a person King Nandi was most likely to name, when asked to name at least one of his friends.

Mooni was bald with a bulbous nose and rusty handlebar moustache. He had villainy to his face and looked as if he had just walked out of mythical books. He took pride in his looks and nurtured it with coconut oil.

Mooni lived in one of the many outhouses in Pushkar Mahal. He cooked his own food, washed his clothes, cleaned his dishes and did all his daily chores himself. He was a self-reliant man who did not need assistance of a woman to survive.

If man is a social animal, Mooni did not meet that criterion. As a child, Mooni tried to be social and friendly, but that never worked. When he was young, he considered the possibility of inadequacy in his efforts to make friends, but after numerous attempts, he was certain nothing was wrong with him. It was as if entire world was against being friends with him.

Mooni believed in himself, and in God, but mostly in himself. He was a devout Hindu and practiced Bramhacharya. For a Brahmachari, a mere thought of woman is forbidden and celibacy is not optional. Mooni chose this path for himself. He never married. He believed he had seen many wise men getting lost in obscurity after marriage.

The truth was that he knew a wife would be a lifelong opposition and he was a man who hated everything that opposed him. There was not enough space in his life to love someone else other than himself and the royal family.

So womankind had very little role to play in his life and that was limited to his grandmother raising him as a child. For these very reasons, he had grown into a bitter old man. He had no interest other than that of the Chakrapani family.

Mooni had been working with Chakrapani's since he was a child. Although always in an outhouse, he grew up with Nandi. His grandmother worked for the royal family and when she died, she asked Mooni to serve the royal family. As he grew old, Nandi treated Mooni more like a distant family member than one of his trusted servants.

Mooni was more loyal to Nandi than to himself. He never went to school, but he managed all the finances for Nandi. Book-keeping was done by the managers of the oil mills Nandi owned. Mooni simply collected money and deposited it in banks.

King Nandi and Mooni met every evening unless Nandi was busy with something more important. Mooni informed Nandi of all the happenings of the day and provided him with the numbers he had gathered from sales. Nandi took advice from Mooni on many matters including those that were personal.

Shubhangi was like a daughter to Mooni. She was the only child he ever liked. Not that he hated other children, but they always seemed to have a different impression of Mooni. For them, he was hostile and scary at the same time.

It was not just children, even grownups felt the same way about Mooni. Mooni never made efforts to make someone like him. He was free from the obligation of being a likable human.

In Mooni's old car that was a gift from Nandi when it was too old to drive, Shubhangi sat quietly. Furor in her silence was obvious to Mooni.

She did not speak to him. He had no business threatening Satvik, more so pushing him with such hostility. She knew Satvik wouldn't have reacted to Mooni.

She was scared for different reasons. It was only a matter of time before Mooni would tell her father about her love affair. Shubhangi knew her father never truly behaved like a king. Never gave more importance to the prestige than to his family.

But this was different. She wasn't sure about her father's reaction. He would be angry. On the other hand, he may just talk to her and would ask more about Satvik. Whatever happens, she knew, was not going to be easy.

The hard thing for Mooni was to find his own fault but even harder was to admit one. He believed that in the incident that happened with Shubhangi and her friend, he reacted courteously. He did not attack Shubhangi's friend. He just pushed him a bit. That too because he couldn't control his anger when he saw a stranger cozying up with princess Shubhangi.

He glanced at Shubhangi who was looking outside car window avoiding him. Her hands were tightly folded to her chest.

"What am I supposed to do? I don't know how else I would have reacted?" he tried to break her silence.

Shubhangi did not say a word.

"This behavior does not suit you. This incident will bring pain to his highness. He wants to marry you in a royal family, a family that is a match for Chakrapani," he tried to console her while carefully driving the old car.

If there was anyone else after her father whom she respected, it was Mooni. That did not mean he could misbehave with her friends. Especially the one she loved. Shubhangi thought. She continued looking outside the window.

She knew that was not going to help her. If Mooni wanted, he could keep it a secret. He can choose not to talk about the incident with her father. That was unlikely if she did not talk to Mooni nicely and did not convince him.

"And do what? Just because I am a princess, I can't fall in love? That is so stupid," she protested.

85

"I know. Would you tell that yourself to your father? He has a weak heart. He already suffered a heart attack. You know it. The future of the Chakrapani dynasty worries him. He sees a son in you," he said.

Shubhangi knew Mooni was partly right.

"Uncle, would you keep this from my father?" Shubhangi requested Mooni.

"I am not going to tell your father. Not so soon. But only if you promise to not see your friend again."

"I love him. And he loves me. He is a nice man. He makes me happy. Like my father does, you do. He treats me like a princess."

"You are too young to know a person."

"I have known him long enough."

"I doubt. What does he do for a living? Who are his parents?"

"He doesn't have parents. He is orphan. And he ..." before Shubhangi could finish her sentence, Mooni brought his car to a screeching halt.

"What? Orphan? Forget it Shubhi. It's never going to happen. Did you just go out and fell in love with a roadside beggar?"

"Uncle! He is not a beggar," she said looking at him with an evident anger in her voice.

"Then what is it that you saw in him? Make me understand, why would a princess of Chakrapani dynasty fall in love with an orphan?"

"I am not going to talk if you are not even ready to listen."

"Well then what choice do I have but to tell your father?"

"To start with, instead of hitting Satvik, you could have talked with him like a normal person."

"I did not hit him. I pushed him. There is a difference. And I feel sorry for that, I was angry, but who wouldn't be," Mooni tried to cover up for his mistake.

Shubhangi did not speak for a while.

Mooni was obliged to listen to her. After all, she was a princess and he was merely a royal servant. Mooni knew King Nandi would not be very happy to know about her boyfriend especially when he is an orphan.

Mooni just met Satvik and he already hated him. He wanted to make every effort to get him out of Shubhangi's life before it was too late.

"You are right. I am sorry I reacted the way I shouldn't have," Mooni said.

Shubhangi looked at him in surprise.

"I want to make it right. Want to give him a chance and not tell your father," he said.

"You would?" she asked.

Mooni nodded.

"Would you arrange a meeting with your friend? Just him and me. I would like to know more about him. But promise me, if I did not like him, you would stop seeing him. And if you didn't, I will have no choice but to tell your father," he said.

That's what Shubhangi wanted, to stop Mooni from telling the news to her father.

She was happy that Mooni was ready to meet Satvik. Mooni may not approve of Satvik but she could use some time before her father comes to know about them. Besides, she knew Mooni's opinion would not matter to her father if he met Satvik without her father's permission.

"I will arrange a lunch between you two," she said hiding her delighted expressions.

Mooni had no intentions to hide the news from King Nandi. In fact, he was eager to tell him as soon as possible. He knew he had to act quickly or the budding love would soon become rebellious. He could already feel a revolt in Shubhangi's manners.

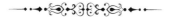

Satvik felt like a person who was robbed of his life's saving. His mind was still in disbelief, vaguely remembering the events that transpired in the afternoon.

He felt as if he never deserved Shubhangi. It had all been so much like a fairytale, a princess falling in love with an orphan. He never truly believed he would have her forever. The dream had come to an end.

When he told Sindbad about what happened that afternoon with Mooni, Sindbad laughed and congratulated Satvik shaking his hand vigorously.

Surprised by his gesture, Satvik asked, "I don't understand?"

"What were you expecting? It had to happen one day. It's good that it happened this way. This is the icebreaker. Now it's time to prove your love to the world," he said.

What Sindbad said made sense to Satvik. Someday it had to be known to the world. Maybe it was time. Maybe what happened that day would lead their love to more meaningful destination, Satvik thought.

But he was not prepared. Neither was Shubhangi. They never talked about it. They were busy nurturing their love, unaware of the world.

Gradually his mind accepted what had happened that afternoon. He could vividly remember it. He went over and over again on how Shubhangi declared her love for him. Every time he thought about it, a wave of happiness filled his heart.

He was determined to have her, to fight with all obstacles in every way possible, to hold her in his arms.

────※───

King Nandi sat in his study after having his afternoon nap. He was thinking about his daughter, princess Shubhangi.

He couldn't believe Shubhangi was turning twenty-one. Time flew fast. Soon she would be married. Thought of her marriage worried Nandi. She was the only heir to the Chakrapani dynasty.

Despite her not caring about the outwardly beauty, Shubhangi had turned in to a finest young woman, one of the most beautiful princesses. There were not many royal families and finding a princess as beautiful as Shubhangi was impossible. Nandi knew any prince would be more than happy to marry her.

Nandi was a proud father. He could never imagine not having her around. But such are the ways of the word. She must leave her home after marriage. He would be happy to send her with her husband, but only in a royal family.

Many a times he imagined having her married to a man who would stay with him as a son, who would look after his business and most of all, who would name their first son after Chakrapani and carry forward the name of the Chakrapanis.

To find a man who is worthy of marrying one's daughter is never easy. It is a difficult task even for a king. He had to do it. One of these days, he decided to visit Makhan Baba and talk with him about Shubhangi's marriage.

After his heart attack previous year, he hardly went out. He had grown fat and his weak knees complained when he walked for long. He could not visit his businesses or manage his finances well. Mooni handled that part well. He trusted Mooni. He was a loyal servant. Almost like a friend. Without Mooni, it would be difficult to manage the operations of his oil mills.

If he had a son, he would have assigned him with all the responsibilities. He wasn't willing to burden Shubhangi with manly affairs. He wanted her to live a happy life and never worry about earning money.

Nandi was lost in these thoughts when he heard a knock on the door. It was time for Mooni's evening visit.

As a routine, servant offered them an evening tea. Mooni provided Nandi with details of daily business. He was eager to be done with it to share important information. Finally, when they finished discussing usual business, Mooni cleared his throat and croaked in his unique style.

"I have some news about princess Shubhangi I should share, if you permit," he said.

Alarmed by mention of Shubhangi, Nandi asked with curiosity, "What is it?"

"Nothing Serious, but it must be attended before it becomes one."

Nandi kept looking at him awaiting him to share the news. Mooni hesitated for a moment before saying, "Shubhangi is in love."

No one spoke for a minute. Nandi was not expecting this news. He wasn't sure how he felt inside. He was neither sad nor happy. He felt curious.

"Who is it? Tell me more," Nandi said.

"I don't know anything about him. I saw them together. They were holding hands in a restaurant."

"They could be friends," Nandi said unwilling to accept Mooni's inference.

"I asked them about it. They said they love each other."

"Shubhi said that?"

"She did."

"Who is this man? Do you know?"

"I met him for the first time. All I know about him is that he is not worthy of Princess."

"Why? What makes you say that?"

"He is an orphan and not a match for Shubhangi."

Mooni narrated Nandi the complete story about how he caught them displaying their affection in public. In his narration, the man with whom she was in love was a conman who may have deceived Shubhangi to fall in love with him.

Nandi was alarmed. A moment ago, he wasn't sure how he felt about the news, but after Mooni's narration he was certain he was not happy with the situation.

The daughter of the Chakrapani dynasty can only marry in a royal family of equal stature. Marrying an orphan would be a shame to the Chakrapani dynasty. Such a marriage is unthinkable. Just a rumor of such a possibility could malign generations of name and respect for the Chakrapani dynasty.

Nandi trusted Shubhangi to be a reasonable young woman who wouldn't fall in love with a commoner. But he knew young age is unreasonable. Even the wise make mistakes in youth. Shubhi was just an innocent girl, unaware of the ways of the ordinary world. She wouldn't know better. Besides, it wasn't a secret Shubhangi was a princess. There were men who would do anything to get married to her for her money.

Father in him justified Shubhangi's innocence and proved Satvik's cruelty.

"This must be stopped before it gets out of hands," Nandi spoke after a long silence.

"I couldn't have said it any better. Shubhangi is innocent. He must have lured her in to it for money," Mooni said.

"Does Shubhi know that we know it?"

Mooni narrated Nandi the discussion he had with Shubhangi and how Shubhangi wanted to hide the news from her father. Mooni felt he proved his loyalty to the king by letting him know the truth.

Nandi was angry with Satvik because Shubhangi wanted to hide it from him. He saw how an unknown stranger could turn his own daughter against him. Nandi was certain that the man she loved was not the right choice for her. They needed to do something about it.

Mooni and Nandi discussed about what they could possibly do to make Satvik leave her alone. They both had no experience in the matters of love. They were men who could hardly speak of love. They knew such things could go out of hand, if not handled carefully.

They decided Mooni would meet Satvik alone over lunch to know more about him. He would then amicably ask Satvik to stay away from Shubhangi. If it comes to it, Mooni would threaten him of dire consequences.

"I don't want to involve Shubhangi in this. She shouldn't know a word about it." Nandi said.

"Be no worried about it your highness, she wouldn't know a thing." Mooni Said.

After the news Mooni shared, Nandi wanted to act fast and ensure that he took Shubhangi's marriage on priority.

"Find the best marriage bureau experienced in providing matchmaking services to royal families. I want to start looking out for the grooms."

"That is a great idea. I will be on it right away," Mooni said.

There was one more thing Nandi decided. He wanted to talk to Makhan Baba at the earliest possible.

Makhan Baba was his spiritual Guru. Nandi was a devotee of Makhan Baba and took his advice in all the matters. He trusted Makhan Baba more than anybody else in the world. He had seen Baba's divine powers many a times. There was no problem in the world that Baba could not solve.

Nandi knew if nothing worked, Makhan Baba would be his only hope.

———•→•◦•⊹⟨⟩⋄⟨⟩⋄•◦•←•———

After what seemed like a dreadful afternoon, Shubhangi eagerly waited for the night to talk to Satvik. She wasn't worried about the revelation of their love to Mooni uncle anymore. She had talked with Mooni that evening. She was happy Mooni did not tell about them to her father. Mooni offered to meet Satvik to know more about him. He had become their confidante.

When she called Satvik that night, she was more drawn to him than ever. A little obstacle had brought them closer than ever. They talked as if they hadn't talked in ages.

She felt sorry and apologized to Satvik for Mooni's behavior. She asked about his elbow. He chuckled about injury so she wouldn't worry about it a bit.

"Did you at least visit the doctor?" she asked.

"It was nothing I couldn't handle," he said.

Satvik had angered her by not visiting the doctor. She blew air on his elbow and kissed it over the phone. He thanked and told her that the bruises healed with her magic kiss. She laughed.

"Elbow wasn't the only thing, you know," he said.

"Really, what else?" she asked.

"I bit my lips when I fell down. If you could work your magic there too."

"You are shameless. You are sentenced to a month without kisses."

He pleaded guilty and asked for forgiveness. She generously reduced his sentences to a week. Satvik praised her generosity.

"Mooni uncle was sorry about what he did to you. He did it in anger," she said.

"You don't have to do this for him. It's alright. I can imagine why he was so angry."

"Well, that's not the only good news. He offered to help us. But before that, he wants to meet you and know more about you."

"What does that mean?"

"It means he wants to talk to you over lunch."

"Like a date?"

"Yes, like a date."

"And you would be there?"

"No, he wants to talk to you alone. You know, man to man. It's better if I am not there, you can talk frankly."

"I don't have a good feeling about this. But I will think about it."

"You have to meet him. If he likes you, he would help us. My father listens to him. When time is right, we will tell my parents. He could help convince them. Just make him feel comfortable with the idea that you are the right man for me."

"Well, I don't think I am the right man for you. No one could ever be."

She giggled, "I am flattered, but that's not up to you to decide."

Shubhangi kept insisting until he agreed to have lunch with Mooni. Satvik had no options. He was ready to do anything that would help him be with her.

She insisted Satvik must make a good impression on Mooni. She knew convincing Mooni was not easy, but it was not impossible either.

As they went to bed that night, they were happy and hopeful about the future of their love. Unaware of the fact that Nandi and Mooni had already planned their future.

Chapter 8

Mornings were busy for Makhan Baba. Every morning, hundreds of devotees gathered in the *Ashram* for his blessings. Makhan Baba was preparing himself for morning prayers when his close disciple Pandit knocked on doors of his chamber.

Pandit was not really a disciple. He was Baba's associate. He could be called confidant since he knew Baba's many secrets. Baba knew Pandit's secret too. Pandit was wanted by the police for a bank robbery. Their secrets were safe with each other.

It was long time ago. Back then, Pandit was known as Pandurang. No one believed Pandurang when he said he robbed a bank but did not take the money. He told the truth. He managed to break in to the bank but could not break the safe. He ran away without taking any money.

In the morning, the bank manager emptied safe before calling Police. Pandurang had left all the evidence for the Police to book him for a bank robbery. It was impossible for Pandurang to prove his innocence. He stayed away from police and became a part of Baba's *Ashram*. After assuming a new name as Pandit, a long beard and saffron gown, no one could recognize Pandurang.

"Who is it?" Baba asked without giving him permission to enter his chamber.

"It's the King of *Palam*," Pandit said winking at Baba.

Baba hurriedly snatched the phone from his hands and signaled him to go out. Pandit complied.

"Your majesty, what an auspicious morning," Baba greeted Nandi.

"Good morning Baba, I want to meet you. It's urgent," Nandi said.

"Anytime, I can always make time for someone special like you."

"I am thankful. I should come by in the afternoon."

"I will wait for you. Is everything alright?"

"Things are fine. Something important has come up. I want your blessings. Only you can guide me on the right path."

"My blessings are always with you."

"I know and I thank you for that Baba. I shall see you as soon as possible," Nandi said.

It was not always that Nandi himself called Makhan Baba. His servants arranged meetings with Baba for him. Baba knew something was bothering Nandi, which only meant easy and good money.

King Nandi had been Baba's devotee for many years. He came to see Baba every month and sought his blessings. He was one of Baba's most lucrative devotees and donated huge amounts of money to the *Ashram*.

After a sumptuous lunch, Baba awaited King Nandi while relieving stress by watching songs on a large television in his closet. The closet was full of modern electronic gadgets. It also encased a big liquor cabinet full of imported liquor bottles.

Baba knew the world around him was changing fast. There was huge competition when it came to being a practicing Baba. He had to keep up with trends to keep his devotees. He believed one way to do that was to watch television. Especially watch other Babas who appeared on television and learn preaching.

Baba knew it ought to be bad for his reputation, if someone saw him feasting on *kebab* with imported rum while watching dubbed English movies. That's why no one was allowed to enter Makhan Baba's room without his permission. Not even Pandit.

Makhan Baba had been living his dream. It wasn't easy to become the famous Baba he was.

Baba had always been a lazy man who indulged in pleasing his senses. Since childhood, he respected secluded laziness. He was secluded mostly because he had no friends. Other children of his age bullied him and taunted him. They called him 'Chor, chor, Makhanchor.' It was not his fault that his name was Makhanchor. It was not his mother's fault either. She was the only person who loved Makhan. She named him Makhanchor after one of numerous names of Lord Krishna.

When Makhan was old enough to be someone but was no one, his mother thought marriage would bring a change in his estranged life.

It did.

Laziness made Makhan believe in luck. Makhan thought he could try his luck with marriage. Instead of bringing comfort in his life, marriage brought him discomfort. His wife made him work and earn for his family.

He became a postman. It was the only job he could get with his slight qualifications. It did not allow him any rest. Through the day, he peddled his bicycle and went door to door to deliver mail.

One night after surviving a year into marriage, the postman had a self-realization. He knew he was born for a special purpose that did not include delivering mails. Makhan ran away from home. This was just before local post office started receiving complaints about undelivered money orders for that month.

Before realizing the purpose of his scrawny body in this world, Makhan spent six months among a gang of saffron clad Babas. They were on a perennial pilgrimage to nowhere.

He was amazed by their lifestyle. They did not do any work. They slept for most of the day. Everywhere they went, people worshipped them, touched their feet and offered them good food, money and gifts. At that moment, he knew he was born to be a Baba.

Even before his beard could grow long enough to testify to his saintly status, he wore a saffron gown. It felt good, as if he was a part of the band of carefree, bearded yet powerful men.

When he thought he was ready, he distanced himself from the gang. He came to *Pune* in search of a place to setup his own *Ashram*.

He found an old temple of Lord *Shiva* on a hill at the outskirt of the city. It stood majestically amidst an atmosphere of divinity. It had a beautiful structure with a large courtyard. The tall structure of front gate was magnificently carved in black stone. The temple was not well kept but there was a soothing calmness to it. It was a perfect place to start his *Ashram*.

Soon he found an associate who kept the temple clean, offered pujas in the temple with him and kept the rumor mills running. His name was Pandurang. He was running away from the police after a bank robbery. Baba took him under his wings and changed his name to Pandit.

Pandit was street smart. He quickly gathered few more associates for Baba. They helped him erect his *Ashram* on the hill around the temple.

Rumors about Makhan Baba started spreading like a wildfire. It told about his divine power of curing chronic diseases and helping people fulfill their wishes. The rumors said Lord *Shiva* took time to come in Makhan Baba's dream and asked him to setup *Ashram* and cure people of their misery. Rumors believed Baba once was a rich man living a luxurious life before he came there to serve people.

Makhan felt humbled when he heard a rumor that he could burn anyone who angered him. It also worried him thinking about if he would ever be put to test. But nothing really angered him. Thing that he learnt from his pilgrimage was to always have a perpetual expression of happiness on the face.

His group of associates led by Pandit closely guarded Baba's secrets. They devised ideas to impress devotees during prayers. They spied on rich devotees and made Baba a fortuneteller. In turn, Baba rewarded his associates generously.

Over time, the list of Baba's devotees grew in number. It included big names in the city. They kept Baba happy by bestowing him with money and gifts.

———•••◆•◈◦◇◦◈•◆•••———

King Nandi truly believed in Makhan Baba. He confided in Baba. Baba's blessings had helped him through good and bad times in his life.

Nandi's father King Yashvardhan spent most of the royal wealth in pursuit of his happiness. When Yashvardhan was old and about to die, the future of the Chakrapani Dynasty worried him. He wanted a grandson from Nandi.

Nandi was a proud father when Shubhangi was born. His happiness couldn't last long as his father, Yashvardhan, showed clear disappointment. He wanted a grandson who could take the name of the Chakrapani dynasty forward.

Yashvardhan died soon after. He made Nandi promise him that he would carry forward the name of the Chakrapani dynasty. For many years, he and his wife Devyani tried for a son but she couldn't conceive a second child.

Nandi suffered from sleeplessness. He visited numerous doctors and finally gave up on good sleep.

It was then that Nandi heard of Makhan Baba's miraculous powers to cure any disease. He turned to Makhan Baba. It did not take long for Baba to know the reasons he couldn't sleep well. Baba told him that his daughter would grow up to marry a prince. That she will bear a courageous son who would take the name of Chakrapani. He blessed Nandi and gave him powdered ash to drink with water every night before sleeping.

That night Nandi slept well in years. Nandi was so pleased with Baba that he bestowed him with lavish gifts and became his devotee. After that day, Nandi did not take any major decision without consulting Baba.

Nandi knew Baba would find an answer to the problem Shubhangi had created. That's why he did not waste time in arranging a meeting with Makhan Baba.

Nandi entered Baba's chamber in a hurry. His nostrils filled with the familiar aroma of incense sticks. Baba greeted him as Nandi touched Baba's feet.

Nandi narrated him his royal predicament. Baba had predicted that Shubhangi would marry a prince and fulfill the last wish of his dead father. Instead of a prince, she was falling in love with an orphan.

Makhan Baba saw an opportunity. His eyes widened. He wanted to look sad, but a wave of happiness spread across his face. He knew his facial hair had grown wild enough to hide his expressions.

"*Beti* is in love?" after what felt like a long silence, Baba spoke.

"With an orphan," Nandi said emphasizing every word.

Baba pondered, staring in the blank. Nandi stared at Baba's divine face.

"Such have become the ways of the world," Makhan said still staring in the blank.

Nandi kept looking at Baba's face. It was difficult to judge what Baba was thinking. He waited eagerly, "Baba, say something. I don't want her to ever think of him. Ever. I am ready to pay whatever it takes," Nandi said.

Baba closed his eyes. He kept his eyes closed for a long time. Nandi kept looking at him, awaiting his eyes to open.

Finally, Baba opened his eyes and smiled.

"What is it Baba?"

"It is the time, the time, mightiest of them all. It has come. The time has come to marry your daughter. Prepare yourself for her marriage and you shall find a royal match you always wanted," Baba said enlightened by his visions.

A wave of happiness ran through Nandi's body. Once again, Baba knew what was on his mind. He had already started preparing for Shubhangi's marriage by asking Mooni for a marriage bureau. With Baba's permission, his determination was strengthened.

"What about Shubhangi's willingness? What if she doesn't agree to marry anyone other than that orphan?" Nandi asked.

"We must perform a *Jaap*, a prayer, to get her mind away from the bastard. Only if you want. I will perform the *Jaap* and request Lord *Shiva* to clear her mind. It takes three days to complete the *Jaap*. I would not be able to serve any of my devotees. They will be disappointed."

"Baba, I request your help. I always believed in you. Please help me," Nandi requested.

"I know this is a sensitive matter. You are a king. You have a name to keep. Going to the police will not help in this matter. It will destroy your reputation."

"Baba, you know everything. I have come to you with hope. I know it will not come without a price. I am ready to pay the price Baba, forgive me if I have spoken more than I should."

Baba thought for a while, "You are my devotee. I don't treat devotes based on their status. But you have been a strong believer and that's why I will spend next three days for your cause. You must help my other devotees and my associates who help to spread the happiness."

"Baba, you name the price, I will arrange for money"

"Your daughter is like my daughter. To please God, we must not worry about money spent on prayers. My assistants will tell you the amount they need to arrange things."

When Nandi left Baba's *Ashram*, he was a happy man. He was confident Baba's *Jaap* would solve all his troubles.

With Baba's blessing, he decided to start preparations for Shubhangi's marriage.

———◦—◦—◦⟨◉⟩⟨◉⟩⟨◉⟩—◦—◦—◦———

Satvik dreaded visiting Mooni as the day of their meeting approached. Shubhangi had arranged their meeting that weekend. She wanted Satvik to win Mooni's heart but Satvik was not confident about it.

A night before their meeting, Satvik was hesitant.

As night progressed, he kept thinking about his visit to Mooni uncle and ways in which he could win his heart. He was scared of Mooni. His first introduction to Mooni did not go well. He wanted to make this meeting work. He needed Shubhangi's help to give him confidence.

Finally, he decided to head to Pushkar Mahal. In the darkness of night, he neared the gates and saw Mooni seated on the porch of his outhouse with a thick wooden stick in his hand. Satvik looked at Mooni's face. Moonlight reflected from his bald head. Mooni's furious eyes met with Satvik's eyes. Satvik turned and ran away from the gate. As he ran on the road, he heard Mooni's footsteps. He saw Mooni chasing him with the stick in his hand.

"*Chor, Chor*! You will not escape today, *har har mahaadev*," Mooni shouted running behind Satvik with his loud shouts.

People must be too tired or they knew Mooni well. Not a single window was lit. Satvik hid behind a tree and looked back. He was amused at Mooni running on the dark road barefooted, shouting alone. He knew he could outrun Mooni and if it came to using hands, he could take advantage of the darkness and beat him.

Mooni ran haphazardly, huffing and puffing. Then he turned back and returned to palace. Satvik was relieved. It was all over.

Satvik had underestimated Mooni as moments later Lemony came running, barking as loud as she could. It took only a few seconds for Lemony to detect the target. A quick sniff and she ran in Satvik's direction like a ferine beast hounding for a prey deep in the woods. Mooni followed her, still shouting profanities.

Satvik haplessly ran on the empty road with all his strength. His morning running routine in the gym came to his rescue as he managed to escape Lemony quicker than he imagined. Lemony's loud bark faded.

He stopped in the middle of the road. He was catching a breath with his hands on his knees. Before he could enjoy his freedom, he heard quick footsteps. As he turned, his eyes met Lemony's shining eyes. An evil smile spread across her face. She jumped on him and pushed him on the road.

The moment froze in his mind when she was in the air pouncing on him. Her teeth sparkled in the darkness like those of werewolves. He went numb and before he could gain his senses, her sharp teeth penetrated his flesh. She took a big bite of his thigh.

He felt he was falling in an endless tunnel. Then his head hit the ground. He opened his eyes in darkness to find himself on the floor. He was panting hard, his forehead full of sweat.

It took him moments to realize it was a dream.

He was relieved. It was around 2.00 AM in the morning. Mooni and Lemony managed to create a nightmare he wouldn't forget soon.

─────•◦•◦◦⊰⊱◦•⊰⊱◦•◦•─────

Morning brought peace to Satvik's mind when Shubhangi called him. He needed her help in preparing his mind to visit Mooni.

"Are you ready to meet Mooni uncle?" she asked.

"I am not sure. I don't feel confident."

"It will be okay. Just be yourself, don't worry about it."

"I really want to impress him. But I am not sure how."

"I know. Mooni uncle is a difficult man. Just keep talking to him and keep listening to what he says with a smile. Show him respect and that you believe in our culture, in our traditions."

For next few minutes, Shubhangi gave Satvik tips on pleasing Mooni. She really wanted Satvik to change Mooni's mind. She knew convincing her parents would be lot easier with Mooni's help.

Satvik took time to prepare himself. He neatly dressed his long hair and wore a traditional *kurta*. He prepared himself as best as he could.

Just when Satvik was ready to leave for the date with Mooni, Sindbad entered with a big frame in his hands. Looking at Satvik's nervous state, he gave few tips to Satvik on how he could impress Mooni.

"This is a painting of Chinese 'Om' which I think you should gift to Mooni," Sindbad said handing over the painting to Satvik.

It was a painting of one big Chinese word. Or many words. He couldn't tell for sure. It had tediously entangled lines hand painted in red on a big canvas with fading layers of saffron shades surrounding it, creating an effect of an auspicious aura.

"What is it?" Satvik asked.

"It's a Chinese 'Om'!" Sindbad reiterated. Satvik noticed a mischief in his eyes and knew he was up to something.

"What?" Satvik asked.

"It's Chinese equivalent of 'Om," Sindbad said.

"Tell me the truth," Satvik asked.

"Look, after you told me about your encounter with Mooni and his offer to help you, I did some research from the oil mills he manages. Mooni believes in the power of 'Om.' They also told me that Mooni believes in Chinese astrology. His house was done according to Feng Shui, a Chinese version of *Vastushastra*. He will love this painting."

"Chinese 'Om?' I have never heard of such a thing. Is this for real?"

"What do you mean is this for real? You know there is nothing that's not there in Chinese. Besides, it's just 'Om' spelled in Chinese."

"I don't have a good feeling about this. I don't think this is such a good idea."

"You think going empty handed is? You must gift him something. Trust me. This would be a perfect gift."

"Alright! You are right. I should have thought about a gift."

"You should have, but, I knew you haven't. That's why I brought this."

"Thank you for this," Satvik said taking the painting.

"You bet."

With a hidden mischief in his eyes, a devilish smile spread across Sindbad's lips as Satvik prepared to leave.

Chapter 9

The street was full of restaurants and sweet marts. Satvik reached on time at the restaurant Mooni had suggested. He decided to wait for Mooni outside the restaurant and stood there holding the painting in his hands.

Mooni came in long strides after parking his old car in a nearby parking lot. At first Satvik did not recognize Mooni, but when he did, he bowed his head and smiled at him. It did not have any effect on Mooni. He did not say a word and entered the restaurant. Satvik followed him.

Without taking help from any of the restaurant staff, Mooni selected an empty table in the corner and sat. Satvik followed and sat opposite him.

Mooni pulled out his kerchief and wiped his bald head. He did it for few times until his head glistened. Then he poured water in the glass and drank it in haste. He looked at Satvik only when he was comfortably settled.

"*Namaste* uncle," Satvik said, without letting the moment of encounter go waste. He joined his hands and bowed his head in respect.

Mooni just shook his head as if receiving well-deserved respect Satvik offered to him and said, "Hmm!"

Satvik thought it was the right time to present him with the painting of the Chinese 'Om.'

"Uncle, this is for you," he said handing over the large frame to him.

Mooni quickly grabbed it and looked at it carefully.

"What is it? Some Chinese gibberish?"

"It's 'Om' in Chinese."

"Om?"

Satvik nodded.

Mooni bowed his head to the painting and muttered with his eyes closed. Satvik noticed a fleeting look of approval in his bulbous eyes. Mooni was pleased but he did not show any signs of emotions on his face.

A waiter appeared out of nowhere and took a deep breath as if he hated his job more than he hated anything else. He threw the menu cards on the table, hardly gently.

"Order sir?" he asked Satvik in his disrespectfully coarse voice, with an almost invisible stoop.

Satvik picked up the menu card but the waiter did not wait and vanished as quickly as he appeared leaving them waiting for his reappearance.

With both his hands resting on the table, Mooni sat staring at Satvik as if trying to penetrate his mind. He finally took his eyes off Satvik's head and started setting his countable greasy hair at the back of his skull. He massaged his dome with all his fingers and disgusted everyone around him.

Mooni made it obvious without speaking a word that he was not pleased with Satvik. He was more than obvious in showing his dislike towards him.

"What would you like to order for lunch, uncle?" Satvik asked the old man respectfully.

"Your choice, just add curd for me," Mooni said.

"Would you like some soup?"

"Tomato soup," he said without looking at him.

A few minutes later, the waiter showed up again with a mastered skill for sudden appearances like one of those in mythical movies, this time with a pen and a pad.

Satvik ordered soup and appetizers. He also ordered veggies and chicken for the main course as quickly as possible lest the waiter disappear again.

Satvik's taste for chickens was about to prove detrimental. Shubhangi forgot to tell Satvik that Mooni was a devout *Brahmin* and a strict vegetarian. It barely occurred to Satvik to ask Mooni About it.

"I thought you were a vegetarian?" Mooni asked raising his eyebrows to form wavy lines on his everlasting forehead. It rendered an extra villainy to his pompous face.

"Umm…yes, occasionally I am a non-vegetarian," Satvik said and laughed trying to sound funny.

Mooni didn't find it funny.

"I am a strict vegetarian," he said twisting his face in disapproval.

"My conscious will never allow me to eat animals," he added to make Satvik feel guilty for being a chicken eater. Mooni's face reading failed but he found something to put Satvik down.

"We can cancel the order." Satvik suggested. Mooni completely ignored him.

"How can we kill them? We should never forget we too are animals," Mooni pushed him further in the depths of despair and dismay.

Satvik wanted to remind Mooni that he asked him to order anything and cannot rant about it. But that would be rude and against his mission to impress Mooni.

"I agree. Shall we cancel the order?" Satvik asked politely trying to save the situation. Although he really wanted to tell Mooni that chickens are birds and not animals.

"It's okay now, the chicken is already dead," Mooni said with a stern voice.

Satvik didn't know how to react and shook his head in agreement. The man was indeed difficult to converse with. Mooni took a sip of water, looked upward and gurgled like a wolf howling on a full-moons night, before taking it in.

"You know, our eating should never cause any deaths," he preached Satvik and then sighed with a demeanor of a great philosopher.

Satvik nodded and tried to smile but it came out lopsided and dismal. It was difficult for him to be modest and not laugh at him. He decided to let Mooni ride the high horse.

Satvik's mind wandered ignoring what Mooni had to say about the holy chickens. He curiously wondered what animal Mooni's face resembled. Despite having front teeth like rabbits, Mooni's face gave an impression of an ugly green frog for his widespread thin lips, baldhead and bulbous eyes. He almost had no neck. Like a frog, his flat nose was a prominent feature of his face. The facial skin was pulled over his bright, shining nose and was wrinkled all over his face.

But he was not green. That was the only differentiator. But then, not all frogs are green, Satvik argued with himself. To prove Satvik right, Mooni even croaked periodically.

"What's with your hair?" Mooni asked bringing Satvik back to reality.

Finally, Mooni left poor chicken aside, his own few hairs aside and shifted his focus on Satvik's long hair. Satvik thought, for a man as baldheaded as him, his long hair should be the most envious thing.

"What about it?" Satvik asked.

"This hippy cut, do you ever cut them?"

Satvik felt he should tell him that princess Shubhangi liked his hairstyle. She was the one who wanted him to look like a Jesus.

A mere thought of Shubhangi reminded him of her bright smile. It reminded him of his mission with Mooni. He decided to focus his attention on his mission to win his heart.

"I have been busy lately. I was about to cut them today," he lied.

Thankfully the waiter appeared, in a flash again. He brought everything and served a four-course meal at once.

The moment the food was served, Mooni jumped on it. He slurped on soup and chomped on vegetable starters. It is acceptable to an extent if you make some noise at the dining table. In India, that extent is large. But the munching sound that emanated from Mooni made people dining on other tables stare at Satvik with anger, as if he was responsible for it.

Mooni directed Satvik's personal interview to his family background. Among those various unheard noises, he produced with his mouth, he asked him questions about his family.

"What do your parents do?" Mooni asked although he knew Satvik was an orphan.

"I am an orphan. My parents died when I was very young. I grew up in an orphanage," Satvik said.

"So there is no one in the name of family?"

"No sir, there is. I have a big family. I have twelve children. Not my own, but they are like my own children. I have few very close friends who are like my brothers."

Mooni wasn't aware about the children. He was shocked to know Satvik had children. Twelve! Mooni didn't know how to react. Satvik was not expecting Mooni's appreciation.

"So you run an orphanage to help orphans because you are orphan?" Mooni asked.

His question angered Satvik.

"It's not an orphanage. They are not orphans. They are my children. I don't take any help from others. I take care of my children all by myself."

Mooni felt the frustration in his voice.

"Shubhangi knows about it?"

"Yes. She has met my children. They love her. And she loves them."

Mooni realized the closeness between Shubhangi and Satvik was more than he believed. He wasn't happy with the new information.

"What do you do?" Mooni asked changing topic.

"You mean job?"

"Yes."

"I am a software engineer. I work with an international software company."

"How much money you make?"

"Enough to take care of all my children and live a happy life," Satvik replied not allowing him to get into details.

Mooni knew that with twelve children to take care, no job should be good enough.

"Do you know Shubhangi is a princess? That she is the only daughter of her rich father," he asked without being sympathetic to Satvik.

"Yes, I do. That has nothing to do with why I fell in love with her," Satvik said.

It did not matter to Mooni. Mooni did not believe in love. He believed it's a lust disguised in love. Love out of marriage was a sin for him. Satvik's confession of love for Shubhangi angered him.

They did not speak for a while.

"Look, I am meeting you because princess Shubhangi insisted. To tell you the truth, you are like my son. I will give you this advice. These are big people, out of our reach," Mooni said looking directly into Satvik's eyes for the first time.

Satvik knew where he was going with it. He did not say a word.

"Forget Shubhangi. She is not for you. You will get a good girl. Love is nothing. In your age, you will fall in love with every young girl walking down the road. That does not mean you have to marry all of them. It is not love. Love can happen only after marriage," he said.

Satvik did not know how to react to Mooni.

"Princess Shubhangi is young. She does not understand what love is. Her father is a king, rich and powerful man. You don't want to piss him off."

Mooni kept suggesting Satvik never to think of Shubhangi for it could only land him in trouble. Satvik was lost in Shubhangi's thoughts. He couldn't imagine not having Shubhangi in his life. In those moments, he realized how worthless his life would be without her in it.

"Well then, it's all settled. You will not meet Shubhangi again. You will forget her and tell her that you don't love her.

In return, you can always ask for any help you need from me," Mooni concluded.

Satvik did not want to say anything. It was not worth it.

Mooni's face brightened as if he had just won the battle. He was happy that Satvik heard him and understood what he was trying to tell him. He finished his lunch with enthusiasm.

Satvik felt relieved when they were done eating.

While Mooni walked away with the painting, Satvik knew he had failed miserably in his mission to impress him.

——•→•⟨⟩⟩⟨⟨⟩⟨⟩•←•——

The only time the Chakrapani family visited their kingdom, *Palam*, was during yearly celebration. *Palam* celebration never started without head of the Chakrapani dynasty, King Nandi. People of *Palam* eagerly awaited their royal family. King Nandi lighted candles, performed prayers and inaugurated a weeklong *Palam* celebration.

As a child, Shubhangi enjoyed every day of the *Palam* celebration and stayed in *Palam* for a week. That was then. In the recent years, she had been to *Palam* only on the inauguration day.

The royal photographer clicked the Chakrapani family before they went to *Palam* for the yearly celebration. It had become a tradition. Over a week, he took photographs individually and then as a family.

The *Palam* celebration was months away yet the photographer was invited. Shubhangi was told about the photo-shoot in advance. Her preparations for the shoot always started a week in advance with multiple visits to her beautician.

It took more than two hours for her maidservants to prepare her. With the help of her maidservants, she adorned herself with ornaments and royal garments studded with shimmering stones. With an ease of familiarity, she allowed the photographer to capture the essence of her maturing beauty in the backdrop of the royal household. In a honeyed lighting, her face shined with radiating glow.

Her mother was proud of how her little princess had turned into a beautiful woman. Completely enamored by the beauty of her nubile daughter, Devyani performed a ritual to ward off evil spirits by cutting lemons and throwing them in all four directions.

It made Shubhangi laugh. The chirpiness of her innocent laughter melted the heart of her mother.

"I should tell you this," Devyani said.

"What mother?"

"You father warned me not to tell, and to keep it to myself."

"What is it? Tell me."

Despite Nandi's warning not to tell Shubhangi the purpose of the photo-shoot, she let the secret out.

"These pictures are for your marriage profile. Your father wants to find you a prince."

The disclosure of this information infuriated Shubhangi. She didn't say a word and ran to her chamber. Thinking her daughter was abashed at the news, Devyani laughed. She was happy and took Shubhangi's gesture for her approval.

It all came to Shubhangi. She felt stupid. How could she think Mooni uncle would support her in her secret love affair? He was more loyal to the king than to anyone else. She should have known Mooni would never keep a secret from her father.

Shubhangi was angry. She was angry at her mother for not consulting her before they thought about her marriage. She was angry with her father for not confronting her about her relationship with Satvik and for trusting Mooni over his daughter. She was angry on Satvik for being so naive that his charm wouldn't work on Mooni or her father.

Chapter 10

"I failed to impress Mooni uncle," Satvik told Shubhangi as they talked over the phone that night.

Satvik narrated his meeting with Mooni. Shubhangi was not surprised to know Mooni warned Satvik to stay away from her. It only confirmed what she knew.

"I don't know Shubhi. What if this all ends soon?" Satvik asked.

"Well, if you think so, it will definitely come to an end. No one ever said marrying a princess was easy. And here you have already given up on us."

"I am not giving up."

"Then why are you so discouraged?"

"Because I don't know how else I could have convinced Mooni uncle. He had made up his mind long before I even opened my mouth. There was no way to convince him."

"I know you tried. That's all that matters to me."

"He threatened me. How can he do that? Isn't he just a royal servant?"

It was a difficult question for Shubhangi to answer. He was right. Mooni was just a royal servant. But she also knew he wasn't acting on his own. He was just a messenger of her father.

"Just forget what he said. It doesn't mean much."

"Is he going to tell your father about us?"

"If we kept meeting," Shubhangi said not wanting to tell Satvik her father already knew about them.

"What do we do now?"

"I don't know either. I don't think we can keep it away from my parents. They will come to know soon. But that doesn't change a thing. I love you and I always will."

Shubhangi was scared but determined. Satvik felt relieved talking to her. As long as she was with him, he was ready to fight the battle.

When Satvik told Sindbad about his meeting with Mooni, he just laughed it off. He told Satvik he wasn't expecting any other outcome. Although he did eagerly listen to how Mooni received the painting.

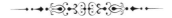

Satvik did not care about Mooni's threat. Neither did Shubhangi about her parent's attempts to find her a royal suitor. They kept meeting each other as if nothing ever happened. As days passed, things seemed peaceful again.

Over one weekend, Satvik and Shubhangi met in a park. They spent the beautiful evening together. When sun set and the dusk started spreading the darkness, they started for home.

They were walking on a seemingly empty road by the side of the park towards the car when they heard a loud sound. It was a motorbike revving up towards them.

Instinctively, Shubhangi looked back just when the motorbike came dangerously close. When it was about to run over Satvik, she quickly pulled him towards her. They both fell on the road as the bike passed by.

The bike stopped at a distance. Two men in helmet got off the bike and ran towards them. Before Satvik and Shubhangi could get on their feet, they reached them.

One of the men kicked Satvik in his stomach. Satvik fell to the ground again.

The other biker pulled Satvik by his collar and said, "Keep your words or you will die. Stay away from her."

Shubhangi was still in a shock. She didn't know how to react. Then it came upon her. She never had to use it but it was the right moment. She pulled the gun out of her purse. Without waiting for a moment, she fired a gunshot in the air and startled both the bikers and Satvik.

She pointed her gun at them. Looking at the gun, both the bikers raised their hands. Shubhangi looked at Satvik. His face was distorted. He was struggling to get up holding his stomach.

"Oh my God, are you hurt?" Shubhangi said and helped him get up on his feet. Satvik regained his composure.

"I am alright," he said.

When she turned towards the men in helmet, she saw them running towards the park.

"Rascals," Shubhangi screamed.

She raised her gun and aimed towards them. Before she could fire a shot, Satvik held her hand and brought it down.

"What are you doing?" he asked.

"They can't just come and attack us. No one can. It's our right to protect ourselves," she said with teary eyes.

"It is. But you are shooting towards the park. And they were not random strangers. Remember what he said. Stay away from you. I know who sent them. It has to be Mooni uncle."

Shubhangi knew he was right. But it can't be Mooni alone. Her father had to be party to it. Mooni wouldn't do anything like that without her father's permission. She ran into Satvik's embrace and held him tight. Tears rolled over her cheeks.

"I am sorry, I am so sorry," she said.

"Why are you sorry?" he said.

He held her face in his hands. Looking at tears on her face, his eyes were misty.

"I love you," she said and kissed him on his mouth for a long time. When the wave of overwhelming emotion receded, she regained herself.

"I am not the kind of person who would put you up against your family. I just want you to know, whatever happen in the future, I will always love you, always." Satvik said holding her hands.

Still shaken from the attack, they walked carefully on the road.

"Do you remember the place where you first said I love you to me?" Shubhangi asked.

"I can never forget it."

"Let's meet there tomorrow and relive those beautiful moments again. Would you come?"

"I will."

That night when they parted ways, they were still shaken. Satvik was yet to come to terms with events of that evening.

Shubhangi was determined to retaliate. She was not willing to let go of the love she had found. If she could have any man she wanted, Satvik was the man she wanted and there was no one who could stop her from having him.

In one's life, there are places which, have witnessed life changing moments, places which are like roots from where an entire new life had sprung, places worthy of repeated visits. For Shubhangi and Satvik, that place was where Satvik first declared his love for her, The Blue Lagoon resort, under a young Banyan tree by the lake.

Satvik waited there for Shubhangi. It was only yesterday they met, but it felt like years. His love for Shubhangi grew with every passing moment. He felt he was more in love with her than he was when he came there that day.

He smelled her fragrance; more enchanting than thousand fresh blooming roses. She walked gracefully holding her long royal gown in her hands. He could see her smile, more beautiful than ever.

He walked towards her in a trance. As he held her hands and moved forward to embrace her, she kneeled on her knees. The frills of her delicate gown rested on the grass.

She raised her face towards him and took a deep breath. Before he could realize what she was up to, she spoke, holding his hands, looking directly in to his eyes.

"Will you marry me?"

A lump full of infinite blooming emotions rose in his throat. He went on his knees next to her. Her sublime face radiated her beauty in the twilight. He held her hands, weaved his fingers with her fingers and looked into her bright eyes.

"Yes, a thousand times yes, for a thousand lives yes, for a wait of million years, yes, I will marry you. I always wanted to, for you are my soul, for you complete me. Without you, I am lifeless. Without you, I would die," he said with choked voice vitiated by emotions.

As they rose on their feet, he pulled her towards him and embraced her tightly. She buried her face in his chest. The smell of her hair intoxicated him. The warmth of his body melted her in his arms.

He held her face and came close to her unblemished face. Her eyes sparkled like a precious crystal. Their breath mingled, lips whispered before they touched. He shivered with soft touch of her lips. Warmth of her kiss brought him to the life. His tongue talked how deeply he loved her and she reciprocated his ardent kiss.

As he kissed her holding her tightly, her tender breast heaved beneath his warm chest in unison. His reassuring kiss took away all her fears. Tears of happiness rolled over her cheeks. The charm of her delicate kiss made his heart beat differently, as if it had found a new rhythm to beat. He could stay there his entire life osculating her tender lips.

As they kissed, he felt his existence vanished. As if gravity had no effect on him, he felt like he had become an invisible center around which entire world had started revolving.

That moment brought them together for life. They were more determined than ever. She would never let him go. He was ready to fight with any force in the world that would stop them from being together.

They were lost in unending space and time, until she slowly pulled away and broke the kiss.

"That's enough for today," she said with a bashful smile on her face.

With teary eyes beaming with love and lips reddened with osculation, she smiled a smile of a new bride. He smiled back at her. He was a changed man.

He looked in to her soft and loving eyes. Without a slightest doubt in his mind, he knew she was the most beautiful woman in the world. Her face was divine, her skin sublime, unblemished like milk, smooth like a marble. He pulled her again and took her lips in his mouth.

Satvik had another surprise waiting for him. Shubhangi took him to the clubhouse in The Blue Lagoon resort. As they jauntily entered the club-house, Satvik saw all his friends - Sindbad, Amit, Gopal, Chahek and Gunjan waiting for them.

It couldn't have been a coincidence. He looked at Sindbad inquisitively.

"So?" Sindbad asked Shubhangi raising eyebrows.

"He said, yes!" Shubhangi said with a cheerful smile.

They clapped and cheered and congratulated the couple.

Satvik looked at Shubhangi trying to gauge if she had invited friends there. Sindbad helped to clear the confusion by letting him know they all knew what was about to happen.

Sindbad had talked with Shubhangi after Satvik told him about biker's attack. He was worried. He wanted to ask Shubhangi if she was serious about Satvik and if she loved him enough to put his life at risk. Shubhangi told him she was planning a marriage proposal the next day. Together, they planned to invite their friends and celebrate after she proposed to Satvik.

Sindbad escorted everyone to reserved table by the pool. Gunjan, Chahek and Shubhangi quickly got together and had their girly talk going on in titers and whispers in the surrounding chaos. As the girls talked, Shubhangi's face turned a bashful crimson.

They all celebrated the occasion with drinks and food. His friends expressed envy and made fun of Satvik for the princess had to propose to him. Satvik expressed his anger for the kind of friends they were to not let him know what was coming his way.

Everyone was happy for them and enjoyed that hour of celebration.

"Of all the people in the world, you couldn't find anyone better than him?" Amit asked.

"I know, right? On top of that, I had to propose." Shubhangi said.

"You are the luckiest man on earth," Amit said to Satvik.

"Couldn't agree more," Satvik said.

"He is not the only one lucky. I think Shubhangi too is lucky to have him. He is the best. A noble soul," Gopal said to Shubhangi. He was already drunk.

"I know, that's why he is mine," Shubhangi said wrapping her hands around Satvik's arm.

"So, when are you getting married?" Gunjan asked.

Before Satvik could say they haven't thought of it yet, Shubhangi spoke.

"Soon, in a month or two."

Everyone cheered. Satvik was taken aback by what she said. She had already thought of it without talking to him. He looked at her. She gave him a reassuring wink.

"This calls for another round," Amit said. He was drinking pineapple juice yet behaved as if he had been drinking for hours.

"My father knows we are in love. He is going to do everything possible to get me married in a royal family.

I can't stop him for long. So, we don't have much time," Shubhangi said.

"Your father knows about us?" Satvik asked in shock.

She nodded her head in agreement. She let the secret out that it's not just Mooni, but her father knows about them too. It made all sense. Satvik understood why she couldn't wait till he proposed to her, why she was insisting on getting married in a month.

"You said your father would do everything to stop you two from marrying. And your father is a king, a powerful man. When he tries, my guess is that things happen," Amit said hinting at odds stacked up against them.

"I know. But there is nothing more powerful than love," Shubhangi said.

"We are with you. Nothing can stop you from getting married. We promise you," Sindbad said.

"Yes!" everyone echoed.

"I know what exactly needs to be done. The court marriage. First thing you should do is to apply for marriage at the registrar's office. It will take a month before you two could get legally married," Sindbad said.

"That's a great idea. I never thought of it. Thank you," Shubhangi said.

"My pleasure, your highness," Sindbad said bowing his head.

Shubhangi didn't want to waste time in applying for the court marriage. She knew convincing her father would not yield results. Satvik wasn't sure if it was a good idea. He wanted to meet her parents and talk to them first. Shubhangi snubbed him. She insisted they could use court marriage in case her parents did not agree.

When Shubhangi persisted, Satvik agreed to visit the sub-registrar's office.

Like any other government office, it had a rustic smell of unyielding atmosphere. Everything there shouted that no charm except that of money works here.

Satvik had no experience when it came to working with government officers. Shubhangi did all the paper work while he stared at the people. Shubhangi's charm worked well.

They spent next few hours completing numerous forms. Shubhangi did most of the work, running around enquiring, getting affidavits done and furnishing details. Not to mention she had no apprehensions paying money to rotund officials.

"This is the law of the land. Consider I paid them a tip for helping us to get married. I am a princess. I pay a tip for every damn thing," she tried to console Satvik looking at his disapproving face.

"Paying a bribe is no less a crime than taking it," he protested.

"Okay. I know that. You don't have to make me feel guilty about it. And you did not pay the bribe, so don't feel guilty yourself," she said.

Finally, the clerk at the counter with his mouth filled with tobacco nodded that they were done.

"A notice would be placed on the board for thirty days for anyone to object. You are free to marry any day after that. Madam has paid the money, so, call me on my number a day in advance when you are ready. I will send someone there. You will get the marriage certificate the same day. You can go now. Next!" he said with constant inertness in his voice.

As they walked out, Shubhangi held his hand. She looked in his elated eyes. Her gray eyes shined with cheerfulness.

"Congratulations Mr. Bharat! We are engaged," she said.

"Your highness, congratulations to you too," he said.

She walked gracefully, holding his hand, waving her fingers in his fingers. The feathery touch of her hand sent a shiver through him. His heart throbbed with excitement. He couldn't believe he was getting married to a princess.

He felt he was indeed lucky to have her.

When one believes in luck, one cannot have a control over things that follow. What the clerk at the counter did not tell them was that a notice would also be sent to their homes.

Chapter 11

'The Royal soul-mate' matchmakers specialized in connecting royal families in holy matrimony. The royal charm of Shubhangi made her the face of their business. Their matchmaking services were never used for a princess so beautiful. Executives at the matchmaking agency were busy visiting royal families in the Indian sub-continent carrying Shubhangi's exquisite marriage profile.

Unaware of an extensive search launched by matrimonial agency, Satvik and Shubhangi continued relishing their strengthened bond after their engagement.

Every night they talked with enthusiasm for hours together. They met over weekends and spent time with children. They had their entire life planned together, the life they would spend together, the places they would visit together. They talked about their children at Chhaya Sadan and having their own children.

Time flew when they talked. Days passed and with every passing day, their bond became stronger. Eventually the time, when their love would put to test came around.

—•→•❦❀❦•←•—

Visiting the gym every day was monotonous and took great discipline. Satvik did it so earnestly that he was addicted to the gym.

He looked in the mirror at his half-naked body. His long hair was appropriately styled and slightly curled at ends after his recent visit to salon with Shubhangi. His new look enhanced his oval face and square jaw.

His gym training was visible. His shoulders were more rounded, chest more squared. His stomach displayed the protrusions of his abdominal muscles. His clean-shaven chest felt itchy with sweat. He would have never shaved it if it wasn't for the gang of musclemen. They had become his friends and helped him build the physique.

He was pleased looking at himself in the mirror. He was certain of fulfilling Shubhangi's Greek Jesus fantasy. His mind shamelessly wandered imagining the ways Shubhangi would appreciate her Greek Jesus.

Future seemed promising and full of excitement with Shubhangi.

There was no *Jaap* performed to cure love-struck Shubhangi in Makhan Baba's *Ashram*. Baba never knew of a prayer that could cure a spell of love. He never rejected easy money that came his way. He believed it to be an insult to Goddess *Laxmi*.

Makhan Baba quickly spent the money King Nandi gave for *Jaap* on filling his hidden cabinet with imported liquors.

He bought enough alcohol to last a year. His skinny body did not resist the effect of alcohol very well.

The blessings, the prayers, the saintly postures and all the controlled movements through the day irked him. In the night, when he was alone and drunk, he unleashed himself and broke those boundaries. He danced to popular music with a dancing style unique to him. No one outside his soundproof chamber could hear him even in the quietness of the night.

Every night, looking at his face in the mirror, he praised the generosity of King Nandi in a loud voice. Then he made ugly faces like drunken Englishmen. "Long live the king," he would shout and offer a tight salute to himself in the mirror. He would then laugh aloud looking at skinny, bearded, drunk saffron clad Baba saluting him in the mirror.

——•→•◦❁◦❈◦❁◦•←•——

Finally, the good news made its way to Pushkar Mahal. Mooni came running early morning and shared the good news to Nandi.

It was the news that Nandi had been eagerly waiting for many days. The news that made Nandi ecstatic was about a marriage proposal for Shubhangi. 'The Royal Soul-mate' Matchmaker services, which billed unjustifiable money, had found a royal family eager to have their son married to the princess Shubhangi.

As per the royal custom to treat a messenger who brought good news, Nandi took off his golden bracelet and awarded

Mooni with it. For Mooni, it wasn't the golden bracelet but the affection of Nandi that mattered more. He was delighted to bring the news to Nandi.

King Nandi's faith in Makhan Baba strengthened that day. Money that Nandi paid to Makhan Baba for a *Jaap* had paid off. A prince has shown interest in marrying Shubhangi. He closed his eyes and bowed his head in respect remembering pleasant face of Makhan Baba.

Mooni told Nandi about the royal family who sent marriage proposal. Vikramaditya, the prince of *Patti*, was a young, handsome prince from a royal family of northern India. He had just returned from London after completing his education. To the family's delight, he had shown great interest in Shubhangi without much persuasion.

The descendants of Nanda dynasty, *Patti* family had amassed huge wealth in apple farming. The prince, after studying and staying in London with Englishmen, had acquired a modern mindset just the way Shubhangi would want in her husband.

Looking at photographs of the prince in royal yet modernized demeanor and reading his profile carefully wrapped in a silver lined embroidered folder, Nandi was delighted.

"The prince and his family appear perfect for Shubhi," Nandi said.

"Yes, your highness. We shall not waste any time," Mooni said.

"I agree with you."

"I am told, prince said, he had never seen someone so beautiful like our Shubhi. He would like to meet the princess at the earliest possible," Mooni said.

Nandi felt proud of his daughter. He never had a doubt she was the most beautiful princess in Indian sub-continent.

"You don't know how happy you have made me," Nandi said.

"It's my pleasure, your highness," Mooni said.

That moment, only thing Nandi hated about life was his diabetes. It did not allow him kingly pleasure of devouring sweets. It was a daring act for Mooni to offer him sweets, but for the news he had brought with sweets, Nandi broke the rule and gulped few nuggets of the delicious sweets.

With childlike excitement, he called for Devyani, his queen, the mother of his beautiful princess daughter. Nandi's plump face barely managed to accommodate the excitement.

She knew Nandi had some good news to share with her. With a royal sophistication, she waited for her husband to tell the news.

When she heard, Devyani was equally happy. Her face beamed with joy. With an awkward stare, she went in his embrace, vaguely managing to encircle her hands around his barrel like abdomen.

For a moment, he thought he should call for Shubhangi and share the news with her. He hadn't talked with her in days. He never discussed with her about her marriage, never took her permission to start looking out for grooms.

Unaware that Devyani had shared the secret with Shubhangi about their search for a perfect prince, Nandi decided to share the news with Shubhangi later.

"Don't tell Shubhangi yet. Let me share the news with her when time is right," he said.

"It's such a great news. I can't hide it for long," Devyani said.

"It won't be long. I want to be sure we know everything about Prince and his family."

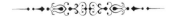

King Nandi's happiness was obvious for a couple of days after receiving the marriage proposal from prince of *Patti*. When the servant brought Nandi mails for that day, Nandi was lost in thoughts of arrangements he would have to make for Shubhangi's marriage.

It was the same daily flow of bills and business mails. But a notice caught his eye.

He opened it and started reading. It was a notice from the office of the marriage registrar, for not having an objection to intended marriage by Shubhangi with some Satvik Bharat.

As he read it, his pleasant mood quickly turned to outrageous anger. His heart paced faster like an aimless, angry elephant. His nostrils flared in anger.

As Shubhangi delicately walked through the large doors of the palace, the bells in her stone studded anklets made a rhythmic music evincing the excitement of a princess returning from visit to her secret lover. Her deep gray eyes sparkled. Her face was still blushful from the possibilities held back in her heart.

She was greeted by her mother. Devyani was eager to share the good news of the prince of *Patti* with her daughter. Nandi had warned her to wait for the right time.

"You look so beautiful," her mother said.

Shubhangi looked at her mother's face to find traces of emotions that could resolve the quandary of the awkward greeting she had extended to Shubhangi. With an obvious remark made about her beauty, she was certain that there was something going on in her mother's head.

"What is it Mother?"

"You were so little," Devyani said showing the span of her forearm, "and now look at you. I can't believe you have grown up so fast. It's only a matter of days before you would be married."

A thought of parting from her daughter rose tears in Devyani's eyes. With feminine proficiency, she quickly wiped minute drops of tears.

Shubhangi sensed it was something about her marriage. Holding her mother's hand, she cautiously sat by her, thinking about how she could ask her mother what had transpired.

Before Shubhangi could ask a question to her mother, a maidservant apologetically interrupted. She informed them that Nandi wanted to see Shubhangi immediately.

Unaware of the things that were about to happen, Devyani thought Nandi had called Shubhangi to tell the good news himself. Devyani smiled at Shubhangi thinking her daughter would be told about the marriage proposal.

Shubhangi greeted her father as she entered his chamber. He did not reply her. His face was stern. His eyebrows crowded his forehead making his anger obvious on his face.

"What's wrong Dad? You seem very upset," she said.

"I never expected it from you. You were such a good child?" Nandi said.

"What is it Dad?"

"Perhaps you can explain it yourself," Nandi said handing her the notice from marriage registrar's office.

She was numbed. Speechless. The reason for her father's obvious anger was written in the letter. The letter screamed she had been planning to get married to her lover secretly.

"My daughter? The princess of Chakrapani? How could you do this?" Nandi asked.

Shubhangi could not say a word. She wasn't prepared to answer any of his questions. She never expected things to unfold this way. She cursed the clerk at the counter in marriage registrar's office. He did not inform that a notice would be sent to home.

"Who is this man, Satvik Bharat? Same orphan you are roaming around with?" he asked.

"So you know about him. Mooni uncle told you. I suppose you know everything about him. Why ask then?"

141

"Because, I am your father. You should know the pain I am going through to search a good match for you?"

"Why are you taking so much pain when I already found a good match?"

"Are you so eager to get married?"

"I was not, until you sent my marriage profile to the world without asking me. I know you deceived me in to the photo-shoot for my marriage profile."

"Shubhi! Mind your language. You have not grown old enough to talk to your father in this manner."

"What wrong I did?"

"If you thought you were not doing anything wrong, why didn't you tell me and your mother about the man you were seeing?"

"Why didn't you ask yourself? Before arranging my marriage with a stranger?"

"Your marriage is not fixed. And the stranger happens to be a prince. You would have known about him at the right time."

"Really? What if I say, I would have told you about Satvik at the right time?"

"On the day of your marriage?" Nandi said pointing towards notice in her hand.

"If you trusted me and not schemed with Mooni uncle to find me a prince, this wouldn't have happened. I know everything about your meeting with Baba, my photoshoot. You even sent men to threaten him?"

"The man you would marry will be a prince and not an orphan. That's final. No one can change that. Neither you, nor me."

"It's my life, I own that decision. I would marry the man I love and if that man happens to be an orphan, so be it."

Nandi's anger rose instantly. All his dreams were at stake. The name of the Chakrapani dynasty was at stake.

"Shut up! Not a word again," Nandi shouted at Shubhangi.

His shout was clearly audible to Devyani. Shubhangi was never shouted at by anybody, not even by her father. He always pampered her, called her 'my princess.' She never saw her father so furious.

Shubhangi never talked to her father the way she did that day. Her face was red. Her eyes were blurry with the gathering of tears. She looked at her mother who came running to the chamber. Devyani embraced her daughter and stared Nandi with wide eyes.

"She is grounded. She is not going out, not talking to anyone without my permission," Nandi ordered as he left the chamber stomping his feet in anger.

Shubhangi sat on the chair with Devyani who was still clueless about why Nandi was angry with his beloved daughter. Shubhangi handed her the notice. She had to know the truth.

As Devyani read the letter from the marriage registrar, her face kept changing expressions.

Nandi's orders were followed diligently. Shubhangi was grounded. Before her mother took her phones away, Shubhangi managed to send a message to Satvik. She informed him she wouldn't be talking to him for few days and would call him when she could.

Shubhangi was kept under a constant, watchful eyes. She wasn't allowed to use her phones or her computer. She roamed freely inside Pushkar Mahal except, her maidservants accompanied her everywhere. She could go outside the palace only in her mother's presence.

What she couldn't do was the thing she wanted to do most. To be with Satvik, to talk to him. The resistance only increased her love for him.

Shubhangi knew her father was disappointed in her. She never saw her father so angered. But she knew, with time, things would get better and then everything would be normal again. Her twenty-first birthday was just days away. In her heart, she believed the anger her father held would melt sooner and he would forgive her on her birthday.

It wasn't very difficult for her to find a phone and call Satvik. But she decided to obey her father. She wanted to give him a sense that his daughter listened to him. In return, she hoped he would listen to her.

Satvik did not know what had happened. Shubhangi's message only confused him. He waited for couple of days and then called her many times a day. It was never answered.

Satvik was worried. He tried hard to focus his attention away from Shubhangi. There was not a moment when her thoughts left him. Many times, he thought of going to Pushkar Mahal. But she had sent a message she would call, so he waited. As her birthday approached, Satvik was desperate. All he wanted was to talk to her on her birthday.

Chapter 12

It was Shubhangi's twenty-first birthday. Every year, the birthday of the Chakrapani princess saw lavish celebrations at Pushkar Mahal. This year was no different. Nandi and Devyani wanted to celebrate Shubhangi's birthday with zest.

Preparations for the birthday party started a week in advance. Servants decorated the Pushkar Mahal. A *pandal* was set up in the front lawn. Plants in the garden were pruned. A special cake was ordered and the royal photographer was invited.

Guarded by maidservants and her mother, Shubhangi shopped for her birthday. She invited few of her friends for birthday party on her mother's insistence, all in her presence.

Shubhangi was about to be twenty-one. She looked more beautiful than ever. Nandi thought it was time the world saw the beauty of his daughter. He invited his royal friends and prominent people in the city. He knew by word of mouth the stories would spread - stories of the beautiful princess of *Palam*. Suitors from all over the world, more prominent than the prince of *Patti*, would line up asking for her hand in marriage.

He did not show any remorse for putting Shubhangi under the constant watchful eyes of her mother and maidservants. He did not relax any restrictions even on her birthday. Shubhangi thought three weeks was enough punishment. She made up her mind to not obey her father if she wasn't freed of all the restrictions on her birthday.

———•—➤•❧❀❁❀❧•➤•———

On her birthday, Satvik called on Shubhangi's phone numerous times. As expected, it was not answered. He could not remember the last time he saw her beautiful face, heard her soft voice.

The only thing he wanted on that day was to meet her. As the day progressed, he felt like a caged animal. By evening, he was tormented. He had lost all hopes. It was as if the dream was over. His friends Sindbad, Amit and Gopal knew how he felt. They knew something must be done about it.

They took Satvik to an upscale bar. As alcohol loosened the tension, Gopal spoke. He rarely spoke first. He wouldn't do so if he wasn't drunk.

"This is bad, very bad. This can't be the twenty first century? Two people in love can't meet, can't talk. What kind of country we live in? I hate it," Gopal said thumping his fist on the counter.

As he did so, his empty glass merrily flung in the air, which was quickly pulled down to the floor by gravity. It shattered into pieces to the familiar clang of shattering glass.

For a moment, the bar was silenced and then quickly came to life.

"You are right. Absolutely right," Satvik mumbled.

Satvik had enough alcohol for the night. Sindbad signaled to Amit and Gopal they should avoid reminding him of Shubhangi. Reading a situation was one of many things Amit didn't know about.

"Nothing can stop true love. There is no force in this world which can stop two people in love," Amit said.

"Yes, no one can stop true love. I am going her home," Satvik said with alcohol-induced huskiness in his voice.

"You can't," Gopal said.

"I can't? Try stopping me," Satvik said as he got up.

Satvik heard loud and quick sobbing which, unexpectedly, came from Amit. It was as if pineapple juice had triggered feminine hormones in him making him emotional. It startled everyone including Satvik who sat down again to attend the urgency he had created.

Sindbad wanted to thank Amit for diverting Satvik's attention. Before he could do so, Amit spoke.

"I can't see them apart. We must help them. That's what friends are for," he said with now weakened, intermittent sobs.

"You are my true friend. I always doubted you. Today, I know you always meant the best," Satvik patted Amit as he got up from his seat.

"Thank you," Amit said wiping his eyes.

Sindbad looked at Amit with wide eyes signaling he was not helping the situation.

"I must go," Satvik said as he started walking away.

Sindbad pulled Satvik down, "Of course, you must. But do you think you can just barge into her palace?"

Not knowing whether to answer him yes or otherwise, Satvik kept staring at him

"We are coming with you. But first, let's finish the drink," Sindbad said.

A smile spread across Satvik's face.

"I knew it. You are the best friends anyone can ever have," Satvik shouted.

Only possibility of Satvik and Shubhangi meeting each other that night was at Shubhangi's house. That was if they could break into Pushkar Mahal.

Satvik told them he had been to Pushkar Mahal and knew it well. They all, except him, were certain that trying to break in to her palace was a bad idea. They wanted Satvik to come to that conclusion.

After finishing their drinks, they walked out of the bar and left for Pushkar Mahal in Sindbad's car.

Shubhangi's birthday party was attended by close family friends and prominent people in the city. Mooni received

all the guests, except for Makhan Baba whom King Nandi received himself.

Shubhangi shook hands and smiled at the familiar faces of those wishing her. Among the heard of exquisitely dressed men and women and dazzling lights, her heart longed for him. She felt alone in her own birthday party. Her mind kept thinking about Satvik.

She knew Satvik must have been feeling frustrated for not being able to wish her. He must have thought about numerous ways to make her happy. Was he planning to kiss her, hold her close to him in his arms, for long? She wondered.

She was angry with herself for complying with her father, for not being able to find a way to talk to Satvik. Her otherwise cheerful face was not at the happiest best on her birthday. Yet she was the most beautiful woman in the gathering.

———✦•✦•❦❁❦•✦•———

Satvik had been to Shubhangi's house before. He tried to remember as much as he could, but his alcohol-drenched brain hardly helped.

Satvik was vaguely certain if they could get past the main gate and of course, the guard, they could enter Pushkar Mahal. Once inside, he could climb a big tree by Shubhangi's room and jump into her balcony. Satvik was optimistic about taking a big jump to Shubhangi's balcony. His confidence lasted through journey until they reached the palace.

Pushkar Mahal was lit brightly. Soft music played inside and could be heard from a distance. There was a long queue of cars parked outside Pushkar Mahal. They parked their car at a distance from the palatial house.

They casually walked by Pushkar Mahal. It was guarded by a tall, thick fence wall. Crushed pieces of glass were embedded in the concrete on top of the wall. Climbing the wall and jumping over the fence was an idea that defied rules of physics and biology.

The main gate made a squeaky noise as it opened. They quickly glanced before the lone security guard ran inside after opening the door for the guest. They saw the cheerful guests in the party that was going on in the front yard.

Pushkar Mahal was intimidating. They stood there staring at each other in silence. Their enthusiasm had died down. No one spoke for a while. No one knew what to say.

None of them had prior experience in breaking into a home. This one, in particular, was an unbreakable palace. If they were caught, not only would they be beaten and taken to jail, but Satvik's love story would come to an abrupt end.

Satvik asked, "So, what do you think?"

No one spoke. Not a word. Finally, Amit did.

"I don't think it's a good idea," he said.

"How do you know? You are not the one in love," Satvik replied.

"Well, exactly. That's why I know. I can still think straight," he said.

"Let's go back home. We can discuss it there," Sindbad suggested as he drove them back to home.

———✦✦✧❦❦❦✧✦✦———

If Satvik and Shubhangi were to meet that day, they only had few hours before midnight and many barriers to cross. They needed a plan. They had another round of drinks before they started devising a plan to break into Pushkar Mahal.

When alcohol made its way to their dizzied brains, it boosted their confidence again. Possibilities opened up. Breaking into Pushkar Mahal felt difficult, but not impossible.

"Once the party is over, the guests will return. It will be easy to get inside the palace," Sindbad said.

"It's not just the guard. There are five outhouses around the palace and one of them belongs to Mooni. If there is any man that we should be scared of, then it's him," Satvik intervened.

As if it wasn't enough trouble, Satvik realized Lemony would be on the loose. As long as Lemony was in the compound, there was no possibility of breaking in to the house.

"And I forgot to tell, there is a dangerous, demented bitch, Lemony, a Pomeranian dog on the loose," Satvik said.

No one understood why Satvik called names to the Pomeranian dog. With due respect to the feelings of a man who was down with love and alcohol, it was unanimously agreed that silencing Lemony should be the first thing to do.

Amit took upon himself to do the needful. While others worked in scheming ways to break in the house, Amit prepared himself earnestly and sat for an hour researching on the internet how they could tackle Lemony.

First, the plan to break in was discussed. It was an audacious plan, but not completely impossible. After finalizing it, Amit shared his plan to silence Lemony.

"So what is the plan for kidnapping lemony?" Gopal asked.

"Wait! Are we talking about kidnapping Lemony?" Satvik asked.

"Technically it's called dog-napping. We are not kidnapping Lemony. We are dog-napping her. We will put her in the van. That way even if she wakes up and starts barking, no one would hear a thing and we can put her back in the house when we are done," Amit explained.

"That makes sense, but how do you plan to kidnap her?" Sindbad asked.

"Dognap," Amit reiterated.

"Alright, dognapper!" Sindbad said irritated.

"I have a master plan that can't go wrong," Amit said.

"What is the plan, master?" Gopal interrupted.

"Patience, my dear friend. What are two things dogs like most?"

"You should know," Gopal said and laughed only to realize that curiosity did not allow others to relish his humor.

"Funny! Now, can we focus? Anyone knows the answer?" Amit asked.

No one spoke. They knew Amit well and knew that he would do his thing before he lets out his plan. He was revealing his plan with demeanor of a master thief as if kidnapping Lemony was harder than a bank robbery.

"No one? Alright. The two things that every dog likes are chewing on bone and feasting on peanut butter, instincts, which brings them immense pleasure. What would be irresistible to dogs then? Any guesses?" He asked anticipating a cheerful response.

No one guessed. Intentionally.

"It's simple. A dog bone laced with peanut butter. A dog would jump on it and lick it in a moment. Now, you should ask how this universal fact helps," he said with a sparkle added to his already widened eyes.

"Because, you are planning to mix a sleeping drug with peanut butter?" Gopal said.

"Damn right, you got that one," Amit said.

"Are you planning to kill Lemony?" Satvik asked worried.

Not that he wouldn't have loved to see Lemony dead, but he couldn't imagine how Shubhangi would react if Lemony was dead. It would be a wrong way to put an end to their love story.

"No. No. Who Said that? We are just going to make her sleep. We will give her a dog bone laced with peanut butter and animal sedatives," Amit said with theatrical, mischievous expressions.

Only way to stop Amit from stretching it any further was to praise his plan. They knew it well.

"This is a better plan than any of us could have come up with," Satvik appreciated. Amit blushed with pride.

"So this is how it's going to be. Just before midnight, we will break into the house using a ladder and climbing one of the walls far from the main gate. Then we take care of the security guards and Lemony. We lock the doors of all the outhouses. Then we use the ladder and help Satvik into Shubhangi's balcony," Sindbad said not believing all this could be possible.

"That sounds risky," Amit said who heard rest of the plan for the first time.

"There is no other way. If anything goes wrong we head back," Sindbad said.

"Meow. Meow. Meow. That's our signal," Gopal said.

"Wait, three times the meow of the cat?" Amit asked.

"Yes," Gopal said.

"That's a good idea. I have a feeling we will end up using it before we reach inside the house," Amit said.

"Should we leave him behind?" Gopal asked.

"I was just kidding. You guys never get my jokes," Amit said laughing.

As planned, everyone wore black clothes, as they would help to blend in the darkness. Satvik and Sindbad picked up the van, a ladder and other things from Chhaya Sadan. Amit and Gopal shopped for dog bone, sedatives and peanut butter. They could not find the rug sack so they brought a trunk for Lemony.

When they were done shopping for things required for their plan, they met at the bar. They packed *kebabs* and a crate of beers.

It was an hour before midnight, the time for action.

After a memorable party at Pushkar Mahal, guests returned home. Servants wound up as much as they could before they went home. Content with Shubhangi's birthday celebration, Nandi and Devyani too retired to their chamber.

Shubhangi was dismayed. Her heart was full of anguish. On her birthday, all she wanted was to meet Satvik. She knew Satvik must have felt the same way. She wanted to jump out of the window and run to him.

She could never imagine Satvik, fully inebriated, was coming to meet her.

At about half an hour to midnight, a van stopped near Pushkar Mahal beneath the dark shadow of a tree. The first part of their plan was for Sindbad to enter inside the campus and take care of any threats from guard and Lemony. Amit was not drunk and was an obvious choice to help Sindbad.

Sindbad and Amit stepped outside without making any noise, and climbed up the van using steps on the back door. Sindbad carried the bag containing the dog bone plastered with peanut butter for Lemony. As per the plan, Satvik and

Gopal waited in the van and were ready to run away in case things went south.

Once on top of the van, Sindbad freed the ladder. Plan to rest the ladder on one of the branches of the tree did not work as it kept sliding either on the roof of the van or on the branch. It created noise and disturbed Lemony's slumber.

Sindbad resorted to backup plan of using a rope to climb the tree instead of the ladder. After multiple attempts of throwing rope at the branch that hung outside the fence, they succeeded.

Sindbad climbed the rope and managed to be on the branch that would take him inside Pushkar Mahal. From inside the van, Satvik and Gopal saw it through the window. First step of the plan was completed.

He slowly crawled on the branch towards the trunk, making as little noise as he could. The lights in Pushkar Mahal were switched off, making it easier for him. Sindbad assessed the situation. It was a house bigger than he had imagined. Decorations from the party were not removed entirely. He could still smell the feast. He noticed the outhouses and saw a big doghouse in the front porch.

The guardroom was at a distance. As he climbed down the tree, he saw the guard in the guardroom was drowsy. Sindbad moved swiftly. With dark clothes on him, he felt safe. As he jumped on the grass, Lemony woke up. In a moment, she pushed open the doors of her doghouse and came out. Sindbad froze. He stood there under a dark shadow without making any movement.

Before Lemony could sniff his alcohol drenched breathing, Sindbad took out and threw the peanut butter laced bone at her. She sniffed once, before running and jumping on it. After carefully observing the bone for a moment, she finally licked it. It did not take her a minute to lap up all the peanut butter on the bone. While she licked and chewed on the bone, Sindbad stood still for more than ten minutes.

Lemony kept licking the bone until finally she fell in a deep sleep outside her doghouse.

Once Lemony was asleep, Sindbad swiftly moved towards the guard who was in even deeper sleep. He was snoring. It occurred to Sindbad that he could get extra help to deal with him.

The guard didn't wake up even when Sindbad quietly took the keys for the gate. Sindbad unlocked small wicket gate from the inside and opened it ever so slightly. When he returned to the van, expressions on his face were visible in dim light.

He explained them rest of the plan. One by one, they entered inside and moved to the guard's room. While Amit and Gopal taped the guard's mouth, Sindbad quickly masked him with a black cloth. Before he could put up a fight, they quickly cuffed his hands and tied his legs to the chair.

Sindbad locked the main door of the palace and outhouses with locks they had brought so no one could come out. Amit put Lemony inside the trunk and kept her in the van. Gopal and Satvik arranged the ladder on a large trunk of a tree near Shubhangi's balcony.

Finally, it was time. After shaking hands and exchanging hugs, Satvik climbed the ladder carrying a bouquet with him. Once he was up on the closest branch of the tree to her balcony, he pulled the ladder up. He then carefully placed it on the branch and on the railings of the balcony.

The ladder was inclined and unstable but it was better than jumping from the branch. He crawled on the ladder slowly, balancing his weight. Time was running out. It was almost midnight. He could see the dim light coming through the curtains of her windows.

When Satvik finally made it to her balcony, Amit clapped in reaction. Sindbad quickly stopped him. They cheered silently. Satvik passed the ladder to his friends. As per the plan, he had half an hour to spend with Shubhangi. Sindbad, Amit and Gopal went back to the van to finish the drinks and *Kebab* they had brought.

Satvik took a deep breath in anticipation to see Shubhangi after a long time.

Chapter 13

Shubhangi was still awake. She was thinking about Satvik when she heard footsteps. She was alarmed when there was a light knock on the doors of her balcony.

She carefully walked towards the glass door and slightly moved the curtains aside. She couldn't believe she saw Satvik standing outside the glass door with a wide grin, holding a bouquet of flowers.

She frantically opened the door. Before he could wish her, she pulled him in and hugged him tight. Grabbing his long hair in her hands, she clasped him in a rapturous kiss.

Breaking the kiss partially, he whispered 'happy birthday' and quickly took her lips in his mouth. She opened her eyes in acknowledgement and closed them again.

The kiss reminded him how much he missed kissing her.

"I knew you would come, I missed you," she whispered.

"I had no choice, it's your birthday. I had to come. Happy birthday," he said as he presented her with a beautiful bouquet of flowers.

"Thank you. You made it very special," she said.

Satvik kept looking at her unblemished face. She was tired from a busy day. Yet she looked beautiful than ever. Her lips, reddened from the kiss, glistened in dim light. Her gray eyes sparkled with a joy, like a precious crystal. Her soft creamy skin glowed through her shimmering nightgown.

She pushed him aside and closed the door of the balcony behind him. As she turned and walked gracefully towards her bed, the spellbinding sway of her derriere captivated Satvik's gaze. He followed her with his eyes riveted on her body.

Seating beside her in her bedroom gave him Goosebumps. His inebriated mind wandered in unlimited possibilities.

"How did you come inside?"

"I climbed the tree and jumped into the balcony." He said.

She looked at him with a suspicion. It was hard to imagine anyone could jump into the balcony from the tree. She could test alcohol in his kiss. Sensing her doubt, he clarified quickly.

"I climbed a bamboo ladder. My friends helped me."

"I knew it! Wait, how did you escape the guard? And Lemony?"

He didn't want her to know the guard was tied up and Lemony was sedated.

"It's a long story. We just have few minutes before I leave and I don't want to waste any of that. Just know that it wasn't easy to be here tonight with you," he said.

"But…"

"This could be our last visit," he said interrupting her trying to divert her attention.

"Why you forgot? This can't be our last visit. We are engaged. And I plan to keep my word and marry you."

"We are seeing each other after more than three weeks. We couldn't even talk to each other. Doesn't it say anything?"

"Like?"

"That this could be our last meeting?"

"It doesn't. I will elope with you if it comes to that."

"You will?"

"You doubt? I shall run away with you tonight, if you doubt me again," she said and smiled at him. The charm of her smile made him forget the days he endured without her.

"I never doubted you. I was doubtful about myself. Now I am certain, more than ever. I want to marry you. If I couldn't, I will never marry," he said.

She pulled him and embraced him again. He held her chin, raised her face towards him, and gave her a long kiss. His hands slowly glided over her, feeling an exquisite form of her nubile body.

Outside, in the bus, Sindbad, Amit and Gopal were drinking and munching on the *Kebab*. They were not worried about the guard. His mouth was taped, hands and legs were tied. Lemony was tucked in the trunk pushed under one of the back seats in the van.

When Satvik asked the reason why she couldn't talk to him for three weeks, Shubhangi explained Satvik about the notice from the marriage registrar's office and how her father came to know about the court marriage.

"Things will be normal again," she assured him.

Separation brought them closer than ever. They wanted to spend their lives together and they were more determined than ever.

Satvik handed her his phone so she could use it secretly to talk to him. She refused.

"If I wanted to talk to you, I would have done so," she said.

"Then why didn't you?"

"Because, I wanted to obey my father. I wanted him to realize his mistake."

"Did it work? Has he realized it?"

"So far, no. But he has mellowed. He was the first person to wish me today."

"What if he never allows us to meet again?"

"Then I told you, I will run away with you," she said holding his hands.

"You better. I don't know what I will do without you," he said weaving his fingers in her delicate fingers.

"I think you will do well without me," she said with a mischievous smile.

"I can't, for what I have in my arms this moment, I could give my life for it," he said and kissed on her lips.

"You are looking handsome with long hair. Do I see the Greek God body building up? Can I see it? Take off your shirt."

"No, trust me. It's not yet the Greek God you wanted," he said.

She reached to his shirt and started pulling it up. He resisted her and held her hands behind her.

"You can't stop me," she said spreading her vivacious smile.

"Okay then, on one condition. I can't be naked alone," he said letting her hands free and took off his shirt.

For what he suggested, she punched him with her fists in his chest. He pulled her and kissed her hard on her mouth.

That is when they heard a sound. Three times.

"Meow!"

"Meow!"

"Meow!"

Amit signaled standing below the balcony. He had started getting worried, as it was almost an hour. Sindbad and Gopal were too drunk to realize it.

"Strange, there is no cat in the house," Shubhangi said.

"That's for me. It's signal for me to go."

"Meow? Couldn't you guys just message each other?" she said as she laughed.

"Now that I think about it, it would have been a good option. But we didn't have much time to think it through." Satvik said confused why they didn't think about it.

"Really?" she said laughing as they walked to the balcony.

"I love you," Satvik said looking in to her eyes.

"I love you too," she responded.

"I will wait for your call."

"And I will call you as soon as I get the chance."

"What if you didn't?"

"I will."

Shubhangi promised Satvik that she would call him soon. He held her in his arms and felt her melting in his embrace. The warmth of his embrace made her feel secure. Parting kiss of her luscious lips held him back until they heard 'Meow' again.

Satvik climbed down the rope his friends passed to him. They unlocked the doors while Satvik and Shubhangi blew kisses at each other. She waved to him until they were out of sight. She was happy. Her birthday wish had come true.

Satvik felt bad for the Guard. He wanted to set him free but his friends warned him otherwise. While they were about to leave, Satvik went back to the guardhouse and took the bag off his head. Guard looked at him scared.

"Shh…" Satvik said suggesting him to keep quiet although his mouth was taped.

"Sorry, I can't set you free. Your hands and legs would still be tied. We are going now. Good night." Satvik said. Guard nodded as if thanking Satvik for his kind words.

Amit drove the van back to Satvik's house. Satvik was cheerful. He hugged them one by one, thanking them for being the best friends in the world.

He was happiest person that night. Taste of her kiss, the smell of her bosom lingered in his mind through the night.

The guard was happy that the burglars left him alive. Sense of ease made him sleep through the night.

Beneath the last seat of the van, overdosed Lemony slept peacefully inside the trunk.

———◆•◆◦❀❁❀◦◆•◆———

In the morning, Nandi woke up refreshed after a deep sleep. He walked down to the hall for breakfast. Every morning, he was eagerly greeted by Lemony. It had been like that every day, except that day. That day, Lemony did not run to him. She must be outside in her doghouse, Nandi thought.

Outside, Mooni was about to go for his morning walk when he realized the guard was sleeping. He never slept on his duty. Mooni was shocked when he peeped inside. Guard's hands and legs were tied and mouth was taped. Mooni thought guard was dead. Just when Mooni came close, the guard woke up and stared at Mooni. For the first time in many years, Mooni was startled. Looking at Mooni's face, the guard was scared too. Other servants quickly ran to them. Nandi walked out in the garden hearing the commotion.

The guard narrated the story of four burglars who entered Pushkar Mahal the previous night. Servants were called immediately to check if anything was missing. Queen Devyani, accompanied by maidservants, ran inside and ensured that royal possessions were not stolen.

Everything was in its place. Nothing was stolen. It was a relief. Question remained, what did the burglars steal? Why did they tie up the guard? Then it occurred to Nandi. Lemony had not greeted him that morning. He turned and ran towards the doghouse. He thought he ran, but with his royal paunch, he could only walk briskly.

Lemony was not to be seen. His heart sank. Nandi knew burglars stole the most precious thing next to his family.

"They kidnapped Lemony," Nandi shouted.

Shubhangi came down listening to the chaos. She learnt about the kidnapping. She wasn't worried about Lemony. She thought the gate might have been left open by Satvik and his friends. Lemony may have gone out and would return soon. It had happened in the past.

Nandi was hurt. It was obvious that burglars knew he loved Lemony. He made up his mind to pay a ransom to the kidnappers and bring her back. Servants were ordered to search for her but not to inform police. If the kidnappers learnt about police, he feared they might kill her.

———•—•—◈•⟩⟨◈⟩⟨◈•◈•⟩——

The morning at Chhaya Sadan was cheerful with the children singing songs and getting ready for school. They had a happy surprise waiting for them.

They found Lemony inside a trunk in their van. They believed the dog was a gift left for them by their Satvikpa. The dog was grumpy. But it was clean and well kept. They all took great interest in the dog.

With maximum votes, they named the dog 'Champion.' The dog did not respond very well to the new home and to the new name. With so many children around, it was difficult for the dog to be out of sight. All that dog wanted was to run away.

Satvik's morning was more cheerful than ever. He had been to the gym early morning and started his day with great vigor. When the children informed him of the dog they found in the van, he couldn't believe the mistake they had made. He told the children it wasn't really a gift and the dog belonged to his friend. Promising them that he would bring them a new dog, he asked children to take a good care of the dog.

He feared Shubhangi's reaction. There wasn't much he could do. He couldn't make a mistake to go back to Pushkar Mahal. He decided he would somehow explain it to Shubhangi and return Lemony to her the next time they met. Until then Lemony would be with the children at Chhaya Sadan.

King Nandi sat next to the phone in eager anticipation. He waited for the ransom call from the kidnappers. He never received it.

There was only one call that day and it was from 'The Royal Soul-mates' Matchmakers. They wanted to arrange a family meet with royal family of prince of *Patti*. Even when Nandi was hurt by Lemony's kidnapping, the news brought a smile on his face.

In that moment, his heart weakened. Mixed emotions of joy and pain melted his heart. He felt apologetic for grounding Shubhangi. He realized he had been harsh on her. He knew Shubhangi was angry. She wouldn't agree to meet the prince of *Patti*. Convincing her was difficult. He wasn't sure how he could do it.

If there was anyone who could find a way in that situation, it was Makhan Baba. Nandi knew Baba would listen to the disciple's plea. As he expected, Baba returned his call keeping aside his Godly activities.

He narrated to Baba everything that transpired since their last visit.

"Young blood would always rebel against the odds. Don't forget she has royal blood in her. She is your child. No force can stop her," Makhan Baba said.

It did not make any sense to Nandi. He knew Shubhangi's rebellious nature. That was a reason he paid hefty money to Makhan Baba for a *Jaap*.

"What shall I do, Baba?"

"Remove all restrictions. Set her free. Make her feel you care. Meet her orphan boyfriend. In return, ask her to meet the prince. Once she meets the prince, things would start to fall in place. It's the only way. Only by freeing her, you can convince her."

"What if she refuses to meet the prince? What if she continues to meet that orphan?"

"Then you shall let her. What is harm in that? You don't want to marry her against her will. You just have to change her will so that she wants to marry the man you want."

As always, Baba had found an answer to his problem. Nandi realized his mistake. He knew what needed to be done.

"What about Lemony Baba?"

"She would come back to you when the time is right."

"I trust you Baba. What would I do without your guidance?"

"It's my duty towards my disciples, your majesty."

Talking to Makhan Baba had always helped Nandi to survive difficult situation. His faith towards Makhan Baba always paid off. He knew Baba was right. He must free Shubhangi first to persuade her to marry the prince.

Nandi decided to talk to Shubhangi the next morning.

———•→•◦❖◦❖◦❖•◦•←•———

Champion was well fed and taken care by the children. It was not as friendly as they would have wanted it to be. But they enjoyed its presence. Before they went to bed, they tucked Champion in soft bedding. All of them wished the grumpy dog a good night.

In the morning, they ran to it but the dog was nowhere to be found. It had escaped in the night.

Soon Satvik learnt about Lemony missing from Chaaya Sadan. Not only did they kidnap Lemony, but they also managed to lose her. He knew, Shubhangi wouldn't understand any reasons.

Satvik was surprised when Shubhangi called him that night. Her excitement was evident in her voice.

"What did I tell you? I'd call and I did," she said.

"How did this happen?"

Shubhangi narrated him how Nandi waited to have breakfast with her. Father and daughter had a long chat. Nandi told her how he felt about putting restrictions on her freedom. He apologized to her.

She knew her father was already sad for Lemony. She apologized to him for her behavior.

"What did you do with Lemony?" She asked Satvik.

"Lemony?"

"She is missing since my birthday. I mean she was sleeping in her doghouse the day you came."

Satvik wanted to tell her the truth but hesitated. He could not gather enough courage and decided to tell her the truth later.

"I don't know. When we came in, she was not there."

"Are you sure you and your friends didn't do anything? Because you definitely tied the guard."

"We had to do that, you see. There was no other option. Is he okay?"

"He is fine. But Lemony is missing and you know how much we all love her, not to mention my father."

"Well, I have no idea about Lemony," Satvik said.

"She was with me before the party and if she did not bark at you when you entered, then she must have gone missing during the party. But the gates are always closed. It doesn't make sense."

"She may have gone out during the party and lost her way."

"Maybe. I wanted to put missing posters. I was thinking to go to police but my father doesn't want that. He thinks someone kidnapped her for money and might kill her if police are involved."

"He may be right," Satvik said.

He couldn't imagine police coming with sniffer dogs to his home. He tried to change the course of their discussion.

"So we can meet every day? And your father wouldn't mind?"

"Nope. In fact, there is good news."

"Good news? What is it?"

"My father wants to meet you."

"Meet me?"

"Yes. He wants to meet you. He wants to know more about you, from you."

"Know more about me?"

"Yes, you know what this means? We have a chance. We never have to hide our love. Never have to plan to get married secretly. Of course, they have to like you. Which, they will."

"Why this sudden change?" he asked suspicious of sudden turn of events.

"Well, it's not so simple. In return, I will meet the prince of *Patti* and his family."

"Prince of *Patti*? Who is he?"

"Prince Vikramaditya from the *Patti* family," She said.

Shubhangi told him what her father had offered her. He agreed to meet Satvik. In return, he asked Shubhangi to keep her options open and meet the prince. In a surge of emotions, Shubhangi agreed to meet the prince.

"And if you like him, you would be married to him?" Satvik asked.

"Yes. But, that's only if I like him. Where is the question of me liking anyone other than you?"

Satvik was upset at the possibility of Shubhangi meeting some prince with a prospect of marriage. He couldn't stand the idea of a prince meeting her to seek her hand in marriage. His heart ached.

"There is no match between a prince and me. Why even do this? You could very well marry the prince," he said.

"Except, I will only marry the man I love. And I don't love any prince. I love you," Shubhangi said.

"Then why meet him?"

"That's the only way we have a chance to convince my parents. If I meet him, my father will meet you. All he wants is to be sure that I am not making any mistakes. Any father would want that. If we were married and we had a daughter, wouldn't you want to meet her boyfriend and be sure he is right for her?"

It was that thing about Shubhangi. She could reason with anything she wanted. She could make him feel better with just words.

"I don't know if it's such a good idea but I will do anything to have you in my life. If it meant we go through this, so be it," Satvik said.

"It's difficult for me too. But this is the only option we have."

"What if it doesn't work?"

"Then you know me. I will elope with you."

"Leaving everything behind, just for me?'"

"You always doubt me?"

"Because you love your parents too," he said.

"Yes I do. And they love me. But they are not convinced that I love you and I would be happy with you. I am a strong woman. It is my right to choose the man with whom I want to spend the rest of my life. If I had to meet a prince to be with you, I would do it. And you would do the same for me, wouldn't you?"

"Yes I would, my sweet princess."

"You better, and if you didn't, I will kill you," She said as she laughed.

They talked for hours about the new possibilities. They planned Satvik's meeting with her parents over the next weekend. She decided to make all the arrangements herself at the palace.

———•—•—◦⦉⦊◦⦉⦊◦—•—•———

Satvik called his friends over a party to let them know about new development in his love life. They were happy knowing thing were back to normal and Shubhangi's parents agreed to meet him.

"Who put Lemony back in her doghouse that night?" Satvik asked.

"I don't remember, I was drunk," Sindbad replied quickly.

Amit and Gopal looked at each other.

"I was drunk too. Besides, it was Amit's duty," Gopal said.

Amit couldn't escape. He was not drunk. It was his plan and his duty to put lemony back in the doghouse. For the first time, he realized he had forgotten about Lemony completely.

"I think the dog must be dead by now. I am sure we never took the dog out of the trunk. It was kept under back seat of the van."

"Kids found Lemony in the van. They played with her for a day. Next morning, she was gone. She ran away. We have to get her back before Shubhangi finds it was us who kidnapped her," Satvik said.

"Dognapped," Amit said correcting Satvik. Everyone looked at him in anger.

"How do we get her back?" Amit asked attempting to divert their attention.

"We? I am not going to do anything about it," Sindbad protested.

"Me neither," Gopal said.

"Don't look at me, you are the one who dognapped her," Satvik said in anger.

"Okay fine. If this is what I get for helping my friends, so be it," Amit said in disappointment. He expected someone to offer him helping hand. Nobody did.

"I will find her. If required, I will knock on every door in the neighborhood of Chhaya Sadan. But I will find her," Amit said.

As he promised, from that day onward Amit visited Chhaya Sadan every evening. Children were fond of Amit uncle and his green scooter. Every time he offered a ride in exchange of help to find Lemony, there was more than one of them ready to join him.

Children divided the days and every evening one of them accompanied Amit in his search for Lemony on his scooter. They drove through the neighborhood peeping in front yards. They knocked on neighboring doors and asked about a white Pomeranian dog.

Lemony was not to be found so easily.

As the days passed, Nandi stopped believing he would receive a ransom call from Lemony's kidnappers. He knew why - Lemony was priceless. The kidnappers must have realized that Lemony is worth more than money. They must have fallen in love with her. They must have decided to keep her for themselves.

Chapter 14

Finally, it was the day when Satvik would meet the royal family as a suitor for the hand of the princess Shubhangi. It was also the day that would change their lives forever.

King Nandi was not prepared to meet Satvik. The feeling was like a father meeting a man whom he hated but his daughter loved. For Nandi, he was not just an orphan raised in an orphanage, he was also the man who lured his innocent princess daughter and turned her against him.

The only reason Nandi was willing to meet Satvik was because he wanted Shubhangi to meet Vikramaditya, the prince of *Patti*. If it wasn't for Makhan Baba, he would still be clueless deciding what he could possibly do to convince her.

Neither Nandi nor Satvik liked the plan for the day, but they both decided to go with it.

Satvik's morning was not encouraging. For most part of the previous night, he kept thinking about his visit to Pushkar Mahal. Shubhangi had given him numerous tips to impress her parents but he never felt prepared.

Satvik did not want to ruin an opportunity to create a right first impression. He took time in preparing himself.

His friends helped him get ready for the occasion. Sindbad even offered to go with him as family. Satvik refused.

—·→·→·◈·◦◖◗◦·◈·←·←·—

The day started really well for Mooni. That's just how it started every day. Mooni was in a buoyant spirit as one of his very few old friends visited him.

His proud friend was accompanied by his son, Rakesh. As a child, Rakesh frequented Mooni's house with his father. He had recently returned from China and was visiting Mooni after many years.

After an initial exchange of pleasantries, Rakesh, the young man who was largely disinterested in the discussion between two old and bald men, was amused by the painting on the wall.

It was the painting of the Chinese 'Om' Satvik gifted to Mooni. It hung proudly on the wall in the middle of other pictures of lord *Shiva*.

At mere thought of 'Om,' Mooni bowed his head. For him it was the most powerful word in the world. He believed that utterance of this supreme word absolves one off all the sins.

The young generation does not believe in the power of 'Om,' Mooni thought. One of them must be Rakesh, who was mischievously laughing at the painting. As if something in the painting tickled him.

Mooni noticed Rakesh's arrogance towards the 'Om' but chose to ignore. When Rakesh noted disapproval for his actions on Mooni's face, he spoke.

"Where did you get that painting uncle?" Rakesh asked.

"It was given by one of my friends," Mooni said.

"Friend? Are you sure it was your friend?" he asked suppressing his now obvious laughter.

"Yes, it's 'Om' in Chinese," Mooni Said.

"Om?" Rakesh could barely utter these words as he started laughing profusely.

He vehemently tried to control an unstoppable laughter. When he couldn't, he let go of all his inhibitions and laughed out loud.

"I am sorry uncle, I think I should go," he said getting up from his seat.

"What is wrong with your generation? What is so funny about it?"

"No uncle, nothing funny about 'Om,' but whoever gave you this painting, hates you. I mean really hates you."

"What? Why would you say that?"

"I should probably go, bye uncle" he said and quickly got up from his seat to walk out of the house. His father, still bewildered at his behavior, couldn't stop him.

By now, Mooni understood something was not right with the painting. Rakesh did not look like a man who would laugh unreasonably. He quickly ran behind him.

"You have to tell me what's wrong with the painting?" he asked stopping Rakesh at the door.

"Nothing uncle, it's not 'Om' as you believe it to be. Trust me. I worked in China, long enough to read a little Chinese."

"Then what is it?"

"You really don't want to know."

"Yes, I do. Whatever it is, just tell me so that I can confront the person who gave it to me."

"Uncle, it doesn't say 'Om' in Chinese," he said.

"Then what does it say?"

"Since you really want to know, and I think you should, I would tell you." He said.

Mooni gathered all the curiousness in his bulbous eyes, which appeared to grow in size.

"The painting says," Rakesh paused for a moment as if trying to decide if he should let Mooni know.

Then he spoke, "Fuck you!"

Rakesh left in a hurry still trying to suppress his giggles. Mooni's friend had come out and rushed behind his son.

Mooni did not laugh. He was not good with humor. He didn't find it funny.

Fuck you?

Who says that to an old man? To a man who is a celibate, a *Brahmachari*? What kind of person makes fun of 'Om?' A sick person, Mooni knew.

He came running inside the house and looked at the painting. Every time he saw the painting, he bowed his head in respect. Every morning when he took bath, he lighted incense sticks and asked for blessings in front of that painting.

Mooni's ear lobes reddened in anger. His breathing became noisy. He had rarely experienced such anger. That moment, he wanted to kill Satvik with his bare hands.

He jumped on the sofa and took the painting off the wall. He threw the painting on the ground. Then he jumped on the painting. He kept jumping on it for several minutes.

When he finally opened his eyes, the painting was mangled as if at the hands of a rabid animal. He felt better. He knew what he had to do next.

━━━━•◦❖◦•━━━━

Satvik was lost in thoughts while driving his car to Pushkar Mahal. He had rehearsed everything, numerous times, in his head and wanted to do his best to please Shubhangi's parents. It was one chance, one final opportunity. If he failed to persuade her parents, it was not going to be easy to have Shubhangi in his life.

Satvik was withdrawn to these thoughts when traffic signal turned red. He managed to brake just in time to avoid collision with a biker ahead. As he warned himself to focus on the road, his eyes settled on red light. All moving things on his side of the road stood still.

As luck would have it, after crossing few red signals, his car stalled. Amidst continuous honking and swearing by the people, he managed to pull away from the traffic before it stopped moving. Even after starting well ahead of time, he had wasted much of the time in reaching half way to Pushkar Mahal. He left the car by the road.

The day was serving more obstacles than he could have imagined. Just when he got rid of the car, clouds gathered in the sky quickly turning a beautiful afternoon into an evening.

There was no reason to believe that a drop of rain would fall from the sky in the middle of the winter. Yet the sky made it clear without hesitation that it would pour in abundance. Rain was the last thing he expected to ruin his day. He knew if he did not reach Shubhangi's home within the next half an hour, he would make already bad impression worse.

Standing at the corner, he waited for an auto-rickshaw. Usually, they would come buzzing around but when he needed it most, there was none to see.

Satvik disliked auto-rickshaw drivers. He believed they are deceitful people. The *autowala* brotherhood never managed to correct his opinion. They never ceased to surprise him with the ways to argue for more money. He always avoided them but it was a moment he needed them most.

A smile spread across his face when an auto-rickshaw came maneuvering right next to him. Satvik told him the address. The driver distorted his face, clacked from his mouth and drove off. The gesture meant 'no.'

To add to the misery of the situation, it started raining. Satvik had to act fast and either order for a taxi or get into an auto-rickshaw that came next. When he saw another auto-rickshaw coming closer to him, he decided not to argue with him on fare.

Satvik agreed for double the appropriate fair. He saw the *autowala* could be a savior of his endangered love life and didn't mind paying him an unreasonable amount. For the first time he felt grateful towards the clan of auto-rickshaw drivers.

———•••⦁❈⦁•••———

King Nandi's appointments were strictly followed. Although he had enough time at hand, he judged people by their punctuality. It rarely happened that his appointments didn't show up on time.

Despite Shubhangi's insistence, Nandi walked upstairs to his chamber after waiting for half an hour. He was unhappy that Satvik did not come on time. He gave him one chance and the man couldn't show up on time.

Fully drenched, Satvik and his bouquet finally arrived at the door of Shubhangi's palatial house. He stood composed with a smile he thought suited him best. His heart pounded hard as he waited nervously for door to open.

It was Shubhangi who greeted Satvik with a beautiful smile and a wink. He forgot all the distress he endured reaching there looking at her aphrodisiacal smile.

"Welcome, you are late, and…you are wet. Come inside," She said.

As he entered, his eyes met with an elegant woman seating on a plush archaic sofa. She looked gorgeous. He remembered it was Shubhangi's mother.

"Mother, this is Satvik," Shubhangi said with a cheerful voice. Satvik bowed and touched queen Devyani's feet.

"God bless you *beta*, have a seat," her mother said in a polite voice that suited her royal sophistication.

Satvik handed the bouquet and a bottle of wine to Shubhangi. He sat on the sofa next to her mother. A servant came running with a silver glass full of welcoming sorbet.

"How are you?" Devyani asked.

"I am fine, thank you," Satvik said.

"You are wet. You should dry yourself. Shubhi, can you show Satvik to the washroom?" She said.

Shubhangi quickly got up and took Satvik to the washroom. After a quick hug and a kiss, she left him. Satvik cleaned himself in the luxurious washroom. His fears were gone and he was ready to face her father.

Satvik returned and sat next to Devyani. Shubhangi sat next to Satvik with a shyness that of a bride to be. Her mother looked at them and to the delight of Shubhangi, an approving smile spread across her face.

Satvik felt at ease, everything was going as imagined. That was until he heard the footsteps.

"Father," Shubhangi said looking at the stairs.

185

An old man with gray hair walked down the stairs carefully balancing his big belly on his weak knees. Satvik remembered him from the painting he had seen of him.

Satvik argued with himself whether to stand up and pay him a respect that he rightfully deserved or be seated and wait for him to come down. He got up half-heartedly, slightly tilted his head in respect and said a louder "Hello Uncle."

Satvik was loud. Nandi heard him but turned his face to the stairs below his feet and did not say a word in return. Satvik got up from his seat and waited for him to walk down the stair.

"Walking the stairs is very difficult in this age. If you had come on time, you would have saved me the pain of walking up and down the stairs," he said signaling Satvik was late.

Satvik was unable to decide if he should seat down or wait for Nandi's permission. He looked at Shubhangi who hinted him to seat down.

"I am sorry uncle, I was caught up in the rain," he said.

"You made that very obvious," Nandi said looking at his attire.

They looked at each other. Then there was a long silence. Satvik felt the silence was longer that it should have been.

Shubhangi broke the conversation, "Father, you know Satvik. He is a software engineer. And a philanthropist."

"You have told that hundred times, Shubhi. Will you go upstairs for some time and let us talk to your friend here. I will send for you once we are done talking," he admonished Shubhangi.

With a quick stare, Shubhangi assured Satvik everything will be alright and went upstairs. She was not ready to leave them alone. She looked at them from corridors upstairs. Nandi knew she would be there listening to their conversation.

Satvik introduced himself again and apologized for being late. Nandi did not speak for a while.

"What is your name you said?" Nandi asked.

"Satvik, Satvik Bharat."

"How long you have known Shubhangi?"

"More than six months," Satvik said.

"Do you think six months are enough to know a person?"

"I think so. Sometimes few moments together can bring the familiarity of many lives." Satvik said. He wondered if he had said more than he should have.

"And you think you know Shubhangi?" Nandi asked.

Just when Satvik was about to answer him, Mooni came in haste. He gave Satvik a disgusted look. Mooni carried a perpetual anger on his face, but it was not matched by what he had on his face that moment. Satvik was fearful again.

Mooni requested Nandi to speak to him in private. Nandi and Mooni went in his study. When they were gone to discuss in private, Shubhangi's mother spoke to Satvik.

"I have heard so much about you from Shubhi," she said with a pleasant smile unfazed of what was happening around her.

Satvik smiled back and acknowledged her efforts to make him at ease. While he was still deciding an apt reply, she spoke again.

"Do you love Shubhi?"

He looked at her. He didn't know how to answer that question.

"Yes, I love her. I love her more than anything in this world," words came out of his mouth.

"Then I suppose you would do anything for her," she asked.

"Yes, I will do anything for her," he said.

"I believe you. If you say so, you should be prepared to do whatever it takes to have her," she said.

Satvik nodded his head. Queen Devyani was encouraging. Shubhangi, who had come downstairs and listened to the conversation, smiled bashfully. Shubhangi talked to her mother cheerfully about Satvik and Chhaya Sadan.

After a few minutes, Mooni came outside and stood in front of Satvik. He looked at Satvik with anger. Unaware of the reason which angered Mooni so much, Satvik averted his glance and looked at Shubhangi.

"Come with me, his highness wants to see you alone," Mooni said in his coarse voice.

Satvik stood up and followed Mooni. As he entered the room, Mooni closed the doors behind them.

Shubhangi sat with her mother waiting for them to come out. She was curious to know what was happening inside. The door did not open for next half an hour.

Finally, Satvik came out of the room. His face was red. Tears were rolling on his face. He glanced at Shubhangi and without waiting for a moment, walked out of the door hurriedly.

Shubhangi ran behind him shouting his name but he did not look back. Before she could come out, he was gone.

She knew whatever happened inside the room was not good. She ran inside the room. Devyani followed her. Nandi and Mooni were standing near the door talking to each other.

"What did you say to him?" She asked her father.

Nandi signaled Mooni to go out of the room. Shubhangi had no patience to wait for his answer. Finally, he spoke.

"I asked him what he wanted."

"What do you mean?"

"Your friend demanded money to leave you alone. He threatened he will marry you against my wish if I didn't pay him," Nandi said. Shubhangi kept looking in his eyes.

"I denied," he continued.

"Don't lie to me dad. You have to tell me the truth, whatever it is."

"Watch your tongue. You are calling your father a liar," Devyani said.

"I don't trust you, I know Satvik. You are lying," Shubhangi said to Nandi.

189

"I am not talking on this matter anymore. We are done. You will not see him again. Never!" Nandi said with a stern voice.

Shubhangi turned and ran upstairs. She opened the doors of her chamber and threw herself on her bed. Stream of tears rolled from her eyes.

Chapter 15

Shubhangi tried calling Satvik numerous times but he never answered her call. She was desperate to know what happened between Satvik and her father behind closed doors.

Satvik thought it was better that way. She never should have to know what happened between him and her father. She would be crushed if she came to know about it. It wasn't something Satvik himself would like to remember. He wanted to forget that day, but it kept coming to him.

That day, when Satvik entered the room with Mooni, he saw Nandi in his chair. Mooni closed the door behind Satvik. It was Mooni, who first broke the silence inside the room.

"Fuck you!" he shouted in Satvik's face coming closer to him.

Satvik was taken aback by the sudden attack of profanities. He didn't expect them from Mooni. In that moment, he knew things were about to go terribly wrong.

"Is that how you treat your elders?" Mooni asked.

Satvik did not understand a word Mooni said. It was a nightmare.

"Just because I agreed to have a lunch with you, you thought you could fool me. You said you would never meet Shubhangi. You did. You are a liar," Mooni Said.

Still in shock with hospitality shown towards him, Satvik stood silent.

"You gave me a painting of Chinese 'Om.' You think I would have never known what you did? You are a coward. When you couldn't say it on my face, you wrote it in the painting," Mooni said in a threatening voice.

Satvik was still clueless. He had no idea what Mooni was talking about.

"No one, no one, ever said 'fuck you' to me in my whole life and you have an audacity to give me a painting that says 'fuck you' and lie to me it's Chinese 'Om.' Shame on you", Mooni said without blinking his bulged out eyes.

It took Satvik a while to realize what Sindbad had done to anger Mooni so much. The painting was not a Chinese 'Om' but a swearing in Chinese. Satvik had no defense against it. He just stood there avoiding Mooni's gaze.

"You deceived princess Shubhangi and now you think you can deceive all of us. You can cry your orphan story to Shubhi and gain her sympathy. But I know you. I know people like you. I know your plan. Tell us how much money you want to leave her alone," Mooni said.

Satvik did not say a word. Things had spiraled out of control for him. He was scared of everything that was happening around him.

Nandi signaled Mooni to keep quiet. Then he spoke softly yet with a threatening tone.

"Don't worry. I can understand how hard it could get for an orphan. There is no shame in asking for money," Nandi said standing up from the chair.

It broke Satvik. Tears gathered in his eyes. Satvik had thought of numerous ways to please Nandi so he could accept him. That moment, he knew there wasn't a way he could ever impress Nandi.

"I love her and there is no price you can pay to separate us," he said looking at Nandi. For the first time he looked in to Nandi's eyes.

"You don't understand. If you really love her, you must want to keep her happy. Don't you? You think you can take care of her? Look around and ask yourself if you could ever give her any of these things that she is used to. All this comfort, all these riches you can only dream," Nandi said as he walked up to Satvik.

"You don't think you can marry my daughter without my permission, do you?" he asked.

Satvik did not answer and stood still looking at him.

"Don't fool yourself in to believing you would get everything I have, if you marry her," Nandi said standing next to him.

Satvik felt choked between Mooni and Nandi. All he wanted was to run out of the room and never see them ever again. But he had to stand up for his love. It was being insulted. After taking a deep breath, he spoke.

"You don't understand. I don't need these riches to keep her happy. We love each other. I came to you to ask her hand in marriage, not for your money. I want to marry your daughter. You bless us or you don't, I am going to marry her," he said.

It wasn't a way anyone ever spoke to Nandi. He was king. Dozens of servants worked for him and they never raised their head for the fear they would meet their eyes with their king. Satvik's audacity angered Mooni. He was shaking with anger.

"How dare you talk to his highness like that? Do you even know who you are talking to?" Mooni said pointing a finger at Satvik.

"He is not worthy of standing in front of you. Your highness, if you order, I shall throw him out of the palace right now," Mooni said to Nandi.

Nandi signaled him to stop. Mooni squirmed trying to restrain his anger.

"We know. We know that you broke in my house, tied the guard and stole my dog. I can throw you in jail for a lifetime. The only reason I am tolerating you is my daughter. I don't want to hurt her," Nandi said stressing every word in his kingly voice.

Satvik couldn't understand how they came to know he and his friends broke in Pushkar Mahal. He was taken aback by the sudden disclosure. He could not speak a word.

"The guard identified you. And he would testify against you to put you behind the bars. That's where you belong, in the jail," Mooni explained.

"I am being nice to you. Take the money. Enjoy your life. Run your orphanage. You are doing good work. Leave Shubhangi out of all the hardship you are going through. She is not made for that. If you really love her, let her be happy. Save her from being part of your life. You know better, you wouldn't be able to keep her happy for long," Nandi said trying to reason with him.

With mere mention of Shubhangi's name, Satvik regained his strength. He had to fight for his love. He knew it was his last chance.

"This is a blank cheque, put your price on it and never show your face again to anyone in this home," Nandi said as he slid the cheque in his pocket.

"She would be happy with me as much as I would be happy with her. Your money cannot change that," Satvik said. He pulled out the cheque, tore it in to pieces and threw it in air.

"What did you say? Do you want to die orphan boy? No one will shed a tear," Mooni said coming close to his face.

"I am not afraid. I will marry Shubhangi and no one, no one can stop that, not even you," Satvik said pointing his finger at Nandi.

Those words stung Nandi like a knife. He felt insulted. A stranger challenged him in his house to stop him from marrying his daughter. His hand swung involuntarily and slapped Satvik in his face with a full force.

Satvik never expected it. He almost fell down. For a moment, he thought he should kick the fat man standing next to him. He restrained himself with great effort.

195

"Is that all you can do? Hit a man who loves your daughter?" Satvik retaliated with words.

"Throw him out of my house," Nandi said.

"Get out. Don't show your face again," Mooni said pushing Satvik towards the door.

As Satvik walked to the door, he heard Nandi calling him, "Bastard."

Tears broke the boundaries and rolled over his face. As he walked out of the door, he looked at Shubhangi. His eyes dribbled with tears. He avoided her gaze and hurried towards the main door with quick steps.

Shubhangi knew looking at his face that things have gone wrong. She followed Satvik with long strides. He ran outside avoiding her and vanished quickly.

———•·→•·❧❀❦❀❧·•←·•———

Satvik's world had crashed. He always feared he wouldn't have Shubhangi in his life for long. He knew someday it would come to an end. It did that day. It was a dream that ended abruptly. But it was a dream he would cherish for his life.

After coming out of Pushkar Mahal avoiding Shubhangi, he headed to Chhaya Sadan. Among smiling faces of his children, he tried to hide his pain.

The children gathered around him, played with him and told him stories from their school. For a brief period, he forgot everything. After a while, his mind kept coming back to things happened behind the closed door in Pushkar Mahal.

"So it didn't go as planned?" Jeejee asked.

Satvik shook his head in denial.

"She wasn't for you. You are a good man. I haven't seen many good men in my life. You deserve better."

"It is not her fault Jeejee. It's not because she is a princess, but because I am orphan. Not good enough to marry a princess."

"It's not your fault you are an orphan. Look at these happy faces. Who would say they are orphans? They don't know how it is to be an orphan because they have you. You are their father. They love you. Being orphan has nothing to do with it," Jeejee said looking at children screaming, running after one another.

"You are right. I have enough love in my life. This is my family. No one can take this away from me," he said as he walked towards children.

Three-year-old Nafeesa clung to him shouting at the top of her voice. She wouldn't let him go.

"Satvikpa, will you stay with us tonight for dinner?" Leela asked.

Satvik thought for a moment and nodded his head in agreement. They all cheered. Satvik stayed at Chhaya Sadan and had a dinner with his children. It reminded him how much he loved his children. He reminded himself that there is nothing more important to him than his children.

"Thank you for staying. Children are happy today. Don't burden yourself. Something good will come out of it," Jeejee said while accompanying Satvik out.

"Thank you Jeejee," he said and left for home.

———•→•◦⊰⊱◦•←•———

Sindbad, Amit and Gopal waited for Satvik to return from Pushkar Mahal. They had no doubts about their friend winning heart of the royal family. They were prepared to celebrate the occasion.

Even after spending time at Chhaya Sadan, reality quickly hit Satvik the moment he left. He was sad again. He knew he would never be able to get over it. He would have to learn to live with it.

Sindbad opened the door and greeted Satvik.

"Here comes the future prince of Chakrapani, come inside. We were waiting for you," Sindbad said.

Satvik smiled a pale smile as he entered. Sindbad knew something was amiss. He understood things didn't go well looking at Satvik's face.

"Look at you. What happened to you?" Amit asked.

"It's over," Satvik said as he slumped in the chair.

"What do you mean it's over?" Gopal asked.

Satvik narrated them events of that afternoon. They all listened as Satvik told them every detail of his meeting with Shubhangi's parents. He told them how he was blamed for stealing lemony, breaking in their house and presenting Mooni with a painting of a swearing. He told them about Nandi slapping him in the face and calling him 'Bastard.'

It made his friends furious.

"He slapped you?" Gopal asked.

"He is going to pay for it," Amit said.

"You will marry his daughter, I promise," Sindbad said.

"You gave Mooni 'fuck you' in Chinese?" Gopal asked Sindbad.

Sindbad looked at Satvik and Said, "Yes, I did. I never thought he would ever come to know. I am really very sorry."

"Don't be, that was awesome. The man deserved it," Satvik said looking at Sindbad. Imagining Mooni praying to the Chinese 'Om' every day, they all laughed aloud.

"I knew he will threaten you when you met him over lunch. Knew he will try stopping you from seeing Shubhangi. He deserved it. But how did he come to know what was written in Chinese?" Sindbad asked.

"Dude, how does that even matter? You messed with the old man," Amit questioned.

"It matters. And most of all, how did they know we were the ones to break in that night?" Sindbad asked.

"Because I went back and took off the guard's mask. Remember? I was drunk and did not realize the guard could not scream but he could see me. Mooni must have had him recognize me on my way inside the palace," Satvik said.

"That's why we should stick to the plan. It was not in the plan to remove the guard's mask," Amit said.

"Really? Your plan was to make the dog sleep. Where is the dog now?" Gopal asked.

"It wasn't just my fault. If you guys hadn't gulped the entire crate of beer, Lemony would not be missing. And I am the only one searching for her. Every evening I roam around Sadan to find her and none of you bother to help me," Amit said pointing fingers at Sindbad and Gopal.

"It was none of your fault. You are my best friends. It had nothing to do with what you did for me and Shubhangi. It was just me. Orphan marrying a princess doesn't go well with the world," Satvik said shutting his friends.

"I promise you, no one can stop you two from marrying. I will do everything to see that happen," Sindbad said with a stern voice.

"Me too," Amit Said.

"We all are in it. We all would do everything possible to make sure you two are married," Gopal said.

They extended their right hands arranging their palms one over the other.

"Seriously? A pact? I don't want to," Satvik said.

"Didn't you promise her father that you will marry Shubhangi no matter what it takes?" Sindbad asked.

"Come on? You can't back out. We all made our promises already," Amit said.

Satvik extended his hand over and moved it in unison. They made a promise, a promise that they will do everything they could to bring Satvik and Shubhangi together.

——•→•⁌❀⁍•◆•——

Satvik had challenged Nandi he will marry his daughter. That was his anger, which spoke of the impossible. As days passed, he just wanted to forget everything.

He did everything to forget Shubhangi. He had not answered any of her numerous calls since that day. It helped him distance himself from her. As days turned in to weeks, Satvik distanced himself from everything. He spent most of his time at work, at Chhaya Sadan and in his gym.

Despite all of this, he never really forgot her. There wasn't a way he could forget her for more than few hours. Every night when he went to bed, her smile would flash in front of his eyes opening floodgates of beautiful memories. He wondered if Shubhangi knew what had happened behind closed doors.

His friends didn't know how to help him. Sindbad tried but couldn't convince him to get in touch with Shubhangi. Amit continued his search of Lemony without any luck. Children took happy turns to assist Amit uncle in searching Lemony.

Nandi was still not happy with the situation. Lemony had not returned and her daughter believed he was a villain in her love life. He had grounded Shubhangi again.

Sometimes you must take decisions, which are in the best interest of your children, although they may not like them. Nandi believed he had taken such a decision.

Shubhangi was angry with her father. She was angry with Mooni. Yet, they were the only two people who knew what happened between Satvik and them. She was desperate to know the truth.

Satvik had stopped answering her calls. It angered her. She struggled to hear a word about Satvik and he was not helping. For days, she did not speak to anyone at Pushkar Mahal. Forgetting Satvik was not on her mind. When she couldn't hold herself any longer, she called Sindbad.

Sindbad knew Satvik longed for her. He was incomplete without her. Sindbad told her the truth. For the first time Shubhangi came to know what really happened between Satvik and her father. How Mooni found out they broke in her house, how Nandi offered money to Satvik and how they threatened him. But most of all, how her father humiliated and slapped him.

She was in tears when she heard what Satvik had to go through for her. Her love for him raised many folds. She was more in love with him than ever.

Both Sindbad and Shubhangi knew Satvik needed time. They knew he was miserable but wouldn't talk about it until he was ready.

It was more than a month since Satvik's visit to Pushkar Mahal. He had not spoken to Shubhangi since. There wasn't a moment he forgot her. Whenever he was alone, her thought would slowly take over his mind. In those moments, he would wonder if she had forgotten him, if she had agreed to marry the prince of *Patti*.

He secretly wanted to see her. Know about her without talking to her. There was no way to do so without his friends help. He didn't want Sindbad to believe he still longed for her. After more than a month, in a weak moment, he decided to ask him to check on her.

"Would you do me a favor?" he asked.

"You know I would do anything for you," Sindbad said.

"I… I want to know how is Shubhangi? Is she fine? Is she married already?"

"That's easy. I can do that."

"I know you can. I just want to know if she is doing fine. But without letting her know."

Sindbad knew it was time. He messaged Shubhangi that Satvik was ready. Shubhangi was delighted when she saw the message. Not before long, she managed to find privacy and called Sindbad.

"Here, know everything you wanted to know," Sindbad said as he handed Shubhangi's call to Satvik and quickly dashed out of the house. Bewildered, Satvik took the phone without realizing it was Shubhangi on the other side.

"Hi," he heard her voice.

The purity and gentleness in her voice stirred him. His breathing became heavy. He did not say a word. She could hear him breath in the phone, could feel warmth of his breath.

"Don't you want to talk to your Shubhi?" She asked with a husky voice.

"How are you?" he barely spoke those words. His throat choked with emotions.

"How good can I be without you? You forgot me. Left me alone?"

"I tried hard, but there wasn't a moment I forgot you."

"I know what happened between you and my father. I know why you didn't want to see me again."

"Then you know everything."

"Have you forgotten your promise? You promised me you would always be by my side."

"I have not forgotten a single moment I was with you."

"Then why? Why are you punishing yourself, punishing me?"

"Because that's best for you. Your father was right. I can't give you all the happiness you deserve. I just want you to be happy."

"Can't you see why I love you? You are my happiness."

"That happiness comes with a cost of your father's displeasure. I don't want you to have a moment of trouble, a moment of sadness."

"I am ready to pay that price. I love you. Don't you love me anymore?" She said with her voice filled with emotions.

"I love you too," He said.

"It's been so long I haven't seen you. All I want now is to hold you. Forever and ever."

"I wish I could do so and never ever let you go," he said.

"Don't ever do that again."

"Do what?"

"Not talking to me. How could you not answer my phone?"

"I died everyday thinking about you."

"Good, if you hadn't spoken to me for few more days, I would have come there and killed you myself."

A smile spread across his face listening to her anger.

"I am sorry for what my father did."

"I am sorry for losing Lemony."

"Yeah, you better bring her back. Sindbad told me everything."

"He is against me. He deceived me into talking to you. I had told my friends not to tell you anything."

"No. They are with you. They all want to make us happy. They know we are happy only when we are together."

They were talking after a month. As they talked, anger and bitterness melted away. Love filled a void that was created by many days of isolation. Happiness spread across their faces and their eyes lit with renewed possibilities.

"So where do we go from here?" Satvik asked.

"Well, you have to take me away with you."

"Kidnap you?"

"Yeah right, as if you could kidnap me. I am a princess trained in combat. I would take you down if you tried kidnapping me."

"And I would happily go down," he said with a smile.

"You have to rescue me and take me with you."

"How do I do that? You know what happened last time I broke in your house."

"Who said it would be easy to marry a princess?"

"It's not. I can do anything to have you in my life. We can elope and marry. But are you sure about it? There will be no turning back."

"I don't want to turn back. I was never sure about it than I am now. I just want to be with you. I want to marry you."

As she said those words, a wave of happiness rippled through his mind. The topic of their marriage cheered them.

"You must have dreamt so many things about your marriage. After all, you are a princess. If you elope with me, you may not have the kind of marriage you have dreamt. Your parents may not be there. They will never support us."

"If I was that kind of princess, you wouldn't have fallen in love with me. I don't care about what type of marriage it is."

"You are just saying that because you love me."

"Yes I do, and I can't wait to marry you."

"I can't either."

They talked for a long about their marriage.

"It all feels so good. But it will bring pain to your father, and mother. They will be hurt. They may never talk to you again for bringing the royal prestige down," Satvik said coming back to the reality.

"I know it. It doesn't have to be this way. That's why for one last time, I am going to talk to my father. He knows we love each other. He doesn't have any other option," Shubhangi said.

"What if he doesn't agree?"

"Well, then as I said, come and rescue me. I will wait for you. I will elope with you my knight in the shining armor."

Chapter 16

If there was anyone who could convince King Nandi for princess Shubhangi's wedding with Satvik, it was Makhan Baba. Satvik knew about Nandi's devotion to Makhan Baba from Shubhangi.

When Satvik was insulted by Shubhangi's father, Sindbad started spying on Makhan Baba without Satvik's knowledge. He wanted to find a reason for Makhan Baba to convince Nandi. It wasn't as easy as he thought it would be.

Sindbad had befriended some of the Baba's associates who stayed in the *Ashram*. When they trusted Sindbad, he accompanied them in their shacks. He partied with them and played cards with them. But the things he learnt about Baba from his associates were of not much use.

Then he came to know about Baba's close associate Pandit who harbored all of Baba's secrets. Pandit was Makhan Baba's best man and was the only man who was allowed to enter Baba's chamber. Sindbad knew if there really was someone who could help them, it was Pandit.

After Satvik and Shubhangi's conversation, Sindbad explained his plan to Satvik. He was ready to do everything possible and readily agreed to Sindbad's deceitful plan.

In the morning, they left together for Makhan Baba's *Ashram*. The *Ashram* was set in a serene place and had an air of sanctity to it. When Satvik first entered the *Ashram*, his heart filled with spiritual emotions.

Soon he came to the reality when they were asked to pay a donation for entry to Baba's blessing session. Before Satvik could protest, Sindbad paid the money and got the passes.

Baba's associates were busy controlling the crowd for the morning blessing session. Satvik ensured a place close to Baba's dais while Sindbad sneaked past the dais.

Sindbad moved towards Pandit's shack. He was certain he could enter the shack easily. It was no different from that of other associates he befriended.

Baba and his associates wore saffron gowns separating themselves from the visitors seated next to them. More than a hundred people sat with their hands folded in eager anticipation of Baba's blessing.

Satvik carefully observed Makhan Baba. He was a thin man. He sat on the dais under a big tree. His long hair and a long beard grown over years created an impression of a wise old saint. His legs folded, his hands were lightly resting on his knees. With an incessant smile on his face, Baba unblinkingly stared at his devotees. His smile was unfading as if he wore a mask. For many who believed in him, it was the most pleasant smile.

"You can argue to justify your sense-indulgent ways of living life," Baba's peaceful voice echoed from the surrounding walls.

"But my dear believers, God is mysterious. His ways are mysterious. To know him, to be with him, you must get rid of this unending chain of life and death and achieve the supreme end. You must first break the chain of attachments and believe in good karma. You must first give away what holds you back, your wealth and your earnings, for a good cause and then you will see the miracle. You will see that with the blessings of God, everything is possible," Baba spoke stressing every word knowing his devotees were listening to him carefully.

All of a sudden, Baba looked uncomfortable. His signature smile faded and he closed his eyes. He started breathing heavily. Two of the disciples standing next to him ran and produced a glass of water for him. Devotees eagerly looked at Baba's face. Baba drank water and everything was normal.

Few moments later Baba was restless again. His hands moved across his chest. People started muttering among themselves with augmented curiosity. One of his disciples ran closer to Baba and whispered in his ear. Baba signaled he is alright. Everyone kept quiet as if expecting Baba to tell them what just happened. Baba kept quiet.

Then Baba's face distorted as if he was about to vomit. He was not in a good shape. But everyone just waited, anxiously, as if this was not the first time something like that was happening.

Once again, Baba's stomach moved and rippled upwards. Satvik was certain Baba was about to vomit. Everyone gasped when Baba quickly put both his hands on his mouth. Satvik jumped off his seat but someone seating behind pulled him down.

"Have you come here for the first time? Just sit and watch," the man who pulled him murmured.

Finally, Baba vomited in his hands. He closed his hands holding in the vomit and started shaking his head vigorously. Satvik felt disgusted and turned his head away. Satvik was startled to hear everyone cheering and clapping. He carefully raised his head to an awaiting surprise. Baba was holding what he vomited, a miniature golden idol of Lord *Shiva*.

The crowd was ecstatic. Devotees stood up and cheered. Before Satvik could realize, a long queue formed to touch Baba's feet and receive his blessings.

Satvik was appalled at the reaction of people to Baba's ability to produce gold from his mouth. Baba had pulled his act cleverly. With a divine call through those hiccups, he had given birth to God through his mouth.

While Baba was busy giving birth to the God, Sindbad managed to enter Pandit's shack. He was hoping to find something against Pandit to make him spill the beans. He did not find anything until he opened one of his bags.

Sindbad immediately knew he had hit the jackpot. It contained news articles about a bank robbery. One of the paper cuttings was a wanted poster for someone named Pandurang for a bounty of one-lakh rupees. It took him a while but Sindbad recognized the wanted person was no one else but Pandit himself.

When he received message from Satvik on his phone, Sindbad quickly came out. His work was done in time. He wrote a note on a paper and went to Pandit. After bowing his head, he handed him the note. When he read the note, a smile spread across Pandit's face. Sindbad smiled back at him.

As Satvik and Sindbad returned home, Sindbad showed Satvik the newspaper cuttings. Satvik was happy knowing they found what they were looking for.

"But how would you call Pandit?" Satvik asked.

"He would call us."

"Why would he call us?"

"I gave him a reason and my number. I left a note with him."

"You did? What was the note about?" Satvik asked.

"I wrote him note - if you want big money, I have a small job you can do easily. And mentioned my phone number," Sindbad said.

"I still don't understand."

"This is the man who had robbed a bank. He is wanted. No one but we know his secret. He doesn't have a choice but to share Baba's secrets. That would happen only when he comes out of the *Ashram* to meet us. My note is just going to do that for us," Sindbad explained.

"Let's hope it works."

Pandit did not take much time to call Sindbad. Sindbad had offered him big money for an easy job. It was an opportunity Pandit always waited. He proposed '*Sapna Bar*', his favorite hangout bar in suburban *Pune,* for their meeting when he called Sindbad.

Pandit entered the bar in t-shirt and jeans. If it wasn't for his long beard, Sindbad could not have recognized him without his saffron gown. He introduced himself to Sindbad as if he could rob a Swiss bank all alone, if he wanted. But the brave face did not last long.

Sindbad ordered Pandit's favorite whiskey. Soon Pandit knew he had fallen in the trap. Sindbad told him he knew Pandit was wanted by the police.

"One lakh is a big amount," Satvik said handing him newspaper cuttings he stole from his chamber.

Pandit argued he did not rob the bank at all. He agreed he did break in to the bank but never managed to open the vault. He had left his mobile phone inside the vault making it easier for police to frame charges against him. It was actually the bank manager, who took the money and blamed Pandit. He begged Sindbad to think if he really deserved to go to jail for the crime he did not commit.

Pandit turned out to be a lot easier than Sindbad thought.

"I agree. You should not be punished for the crime you never committed." Sindbad said.

Pandit was puzzled. He had no clue what was Sindbad up to.

"That's why I am returning all the paper cuttings. No one knows. No one has to know," Sindbad said.

That relieved Pandit but he was still confused about what Sindbad wanted from him. Only when Sindbad told him he had no intentions to hand him over to police, he touched the whisky.

"I have nothing against you. I just want to know more about Makhan Baba," Sindbad said.

"What about Baba?"

"You know, the secrets, like these," Sindbad said pointing at the paper cuttings.

"I don't know anything about Baba. He never talks about his past."

"Please don't make it difficult for me. You are my friend."

Pandit was reluctant to say a word about Makhan Baba. He insisted he did not know anything about Baba's past.

"I promise you, neither you nor Baba will be in trouble. I have some other business with Baba. You must trust me. Bank robbery can put you in jail for the rest of your life," Sindbad reasoned with him.

After initial inhibitions, he started talking about Makhan Baba. As whiskey made its way to his brain, he loosened.

Couple of rounds later, he acted as if he drank truth serum. He narrated Baba's biography confirming if he would be in trouble after every few minutes. He told Sindbad how Baba was a postman and how he ran away abandoning his wife and mother.

When Satvik probed, Pandit told about King Nandi's devotion to Baba and the fake *Jaap* performed for his daughter's love affair. Sindbad ordered a full bottle of Pandit's favorite whiskey and handed it to him.

"This is for you. You have helped me a lot. Rest assured you would not be in trouble. You are my friend. From one friend to another friend," Sindbad said touching his shoulder.

Pandit looked at the bottle. Although he was inebriated and it was difficult to judge with his facial hair, he was emotional.

"No one calls me friend. You know? I am not a friend to anyone. You are my only friend. You know? My best friend," Pandit blabbered. His words collapsed one over the other.

"Yes, I am your friend and I need your help," Sindbad said.

"Anything… anything… anything…just say it," he said shaking his head vigorously.

"You have already helped me enough. I need one more favor. Only someone special like you can have address of Makhan Baba's home in the village where his mother and wife lives," Sindbad said.

"You are right. No one knows it. No one but me. Baba sends money to his home anonymously. I go to the post office and use money orders to send the money."

He took out what looked like his wallet full of papers folded and arranged neatly. After spending few minutes carefully looking at the papers, he pulled out a receipt of money order, which had Baba's address from his village.

Sindbad was impressed with the fact that Pandit could find the address even when he was drunk. Sindbad thanked Pandit and requested for one final help, Baba's personal phone number.

Pandit handed Sindbad his mobile, after all, Sindbad was his best friend.

"Search it. His name is Makhanchor. Chor *saala*," he blabbered.

Sindbad noted Baba's phone number.

Pandit requested him to stay longer for the sake of their friendship but Sindbad excused himself for urgent work. Pandit shook hands with Sindbad and hugged him many times. He was confident his new friend would never betray him.

Sindbad left Pandit thanking him and assuring him his secret was safe. Outside Sapna Bar, Satvik eagerly waited for Sindbad. He was happy to know Sindbad's mission was successful.

It had been more than a month and there were no signs of Lemony's return. Nandi knew the orphan and his friends had done something to Lemony. His heart sank with the thoughts of Lemony never returning to Pushkar Mahal.

Besides, Shubhangi was unhappy with him. He did not want to be harsh on her. But he had no choice. It was all for her. He had fulfilled his promise by meeting Satvik. It was

Shubhangi's turn to meet the prince of *Patti* and his family. Nandi was confident that if she met the prince, she would like him. She will forget she ever met Satvik.

Nandi had already communicated to 'The Royal Soulmate' Matchmakers about his readiness. He eagerly awaited a message from the prince's family. Nandi was lost in thoughts when Shubhangi and Devyani entered his study.

The previous night, Shubhangi had talked with Satvik after a month. After knowing about what transpired between Satvik, Mooni and her father, she was determined to talk to her parents. She wanted to make a final attempt to convince them. She asked her mother to join in her conversation with her father.

"Father, I want to talk to you," Shubhangi said.

Nandi shook his head in agreement. Devyani stood beside Nandi.

"I know what happened that day when Satvik came here to meet you. I know what you did to my friend."

"Then, you should know why I did what I did," Nandi said.

"Because you care about me. You love me. And I understand that. But I love him and he loves me. I really want both of you to accept him. At least try to know him. I promise you will like him," she said.

"We already did that Shubhi. I don't want to talk about it. You asked me to meet him, I did. Now it's your turn to meet Prince Vikramaditya. And I promise you will like him far more than him," Nandi said.

"I will meet the prince. But you did not meet Satvik the way you should have. I know it. You know it too," Shubhangi said.

"Oh, so you talked with him despite my orders. Did he ask you to talk to me?" Nandi asked in anger.

"No, he didn't. When he came here, he was our guest. Why did you insult him?" Shubhangi was agitated with her father's responses.

"There are hundred reasons, pick one. He lied to Mooni about the painting and insulted him. He lured you in to loving him. He promised Mooni he will never meet you again but he did."

"What about Mooni uncle threatening him. What about sending men to beat him?"

"The man is a liar. Don't you see? What more reasons you want when he broke in our house and stole Lemony? Isn't it a big enough reason?"

"He did not steal Lemony. And if he ever lied, he did so for love. You lied too. He did not ask for money, you offered him money. And you slapped him? You thought I will never come to know about it?" Shubhangi said.

"Watch your tongue," Devyani said warning Shubhangi.

"I did. I offered him money because I knew that is what he wanted? Can't you see, he is not a match for you, for our family? He knows you are a princess. Everything that I have is yours. And all he has to do is have you." Nandi said.

"If that is what you think, I don't want any of it. All I want is my own life. I have a right to decide what I want in my life."

"No, you don't. Don't forget you are a princess. You are the pride of the Chakrapani dynasty. You don't get to destroy that. If it wasn't for you, I wouldn't have allowed that man to enter in my house."

"And you shouldn't have. But you asked him to come over. Then you insulted him. You slapped him. Called him bastard and threw him out. I know everything."

"If you know it then you should also know that we know he came to meet you the night of your birthday. Meeting him secretly in the night, you brought shame to our family."

"Yes, I did."

"You seem to be proud of it. You did not turn out to be the way we thought. We must have failed as a parent," Nandi said.

As he said those words, Shubhangi felt anger rising in her.

"I would not live without him," she said with tears in her eyes.

"What?"

"I would end my life without him."

Nandi's hand swung and slapped her face. Sudden thrust of his hand pushed her hard. She fell on the ground and lost her senses for a moment.

Nandi stormed out of the room in extreme anger. Shubhangi did not expect him to react in such a way. She had never seen him so furious. He had never raised a finger at her in her entire life. He had never so much as shouted at her.

She looked at her mother with blurred eyes. Devyani was angry too. She walked out following her husband.

Not before long Shubhangi was encircled by her maidservants. They were warned to not leave Shubhangi alone. Devyani took charge and had Shubhangi's phones taken away from her. Shubhangi was quarantined again. Devyani gave her motherly advice to forget Satvik and prepare for the prince's visit.

Nandi asked Mooni to beef up the security of the palace. Mooni did not waste time in installing security cameras around the palace and appointing new security guards.

———•••◈•◈◈◈•◈••———

Satvik tried Shubhangi's phone many times but he never got an answer. When he did not hear anything from her for couple of days, he knew things were not normal.

A week passed without talking to Shubhangi. Satvik was desperate again. He felt as if Shubhangi wanted him to do something. She had told him to come and rescue her if she did not call him.

Satvik's mind wandered in negative thoughts. What if she was forced to marry the prince of *Patti*? What if the marriage was in progress that very moment? His heart sank with such discouraging thoughts. He had to do something before it was too late but he was not certain what could that be.

That's when his phone rang. Thinking it was Shubhangi, he looked at the phone. It was Amit.

"Hey," Satvik answered.

"Guess what?"

"What?"

"I found the dog!"

"What?

"Dude, I found the dog, Champion. Can you believe it?"

"Her name is Lemony. Where did you find her?"

"It was in the nearby slum. The dog is beyond recognition."

"Where is it?"

"She is at Chhaya Sadan. The kids are giving her a bath."

"This is great news. Thank you."

"Anything for you."

"There is one more thing. You have to come home tonight."

"What for?"

"We are meeting tonight. Just come over, it's important."

Satvik's love life needed help before it's too late. He wanted to talk to his friends and ask for their help.

"It's been more than a week since we last spoke. She wanted to try to convince her parents one last time. After that we never spoke," Satvik said as Sindbad, Amit and Gopal listened.

"I promised her that I will come and rescue her if I didn't receive her call. I have to do it and do it fast. Her parents want to get her married to a prince. If I don't do something now, I will always regret it."

"What are you suggesting? We break in her house again?" Amit asked.

"You understand for a third person it would sound like a kidnapping?" Gopal said

"If she could talk to me now, she would want me to help her elope and that's not the same thing as kidnapping," Satvik said.

"We don't have to worry about kidnapping. She is a grown-up, she can go anywhere she wants, marry anyone she wants." Sindbad said.

"Dude, she is a princess. You should know what it means. It means her father is a powerful man. You don't want to piss him off by running away with his daughter," Gopal said

"What if you two marry the day she runs away with you? Once married, the king doesn't have much of a choice, does he?" Sindbad asked.

"Exactly. And the last time I was doubtful about it, I remember you guys promised me that you would do everything to bring us together," Satvik said.

"We did and we will keep our word. Let's get you two married," Sindbad said.

"Let's get you married," his friends cheered as they raised their drinks.

———•·•→•·❧✖❧❊❊❊❧❊❧✖❧❀•◆·•←•·•———

For next one week, they met every night and discussed the plan to help Shubhangi elope. It was necessary that they had better plan than the last time. They also had to plan for the wedding if they succeeded in their plan.

After nearly a week of nightly discussions, they finally had a plan. Every step was meticulously planned, yet the risk of being caught was always there. Bringing Shubhangi and Satvik together wasn't the only thing his friends had promised him. They had promised Satvik a revenge for the slap Nandi had offered him.

Since the day they decided to rescue Shubhangi, Sindbad was working on taking revenge. He had prepared fifteen stink bombs in small pickle sized bottles. It was a stinky mixture of Bombay duck fish, egg yolk, soya sauce and dried cheese decomposed for a week. The bottles were tightly closed. When he slightly opened one of the bottles to show his friends, they all ran to avoid the terrible stink.

Finally, after making all the arrangements to carry out their plan, they were ready to rescue Shubhangi.

Chapter 17

As the sun rose in the sky, birds chirped in the lush gardens of Pushkar Mahal. The colorful Indian bred roosters specially ordered for prince of *Patti*'s feast, cock-a-doodle-dooed one after another. If things went as Nandi planned, it would just be few days those roosters would see the sunrise.

Nandi was seating in the porch seeping hot cup of Darjeeling tea. A servant came running with a phone in his hand. He bowed and whispered to Nandi. It was a call from messenger of *Patti*.

"Nandivardhan Chakrapani," Nandi answered.

"Your royal highness, *Maharaja* of *Palam*, please accept greetings from a humble servant from the court of *Patti*, devotees of *Shiva* and the dynasty of great warriors," voice on the other end spoke with poise.

Nandi could not remember the last time he was addressed like a king. It was not a fashion anymore. Someone associated with a royal family alone could know how to address a king properly. It felt good.

"How are the prince and the family of *Patti*?" Nandi asked.

"With the blessings of the forefathers, the prince and the house of *Patti* are doing well. Forgive me for having called you unannounced. I have come here in the city of *Pune* for making arrangements for the prince's visit to Pushkar Mahal."

"Arrangements? You need not make any arrangements. The prince will stay with us, here, in my palace."

"Yes, of course, Maharaj. But it is my duty to take every precaution for his security. I am here with my two associates for his security arrangements. The world is not as good a place as we think it is."

"That's the price we all are paying for dissolving kingdoms. The chaos around, people love it in the name of freedom and democracy. Anyway, you must come and stay with us."

"My apologies your highness, I would not be able to do so. I am here just for a day. The house of *Patti* has sent sweets and special delicacies for the princess and her family. I am to personally serve them."

"You are a royal guest. You must come and stay with us."

"You are a generous king your majesty. The tales of your generosity are told in all corners of India," messenger said.

It pleased Nandi. He did not know of any charity work he was involved in. But Shubhangi had been spending huge money on charity which was, after all, his money.

"Me and my associates have booked hotel. Our work here will be done by tonight. We all leave for the state of *Patti* in the morning."

"I insist, you must dine and stay with us tonight. You are the guest of the Chakrapani's. You can't possibly stay in a hotel," Nandi said with a firm voice.

"Your majesty, I would not be able to disobey your order. I am but a servant and would love to stay with the family."

"We will wait for you and of course, the delicacies from *Patti*," Nandi said.

"I will not keep you waiting for long, *maharaj*. I ask for one more favor."

"What is it?"

"I am here to arrange for security of the prince Vikramaditya and family. If it wasn't for the prince and his love for the princess, no one would have known I am here with my two associates."

As Nandi heard his words, his face cheered again. The messenger had made a reference to prince's love for Shubhangi. It opened up many possibilities in Nandi's mind.

"My work is that of secrecy. It is beyond my powers, but I request your highness to not mention my arrival to anyone," the messenger said.

"I give you a word. I will not mention your arrival to anyone."

"My king, I shall have the courage and pleasure to see you tonight." The voice spoke.

Nandi was happy. The morning had brought good news. The arrival of a security advisor meant the arrival of prince Vikramaditya. It was just a matter of time.

His wait was about to come to an end.

———·→·→·◈◄◦◄◦◈◄◦◈◄◦◈·◄·→·——

Shubhangi was furious when her mother told her that messenger from Prince Vikramaditya would visit them for dinner and stay with them that night.

It had been more than three weeks since Shubhangi last spoke to Satvik. She was scared at the prospect of meeting the prince sooner than expected. If she met the prince and if he liked her, she could hardly stop things from progressing any further. She knew she must leave the palace at once.

Nandi called Makhan Baba thanking him for his blessings and shared the news of messengers visit. Makhan Baba never understood how his blessings worked for others. Baba told Nandi to show royal hospitality towards the messenger of the Prince for it was likely that he was coming to see his worthiness.

Nandi never thought of it that way. He felt happy he had called Makhan Baba. He believed Baba was right. The messenger might have come to see and gather information about Shubhangi and the Chakrapani family. If he returned happy, he will soon bring the prince to Pushkar Mahal.

On Nandi's instructions, Mooni gathered every member of the house. When all the members including security guards, cooks, gardeners, servants and maidservants gathered, Nandi spoke.

He carefully instructed everyone about the visit of the royal guests from the *Patti* family. He told them the purpose of their visit was to judge the Chakrapani household ahead of prince Vikramaditya's visit.

"The guests must return with praises for the Chakrapani family and bring the prince to Pushkar Mahal," Nandi said.

They all scurried back to their work. It wasn't always that they were rounded up by the king himself. Mooni led all the preparations to ensure the guests were treated well.

———•·•◆•◦⊱⋆⁑⋆⊰•◦•◆•·•———

At Chhaya Sadan, the plan was set in motion. Satvik, Sindbad, Amit and Gopal had their tasks assigned to them. Every step was discussed again to ensure the plan and the back up plans were fool proof.

The first step of the plan was successful. Sindbad had successfully posed as a messenger from *Patti* and managed to be invited by Nandi to Pushkar Mahal.

Amit and Gopal rented a big Ford utility vehicle while Satvik and Sindbad searched for delicacies from *Patti*. Even after researching on the internet, they could not find any famous delicacies of *Patti*. They decided to make apple *halva* the famous delicacy from *Patti* considering the royal family sold apples.

Apple *Halva* brought from the local sweet mart was tempered in the kitchen. Amma and Sakhubai added powdered sleeping pills, which Sindbad and Satvik had brought in abundance. In the end, trays full of *halva* were decorated with silver foil.

While Satvik and his friends were getting ready, the children played with Champion, the dog Amit uncle had found and brought back. Leela told them that the dog's name was not Champion but Lemony and it was going away. The young ones were disappointed until they were told that the dog was going to its home and it will be happy there.

Satvik, his friends and Jeejee discussed about their plan for that night.

"Are you sure you want to do this?" Jeejee asked Satvik.

"I am sure Jeejee. I want this. We both want this,' Satvik said.

"Okay. Then I will start the preparations for the wedding. We can't wait for long once Shubhangi is here. It has to be done immediately," Jeejee said.

"I agree. If we succeed tonight, you two have to get married as soon as possible," Sindbad said.

They decided Shubhangi would stay at Chhaya Sadan with the children. Jeejee took it upon himself to make all the preparations for the wedding. In his old age, apart from being with children, Satvik's wedding was a ceremony he wanted to enjoy the most.

A special dinner was prepared at Pushkar Mahal for the messenger and his two associates. Everybody waited for the messenger. That day, for the first time, Nandi had to wait for dinner for a man who was just a messenger. It felt odd.

Sindbad wore a black tuxedo and prepared himself to look like a royal messenger. Amit and Gopal dressed appropriately as his associates. They avoided excessive make up to make it easier for Shubhangi to recognize them.

Sindbad and his two associates – Amit and Gopal wanted to ensure everybody at the palace ate *Halva*. Everybody, except Shubhangi. That was a difficult mission. Sindbad knew the lesser time they spent with the royal family, the better it was.

They reached Pushkar Mahal at around 9 PM. As Sindbad pulled up the Ford in front of the main gate, guards ran around. The entire Chakrapani household came out and gathered around them. Sindbad, Amit and Gopal were frightened looking at the crowd. Servants took the delicacies Sindbad had brought inside the Pushkar Mahal.

"My name is Shantanu, I am the security advisor and a loyal servant to his highness prince Vikramaditya of *Patti*," Sindbad introduced himself and bowed his head in respect. Nandi presented them with a large bouquet.

Nandi was impressed at the mannerism of the messenger. His attire and his face oozed confidence. If this was the messenger, what would be the prince like, Nandi tried to imagine.

"These are my associates," Sindbad introduced Amit and Gopal who were warned not to open their mouth in any circumstance.

Nandi personally guided them into his palace and then into the grand dining hall. On a big majestic dining table that could accommodate twenty people to a fine dining experience, Nandi enthusiastically talked to the messenger. Mooni and Devyani also accompanied them for the dinner.

Shubhangi joined them late. She was not interested in meeting the prince, leave alone a messenger or his two associates. She failed to recognize they were Satvik's friends.

Nandi was curious to know about the *Patti* dynasty. The messenger didn't seem to mind it. He told stories no one ever heard about the *Patti*'s.

Vikramaditya's great grandfather, Virabhadra *Patti*, had bought one of the first few Rolls Royce, almost a century ago, the front of which was customized to look like a pouncing tiger. The beautiful car still adorns the private possessions of the *Patti*'s. It is said the car is priceless and sought after by many museums and art collectors around the world.

Virabhadra had many famous stories. He was a king until his death and died before independence. His anger towards the British was well known. He did not like the British and their disrespect towards Indian women. He specially ordered a famous French artist to create a life size statue of the British queen. The resemblance was so uncanny that none, who saw it, believed it was a statue. Until his death, the statue stood by his throne and fanned him.

It is said that the British brought the statue from Kumarvishnu, Vikramaditya's grandfather, for twenty elephants.

Even after so many years of independence, Prince Vikramaditya still had many horses, three elephants and a fleet of thirty finest cars. The palace of *Patti* was still the most beautiful palace from the inside.

So said the messenger at the dinner table.

As Sindbad spoke from what he had gathered on the internet, Nandi and Devyani were astonished with the legends of the *Patti* dynasty. Shubhangi was largely disinterested until the end. Although it was difficult for Amit and Gopal, they kept quiet and enjoyed the feast offered by the royal family.

When the dinner was over, the messenger hurried himself.

"It was my good fortune to have dinner with you. We must retire to bed now. We have a flight to catch in the morning," he said.

"When is the prince coming?" Mooni asked.

The Messenger looked at Mooni for any traces of suspicions.

"We want to make arrangements," Mooni explained.

"I am sure once the date is finalized, the Patti family would send a message."

"We had a good time. Give our best wishes to everyone and convey our gratitude for the sweets," Nandi said.

"I would like to serve all of you the famous *halva* myself. So has been ordered by my prince. Each and everyone in the house," Said the messenger.

The servants rushed around and a number of silver bowls were filled and brought over for serving. Nandi's diabetes had not allowed him to touch sweets in a long time. But, he finished the bowl quickly and took another one.

"I've never ate anything like it, this is by far the most delicious thing I have ever put in my mouth," he said and praised the *halva*.

"This is really delicious," Devyani said.

Sindbad, Amit and Gopal were also served big bowls of *halva*.

"I am afraid I am full, and cannot take a bite. Beside, these are for you, we eat the famous delicacy every day," he said laughing.

"No, no, you must share our joy," Nandi said as he scooped the *halva* from his second bowl.

Sindbad could not resist anymore. That would be disobeying the King. Amit and Gopal looked at Sindbad who shook head signaling them not to resist. They finished the *halva* as soon as they could. Shubhangi had not touched the *halva* yet. Sindbad prayed she doesn't eat it.

Nandi noticed as Sindbad looked at Shubhangi's plate. He noticed that messenger had noticed Shubhangi hasn't touched the *halva*. Nandi was alarmed and did not want to give a sense of Shubhangi's displeasure.

"Shubhi, haven't you tried it yet?" Nandi asked.

"Your highness, princess Shubhangi may have it later. After all, she may have to eat this for rest of her life," the Messenger said and laughed. Amit and Gopal joined him.

Nandi laughed at the hint. The comment angered Shubhangi. She looked at the messenger with a stern look. As she looked at him, the messenger stared at her face daringly with his eyebrow raised. She thought that was rude for a messenger, to stare at the princess. It was against protocol.

It took her more than a moment to realize that the messenger was Sindbad and his two associates were Amit and Gopal. Her face saw sudden change of expressions from anger to shock to pleasure.

"Your highness, the word around is that you are the most beautiful princess ever. I confess it is true. If prince had seen her highness in person, he would know you are more beautiful than he thinks you are. It is with love for you, the family of *Patti* has asked to serve this delicacy to everyone in your palace," messenger said and blinked.

It did not take long before Shubhangi realized what Satvik and his friends were up to. She hid her expression of delight.

"Thank you. I will have it later. If it was possible, I would have met the prince today," She said. It surprised Nandi and Devyani. Nandi smiled at himself. The royal charm was already working on his daughter.

"Your highness, all your wishes will come true. Please excuse us, we must leave now. I shall inform the prince that the princess had shared the delicacy herself with everyone at the palace. It will please the prince," the messenger said.

"I shall see to it," Shubhangi said.

"My king, we shall retire now," he said.

"Thank you. Mr. Mooni would show you to the guesthouse. When you see the prince tomorrow, convey our regards and let the family know that the Chakrapani's are waiting to welcome them," Nandi said.

Sindbad got from the seat and bowed his head to the king, to the queen and to princess. He gave an assuring smile to Shubhangi. His associates followed suit. They walked briskly towards the door. Mooni took them to one of the outhouses prepared for their stay.

Shubhangi rounded up all the staff at Pushkar Mahal after their dinner. She asked to serve bowls to everybody and ensured everybody ate the *halva* before they left. Princess feeding them *halva* was a generosity the staff never experienced at Pushkar Mahal. They happily ate it to their hearts content.

It was not long before sleep started taking over the palace.

———•·→•·✥❧⟨❳⟩❧✥·•←·•———

"Hurry up, don't waste time, get everything out," Sindbad said locking the doors from inside the guesthouse once Mooni left.

"What do you mean?" Amit asked.

"I mean, vomit, if you don't want to fall sleep."

Sindbad ran with frenzy to the kitchen and mixed spoons of salt in a glass of water. He drank the solution and signaled Amit and Gopal to follow. They had a sumptuous dinner and hated the thought of vomiting. But there was no other option if they wanted to stay awake.

It was by far the worst experience of their life. They came out fully drained, their faces pulled down.

Sindbad called Satvik to update him once they were sure that the sleeping pills will have no effect on them. Satvik was delighted to know things were moving as planned.

"So they all ate the *halva*?" Satvik asked.

"Yes, they ate it. At least the royal family and Mooni ate it," Sindbad answered.

"Did Shubhi recognize you?"

"Not at first. She wouldn't look at the messengers. It was only in the end she recognized us and understood the plan. Let's just hope she made everyone eat the *halva*," he said.

"So, we are doing it tonight?" Satvik asked.

"Yes, we are doing it. I would call you again. Be ready." Sindbad said.

They needed a coffee to keep themselves awake. It would be couple of hours before they would check to ensure everybody at palace was asleep.

A deep sleep prevailed on the palace sooner than it usually did. The king and the queen both retired to bed early. Shubhangi expected the *halva* to ensure they all slept sound and peaceful until the morning.

At around midnight, both her maidservants were in deep sleep. The delicacy from the *Patti* had done its job. She came out of her chamber and walked freely. She walked out and checked on the guards who were in dreamless slumber.

Sindbad, Amit and Gopal were alert when Shubhangi knocked on their door. They feared their plan was exposed and trouble had reached the doors. With a fearful hesitation, Sindbad opened the door. A smile spread across their faces as they found Shubhangi standing outside.

"Hi," Shubhangi said cheerfully as she entered.

"Welcome!" Amit said.

"I can't thank you all enough for everything," she said.

"Don't be, we are not done yet." Sindbad said.

"Where is Satvik?" she asked.

"We have to call him once everybody is asleep."

"Don't worry everybody is in a deep sleep. But we must hurry."

Sindbad quickly explained the remainder of the plan to her and asked her to pack her belongings.

Shubhangi went back to her room and started packing her bags. Even when she was about to run away, it was hard for her to choose her favorite dresses and accessories. When she was done, she had seven bags full of things she wanted.

Satvik had started from Chhaya Sadan. He was carrying Lemony sedated in a trunk. Before Satvik reached Pushkar Mahal, the plan was set in motion. Amit sprayed paint on the security cameras. Gopal locked Mooni's house first and then the rest of the outhouses. During all this, guards did not allow the smug smile on their faces to fade.

Shubhangi ran downstairs the moment she saw Satvik. As she came out, she ran in to his arms and hugged him. They kissed passionately until Sindbad interrupted them.

"There would be time for that, you must go at once," he said.

"I have a few bags," Shubhangi said.

"Bags? Why?" Satvik asked.

"You don't think I will elope with you without any clothes, do you?" She asked.

"How many?"

"Seven bags. Big ones," she said.

"Seven bags? How big?"

"Each bag needs two of you," She said and smiled.

"What if someone wakes up?"

"No one would wake up. They are all in deep sleep."

"Okay, let's get the bags quickly," Satvik said.

They all went inside. Looking at the bags, they realized what she meant by a big bag. They had to load few bags in the van, as they wouldn't fit in the Ford. When they were finished bringing the bags, they were tired.

"Alright, next up, you two take the Ford and go to Chhaya Sadan. We will do the rest and follow you," Sindbad said.

Shubhangi was at her happiest best. She jumped in the driver's seat and drove the ford herself. Satvik asked his friends to follow them and not do anything more than what they had planned.

Sindbad, Amit and Gopal waved at them with an evil smirk.

———•‣•‣•◈‹‹○››‹‹○››◈‹‹○››•‣•‣•———

Their mission was accomplished when Shubhangi left Pushkar Mahal with Satvik. But there were still a few things to be done.

Sindbad, Amit and Gopal took out the stink bombs and punctured the lids of the bottles. They could smell the terrible stink of rotten mixture. They entered the palace and started planting the stink bombs in the places where no one could find them and even if someone did, no one could remove them.

They planted the bombs inside the sewage pipes, in air conditioning tunnels, below the sofa, in the chandelier, and underneath unreachable corners of furniture.

A stale stench of rotting animal filled the air. They felt better as if they had taken revenge.

"Are we done now?" Amit asked.

"No, not yet," Sindbad said.

"What now?" Gopal asked.

"Don't forget Lemony like we did the last time. We have to put her back. But before that, let's remove all traces," Sindbad said.

They all came out and carefully closed the main door. After unlocking the outhouses, they brought the trunk with Lemony in it to the doghouse. The moment they opened the trunk, Lemony raised her head as if fully awake. All three jumped at once. She was wide-awake as she stared at them.

Amit and Gopal ran out of the gate. They knew that it would not take more than one bark to wake up Pushkar Mahal. Sindbad remained silent and kept staring at Lemony without any movement. When she did not bark, he carefully lifted her from the trunk and put her out. Lemony stayed quiet as if she was in a trance, still dreaming about her old home not knowing she had returned to it.

Sindbad grabbed empty trunk and ran out. He carefully closed the main gate behind him.

Chapter 18

With cool morning breeze, Nandi woke up fully freshened. His head felt heavy from the deep sleep. After the visit of the messenger, he was excited and was ready to prepare for the prince Vikramaditya's arrival.

A strange stench hit his nostril. It felt like vile smell of rotten fishes, something of that sort. He followed the smell as he came out of his chamber. He looked at the group of servants surrounding Mooni.

"What is this smell?" Nandi asked looking at them.

"Your highness, I am already on it. Perhaps a dead rat," Mooni answered.

"How come one rat can stink up entire palace," Nandi asked with curiosity.

Mooni and his men had no answer to his question.

It was in that tense moment, Shubhangi's two maidservants came running. Their faces pulled down in fear. They came and bowed their heads.

"*Maharaj*, Shubhangi is not in her chamber," elder one broke the news. Young maidservant hid behind her avoiding angry gaze of Nandi.

"What do you mean she is not in the chamber," Nandi asked.

"This morning when we woke up, princess Shubhangi was not in her room. We tried searching her everywhere. She is not in the palace. And…" maidservant spoke.

"And what?" Nandi asked with his heart beating faster than ever.

"Most of her clothes are missing from the closets. Her bags are gone. And…" she said

Nandi kept looking at her.

"The Princess left a note," she said extending her hand with her head down.

The note exchanged many hands of the servants standing in circle until it reached Nandi. As Nandi read the note his chest heaved in anger. His eyes bulged out. It scared most of the servants standing there.

'I love you both very much. But I love Satvik too. I want to marry him and not any prince. That is the only way I would be happy in my life. I wish you understood that. Forgive me.

Your rebellious daughter,

Shubhangi'

Nandi read the note and tore it in as many pieces as he could and threw it in the air. His anger knew no bounds. He felt the name of the Chakrapani was ruined forever. All his plans had failed. He had failed as a father.

That's when Nandi heard a frail bark. He stood frozen. His ears couldn't believe until he heard it again.

A frail bark. He was not mistaken.

As Nandi's big belly moved faster, servants made way for him. He stood at the top of the stair. His eyes met her eyes. He was seeing her after numerous days. His already racing heart raced faster than ever. It was Lemony. It had to be.

He ran downstairs barely avoiding rolling himself on the steps. Lemony stood still. She kept looking at Nandi as if she had never seen him. Nandi came closer and picked her up in his arms. Happiness spread across his plump face as he kissed her. The men standing upstairs stared at them in amazement. They couldn't understand the joy Nandi experienced.

Lemony was very quiet. It was unlike her. She did not run to him. She did not jump on him. Her eyes had lost all their sparkle. But Nandi was happy. The sadness that Shubhangi had filled in his heart was reduced a little by Lemony's arrival.

Everyone was still catching up to the things that unfolded that morning. They all walked down to the King and Lemony.

"What did they do to Lemony? Look at her. She looks like a stray dog. Wash her, clean her. Make her the way she always used to be," he ordered maidservants.

The maidservants shook their heads in agreement. They took Lemony with them and went away as quickly as they could.

"Call the vet. I want him to do a complete checkup of Lemony. But first, find where this rotten smell is coming from? Clean the mess. We have lot of things to discuss," Nandi said looking at Mooni.

"Your highness, don't you worry. Everything will be all right. We will get things in order before noon.

————•→•⤙◈⤚◈⤙◈⤚•←•————

The morning at Chhaya Sadan was just the opposite of what it was at Pushkar Mahal. It was the most cheerful morning they had seen.

Satvik woke up to the children playing with Shubhangi. He came out and kept watching her play with his children. Morning glory radiated on her face. She looked ecstatic. As she smiled at Satvik her most vivacious smile, he missed a heartbeat.

He couldn't believe it was just a matter of a day before Shubhangi would be his wife. All his dreams would come true. All the dreams they cherished together would come true.

"Are you marrying my Satvikpa?" young Nafeesa asked Shubhangi.

She shook her head with a twinkle in her eyes.

"Then you will be my mommy, a princess mommy?"

"Yes, a princess mommy," Shubhangi said as she ran her finger in Nafeesa's auburn hair.

"Then I will be a princess too?"

"Yes, you already are. You are my little princess," She said as she picked her up and ran after other children.

Satvik kept looking at Shubhangi. She had brought immense joy to Chhaya Sadan. Suddenly it had become the liveliest place. He wished it stayed that way forever.

———•·◦•❦❈❦•◦·•———

Mooni was clueless. The servants looked at Mooni and waited for his orders. With every passing minute, the bad smell became more prominent. It was everywhere. It added a new dimension to the sad mood at the palace.

It did not take long for Mooni to understand why everything had gone wrong that morning at Pushkar Mahal. Arrival of the messenger, Shubhangi's elopement, Lemony's return, ever increasing smell, everything had to be connected. There was something about the sequence of all those events.

Mooni ran to the guard's room and checked the footage from the security cameras. As he went through the footage from the previous night, his suspicion was confirmed.

"So it was the messenger and his sweets that did the trick," he said as he ran towards Nandi's chamber.

Nandi was feeding Lemony. She sat on his lap peacefully. Even after a long bath that was given by the maidservants, she didn't look like the way she used to. She looked as if it was not her, but her look alike.

"Your highness, it's important," Mooni asked permission to speak.

Nandi signaled him to sit down.

"It was the messenger. And the sweets he brought." He said.

Nandi was confused.

"The messenger wasn't the messenger. He and his associates were friends of the orphan. We did not check about him with the prince. He insisted not to tell anyone about him. He insisted everyone eats the sweets he brought. Everybody did, except the princess. No one knows what happened last night, because the sweets he brought had sleeping drug. He drugged us all. That's when they must have taken Shubhangi with them."

Nandi was shocked. The messenger? He gave him a respect, sat with him and had dinner with him. For all the hospitality and love he had shown towards him, this is what he had to give in return?

"How do you know it was him?" Nandi asked.

"It's on the tape from security camera. Shubhangi came out of palace when everyone was asleep. They blackened the cameras before doing all this. They were friends of the orphan. Last time they broke in, they kidnapped Lemony, this time they kidnapped Shubhi and left Lemony."

"Rascals," Nandi said.

That's when two of the servants knocked on the door. They squirmed looking at the anger Nandi's face radiated. Nandi gestured them to enter.

The elder of them walked closer with two glass jars in his hands. As he brought the bottles close, intense stench filled the room. Both Nandi and Mooni jumped off their seats.

"Take that thing away from us," Nandi shouted.

The man turned around and ran out of the chamber.

"The smell is coming from those bottles," other servant who accompanied him answered.

"What is in the bottle?" Mooni asked.

"It's a rotten mixture of fish mixed with pickles and many other things. They must have been preparing it for days. It's completely rotten," he said.

"Where did you find it?"

"Under the sofa, two of these."

"Bastards," Mooni said and punched his fist on the wooden desk. It hurt more and made less noise.

"How many such bottles?" Nandi asked.

"We've found two. These bottles could be spread all over the palace. We don't know yet."

"Go find all of them. Search every corner of this house and throw all those smelly things out of the palace," Nandi ordered.

He turned at once and ran away quickly.

Every time they found a stink bomb, everybody came to know about it. The smell spread with the air. They packed every stinking bottle they found in a plastic bag and quickly took it out of the palace. But there was no way to know if they had found all the stink bombs to stop scouting for more.

"She is weak, not as cheerful as she used to be. She does not run to me when I call her. As if, she had forgotten her name. Not to mention she is mostly sleepy," Nandi told the vet.

The vet took a good look at Lemony. She was supportive. Nandi thought that was a thing to worry. Lemony cannot be supportive to a vet, for that matter to any stranger. That was unlike her.

"What's wrong with her?" Nandi asked.

"There is nothing wrong with her," he said.

"Then why is she behaving like this?"

"You said she returned after many days. It will take her few days to adjust. And…," he took a pause.

"And what?" unable to wait for him to complete, Nandi asked.

"And she is pregnant," he said.

"Pregnant?"

"Yes pregnant, congratulations," he said winding up his instruments in his black leather bag.

Nandi did not understand how to react to the news. It took him a few moments before his mind realized it was not the news he was very happy about. Some stray dog had impregnated Lemony. He was angry.

He clenched his jaw in anger. Everything that was going wrong was all because of Satvik. Nandi knew it wouldn't be Shubhangi who would bring shame to the Chakrapani, it would be him if he did not avenge what Satvik had done to his family.

—•—•◦❈◦❈◦•—•—

Chhaya Sadan beamed with happiness. All of Satvik's friends had gathered at Chhaya Sadan. As they entered one by one, the children mysteriously looked at each other.

The guests included their favorite Sindbad uncle and his girlfriend, the fair skinned Chahek Didi, Amit uncle who always made them laugh, Gopal uncle who always scared them and Gunjan Didi who occasionally accompanied them on the excursions and sang in her beautiful voice. Children's were happy to see them all and competed with each other to grab their attention.

They had all come together after a long time. Amma and Sakhubai prepared a sumptuous breakfast for the guests. Children quietly listened to the chirpy discussions of the elders. By then, all of them knew about the marriage of Satvikpa with princess Shubhangi.

"When exactly do you get married?" Gunjan asked.

"Tomorrow evening," Satvik said.

"There is just one night in between two lovebirds?" Chahek asked.

"Sooner, the better, if it was possible, I wanted it to be today," Jeejee said.

"Jeejee is right. We have to hurry. Besides, it's been long these lovebirds wanted to get married. Why wait now?" Sindbad asked.

"We are ready," Shubhangi said putting her arms around Satvik. Satvik shook his head in agreement.

"What about the wedding shopping? The wedding dress? After all, princess Shubhangi is getting married. It has to be the best," Chahek said. She could not wait to adorn bride for marriage.

"Don't go there," Satvik said knowing how much Shubhangi loved to shop.

"Thank you. Finally, you mentioned it. And it's not just me. All the bridesmaid need to do the wedding shopping too," Shubhangi said.

All the ladies echoed.

"Yes, she has to be the most beautiful princess bride ever," Gunjan said.

"She already is. For me," Satvik said.

"We ladies will go together and shop for children and for ourselves. I am sure men will take care of their shopping," Chahek Said.

"Groom and his best men need wedding shopping too. We will do our shopping," Amit said.

"Well, you just have till evening. Whatever you want, do it today," Jeejee said.

"We are doing a *Mehendi and Sangeet* ceremony tonight. Just for the bride and the bridesmaids," Chahek said winking at Sindbad.

"Yeah? That is good, because we are having our bachelor party tonight," Sindbad said.

"We are?" Satvik asked.

"We have to," Gopal Said.

"Yes, we are having a bachelor's party. After everything we have done for your marriage, we deserve a bachelor party," Amit said.

"Well, it's settled then. Ladies will have *Mehendi* and *Sangeet* at Sadan. Men will have a Bachelor's party," Jeejee said.

"Jeejee will enjoy the *Sangeet*," Shubhangi said.

"Jeejee, you can't, you have to be with us," Satvik said.

"I wish I could, but I think I will have more fun here with the ladies. Now, let's get started. We just have today to do all the preparations." Jeejee said.

Chapter 19

Makhan Baba received an afternoon call on his personal phone. He quickly grabbed it. It had to be an important call. Only most trusted associates had his personal phone number. It was used for important intelligence on his lucrative devotees.

Instead of his associate, a deep arrogant voice spoke on the other end.

"Makhanchor, good morning! If you don't want your wife and your mother to come to your *Ashram*, listen carefully," Voice said.

"Who are you?" Baba asked baffled.

"It depends," the voice said

"What?"

"If you want, I could be your friend. If not, I could be the worst enemy. It's really up to you."

"Sorry, wrong number," Baba said.

"It's a right number Makhan Baba. You know it. So listen before you put the phone down because if you do so, you will regret it," the voice threatened.

"Do you know who you're talking to?"

"I know exactly who you are. You are a thief. A cheater. Fraud. Your wife and your mother are still searching for you. They are not the only ones. The police are searching for the postman named Makhanchor who ran away after stealing money from the post office. You are famous, but I can make you very famous and for all the wrong reasons," voice said.

Makhan Baba was in a shock. The man on the other side of the phone knew more about him than he had told anyone.

Makhan Baba did not speak for a minute. He weighed his options. The man knew enough about him to destroy him and his reputation he had earned through years.

"What do you want?" Baba asked.

"Not much, it's a very small price in exchange of your lavish life," voice said.

"I work for wellbeing of people. I don't have a lavish life. I am a simple man living in a hut," Baba said.

"You are not a simple man. No man who can produce gold idols from his mouth is a simple man," voice said.

"What do you want?"

"You know King Nandi, your royal devotee. You have already robbed much of his money. Now it's time to stop all that and convince him to let his daughter marry the man she loves," voice said.

"You mean the orphan? That's not possible. The king hates him," Baba said.

"Fair enough, it's your choice. I don't like to force people but I'd ask you one last time. You should not regret your decision. It will make great news, especially with a video. Nothing wrong but just the way you produce the golden idol from your mouth. All news channels will run your story for days. You know people are not very kind with fraud Babas," voice said.

There was another pause for few moments. No one spoke.

"No it is then. Good luck for your new life," voice said.

"Wait," Baba said, "I'll do it."

"You made a right choice. You are not as stupid as your wife and your mother think you are. You have exploited lot of money from Nandi to separate them. Now you have to make it right. I will forget everything I know about you, if you do exactly what I say," voice said.

"Why should I trust you?" Baba asked.

"You don't have a choice. And that is not the only thing you don't have. You don't have time either. You have to do this by tomorrow noon. If you don't do it by then, I will personally bring you mother and your wife to you. And yes, the police and press along with them."

Makhan Baba knew he had no option. Convincing King Nandi to marry his daughter to an orphan wasn't going to be easy. But he can't go back to the life he had left behind. Worse, he can't go to jail.

"Deal or no deal?" voice asked.

"One last question," Baba said.

The voice kept quiet.

"How do you know so much about me?" Baba asked.

"I don't think you understand the deal. You don't get to ask questions. I think you really want to go back to your village," the voice said and disconnected the phone.

"Wait… Hello? Hello?" Baba said.

Baba frantically tried to call back. He eagerly awaited as the phone rang. The man did not answer the phone. A wave of fear ran through his mind.

Baba tried the number again. This time it was answered but a voice did not speak.

"Hello, please don't cut the phone. No more questions. I am ready to do it," Baba said.

"I am not sure you can do it. You don't look confident about it."

"Yes I can. Nandi will do everything I tell him. He will happily bless the couple if I tell him," Baba said.

"He better do so. You know what could happen if he didn't," voice said.

"I know. Just promise me, you will honor the deal. You will never tell anyone about me or my past. You will never tell my wife my whereabouts," Baba asked.

The voice spoke with a serious tone. "Your secret is safe with me. You do your job and forget I ever called you," it said.

"Thank you," Baba said.

"Don't forget the time, before tomorrow noon. I will know when it's done. And yes, this is a public phone, don't call back. We will never talk again whether you do it or not," voice said and then phone was disconnected.

Makhan Baba felt happy that he made a deal with the man on the phone. It was easier to convince Nandi than face his own scary past.

———•·•→•·✦✦✦•·•←•·•———

The day was not pleasant for Nandi. It was evident from his displeased plump face. He never stopped thinking about the events that happened that morning. All of the servants at the Pushkar Mahal were busy scouting for the stink bombs. The happiness that Lemony's return brought was clouded by the news of her pregnancy.

"If it wasn't for Shubhangi, those bastards would be behind bars," Nandi said sipping on Darjeeling tea with Mooni

"I have arranged for two men who are on to it. They will soon find Shubhangi," Mooni said.

"You hired men?"

"Yes, private detectives. These men will help us bring Shubhangi back. They will find that orphan and his friends," Mooni said.

"I don't want any blood, any fight. It's her fault, she took the decision to elope," Nandi said.

"But somebody made her take that decision. To me, that is kidnapping. I just think that somebody should be punished," Mooni said.

Nandi kept quiet. He knew Shubhangi wasn't kidnapped. She loved Satvik and chose him over all the wealth, over her parents.

"Your highness, I think we should go to police and file a complaint of kidnapping," Mooni said.

Nandi kept looking at Mooni. Sometimes it was evident that Mooni was not as bright as he thought.

"What do you mean? What about the prestige of the Chakrapani?" Nandi asked.

"Forgive me for not being clear. But the police will find Shubhangi quicker than us."

"It will be breaking-news on local news channels. Princess of Chakrapani eloped with an orphan. You are not suggesting that, are you?" Nandi asked.

"Your highness, I meant, Shubhangi doesn't have to be a princess. She doesn't have to be your daughter," Mooni said.

"What do you suggest? Say it without riddles," Nandi said.

"I will go to the police. I will register a complaint that my daughter is kidnapped. I will tell them who kidnapped her. They will have to find her. And if it's me, it will not be a breaking-news," Mooni said.

Nandi kept thinking about it. Mooni was beginning to make sense.

"After all, she is like my daughter," Mooni said.

"That will work only if her identity remained secret and police managed to bring her back."

"I will ensure no one ever knows the princess eloped."

"But we must act fast. We may soon hear from prince and his family."

"I understand. I am not stopping till we find Shubhi and bring her back to Pushkar Mahal," Mooni said.

⟶ ⋯ ⟶ ⟶ ⟶ ⟶ ⟶ ⟶

Suddenly Chhaya Sadan had become the liveliest place. Everybody was busy preparing for the wedding. It was a big day for everybody.

Shubhangi and her bridesmaids spent the afternoon visiting parlors and shopping with children. The bride and bridesmaid made sure they shopped for everything they needed to make it a memorable wedding.

Satvik and his friends went for shopping too. They chose a traditional kingly wedding attire, which suited the princess wedding theme.

"Don't you think it's little too loud?" Satvik protested.

"Well, you are marrying a princess. Least you can do is to look like a prince," Sindbad said. Satvik didn't have much of a choice with his friends shopping for him.

When they were done with shopping, they spent rest of the day in arranging for the wedding. They eagerly awaited the bachelor party that night while ladies waited for *Mehendi and Sangeet.*

—•⋆→•⋐⋑⋰⋱⋐⋑•⋆←•—

Sub-inspector Chaganrao Dhumdhere, whom everyone called Chagan, was experiencing the usual boredom of the afternoon. He was the head of a small police station in a rich community near Pushkar Mahal where crime was fairly less. The location did not offer any challenges to his skills and in turn, to his growth in the police department.

By afternoon, Chagan read both the newspapers funded by the police department. He was a rapid reader. It never took him more than two hours to read a newspaper leaving him with spare time. Once, he argued in the staff meeting with chief, whose moustache he envied, that more newspaper should be funded in the station. Newspaper is where one gets to know crimes happening in and around the city and as a policeman, he genuinely liked to read crime stories. He could not see why everyone except him erupted in the laughter that lasted through the meeting.

His mother, a good-natured woman who loved Chagan dearly and foresaw his future, taught him to ignore those who laugh at him for no reasons. She told him that people who laugh without reasons are ought to be stupid. Life offered him many instances to wonder why so many people went stupid at once.

Sub-inspector Chagan had read all the newspapers for the day. Four constables, who worked under him had distributed the pages of the newspapers amongst them and were busy reading.

Chagan always wore an enigmatic face and never talked much. He believed police should be mysterious and secretive about their job, the reasons why he never revealed his hydration routine, a secret to his fitness, to anyone.

His secret was simple. He took a sip of water every five minutes. By the end of an hour, his glass would be empty and bladder full. Besides keeping him busy and his body hydrated, it gave him an opportunity to walk to the urinals at far end of the station every hour. Chagan believed this secret kept him fit and busy.

Mooni reluctantly stood in front of the police station. If it wasn't for King Nandi's rebellious daughter, he would have never stepped in a police station.

In that part of the city, people rarely disturbed the police. When Mooni entered in a hurry, everyone's gaze followed him until he reached Chagan's cabin. Then they continued reading newspapers.

For Chagan, it was a time to get in to the skin of sub-inspector. He cleared his throat and looked at Mooni. A bald man with bulbous eyes, Chagan quickly glanced at the wanted board to be certain Mooni wasn't one of them.

"Sir, my daughter has been kidnapped," Mooni said bringing as much urgency as possible in his voice.

That's when Chagan's watch blinked. It was five minutes since the last blink. He calmly took a sip of water and kept the glass on the table.

"Any suspects?"

"Suspects? I know the man who kidnapped my daughter."

"Really? Interesting. Who do you think kidnapped your daughter?" Chagan said without looking at Mooni.

"His name is Satvik Bharat. He wanted to marry my daughter. She denied, we all denied. So he kidnapped her," Mooni said.

"Okay, tell me from the beginning" Chagan said sensing the urgency of the situation.

Mooni narrated him the story of Shubhangi's kidnapping. He spoke on behalf of Nandi, portraying Shubhangi as his daughter. In his version of the story, Satvik was a villain who wanted to marry his daughter and when she denied, he kidnapped her.

Chagan listened to him carefully except whenever his watch blinked, he took a sip. By the time Mooni finished telling him the villainy of Satvik, Chagan's glass was empty. He felt the urgency to relieve his stretched bladder.

"Mr. Popat," he called one of the constables.

As if losing in the race of reading newspapers, Popat came to his cabin reluctantly.

Popatrao Kale, his badge read. Mooni looked at Popat's huge belly and noticed the irony in his name. There was no chance that Popat could fly even if he had wings of a dragon. Popat did not like the way Mooni looked at him.

"File his complaint. Take the phone numbers, photographs and every other detail. I will come in a few minutes," Chagan said raising his small finger to point his hourly urination break.

Mooni unwillingly repeated the story again, this time with more brutalities from Satvik and his friends. He thought it was essential to spice it up as it was being written by Mr. Popat.

Sub-inspector Chagan stayed outside the station and kept gazing at the road. He knew Mooni had brought him a good opportunity. If he could find Mooni's daughter and nab the kidnappers, it will be good revenge on those who laugh at him in the meetings.

The seniors will appreciate him. He may even get promoted to inspector. But all he really wanted was to have his photograph printed in the local newspaper.

His wife had been asking him to do something that will make his photo appear in the newspaper. One of her neighbor friends scored with her when their family photograph appeared in the newspaper. Though the picture was in a 'funny picture of the day' section where his neighbor rode a scooter with his wife and three kids each dressed as a superman for a fancy dress competition, the family distributed sweets in the neighborhood and also the newspapers to those who intentionally denied having seen their photograph.

Chagan knew if he found the kidnappers, he would be in the newspapers. His wife would be happy. He was excited with the possibilities. He walked briskly towards his cabin.

"Did you get all the details?" Chagan asked Popat in an authoritative tone.

"Yes sir."

"Photographs?"

"Yes sir."

"Phone Numbers?"

"Yes sir."

"Suspect's details?"

"Yes sir."

"Very good Popat. Mr. Mooni, you can go now. I am personally going to work on this case and I will bring your daughter back to you. Call me immediately if you get any ransom calls from the kidnappers."

"Sir, money is not the motive, it's the marriage. He will never get a call from the kidnappers," Popat said proudly.

Chagan did not like his audacity to be so revealing about the investigation, which had not even started. He stared at Popat who quickly remembered to keep quiet.

"We will see that Popat, don't jump the gun. Mr. Mooni, I will call you if I need any information. You may go for now," Chagan said.

Mooni left in a hurry. His work was done. sub-inspector Chagan appeared determined to catch Satvik and his friends.

"Popat, you must learn how to be secretive," Chagan said to Popat when he was sure Mooni had left. Popat shook his head in agreement.

"Anyway, I have thought about a name for this operation to rescue Mr. Mooni's daughter," Chagan said.

"What is it sir?" Popat asked.

"Operation Black Cat."

"Operation Black Cat? Why?" Popat curiously probed Chagan.

"Have you ever seen a black cat Popat?"

Popat couldn't understand the reasons behind such a question. He wasn't surprised, he was used to Chagan's antics. He just kept looking at Chagan.

"We have all seen black cats. They are unique, yet we don't know where they come from or where they go. They are like criminals. we don't know much about them. That's why the name, operation black cat."

"I got your point sir," Popat said not being in a mood to argue with Chagan.

When Popat left, Chagan went in to the slumber. He stopped his hydration routine with 'Operation Black Cat' at his hands. He kept thinking about ways to nab Satvik Bharat.

The two private detectives Mooni hired to find Shubhangi were the best and the costliest private detectives in the city of *Pune*.

Despite being the best, it was the first assignment they had that month. For the first time they did not have to follow someone but find someone. They had never found a person with just a photograph. It was not an easy task in the crowded city.

While the private detectives struggled, it was easier task for sub-inspector Chagan. He had already sent the name 'Satvik Bharat' to search in the police database. It was neither the fastest nor the accurate way to track a person, but it was the only option available.

Police database was full of faulty details. But it always provided something to start with. There was no time limit how soon he could get results. It could take from few minutes to months. Chagan knew he wouldn't be able to get the details faster if he gave his name. He lied and listed the police superintendent for a requestor.

Even with that, it took them few hours to get substantial information. But it worked. They had a hit in the traffic police database. By evening, Chagan had information on Satvik Bharat.

Satvik's name was registered in the traffic department's database. A Volkswagen van was registered in his name. Chagan felt lucky. Few hours in 'Operation Black Cat' and he had an address of the kidnapper.

Chagan gathered two of his best constables, Popat and Bhaskar. He briefed them on 'Operation Black Cat.'

"We have the address of the kidnappers. We cannot waste time. Prepare yourself, we will start at around 7 PM," Chagan said.

Chagan knew catching kidnappers was going to be easy if the address was accurate. If they played safe, 'Operation Black Cat' would be successful and he would be on the front page of the newspapers.

"Kidnappers could be armed, take your rifles," Chagan said.

"Do we really need them?" Bhaskar asked.

"Yes, get ready. It's time for action."

Chapter 20

By evening, Chhaya Sadan shined with numerous lights and was ready for the wedding the next day. The ladies readied themselves enthusiastically for the *Mehendi* and *Sangeet* while the men waited eagerly for the bachelor party.

The delicate hands of Shubhangi were being adorned with intricate design of *Mehendi*. Beautiful *Mehendi* radiated on the fair skin of her hands. She wondered how happy her mother would have been to see her being adorned. Her face saddened for a moment. She secretly wished her parents would come and bless her wedding.

Satvik and his friends, after completing all the arrangement for the wedding, had come home in the evening for the bachelor party. They wanted to go to a pub and celebrate but there wasn't much time left for that.

"We can celebrate at home," Satvik suggested.

"Dude, we are not celebrating at home. It's a bachelor party," Amit said.

"You know how much we have struggled to pull off this wedding. It's just a matter of few hours. We don't want anything to go wrong now," Satvik said.

Satvik looked at Sindbad for help.

"Let's have it the way groom wants it. We will go out for a party after the wedding," Sindbad said.

"As long as we are together, it'll be fun anywhere," Gopal said.

"Exactly," Satvik said.

They all decided to celebrate at home. The bottles were opened and drinks flowed freely.

"To the Greek Jesus," Sindbad raised a toast.

"To the Greek Jesus, cheers!" they all echoed.

Chagan and his two associates did not face any difficulty in finding Satvik Bharat's address. They parked the police van on the street. Chagan locked the gun in the holster. Bhaskar and Popat kept their rifles in the car. Chagan wouldn't allow them to load the rifles. Carrying them without bullets was in vain.

They all stood waiting outside the building. Popat and Bhaskar waited for Chagan to tell them the plan.

"Do we need a search warrant?" Popat asked. He was always more curious than required, Chagan thought.

"To nab the kidnappers?" Chagan asked.

"To enter their home and search for the victim," Popat answered.

"We are the police," Bhaskar said.

"That is the law. Law is the same for everyone," Popat said and raised his shoulders as if saying he just wanted to help.

"I think he is right," Bhaskar said taking Popat's side and then raising his shoulders.

That disappointed Chagan. It was end of the day. There was no way he could get a search warrant.

"We don't need a search warrant. We have to rescue the girl from kidnappers. We must enter the house without search warrant," Chagan decided.

"But if they are kidnappers, they would have weapons. Besides, we are in police uniform. The moment they see us, they will attack us. I honestly think we should at least change our clothes so they will not be alarmed," Popat said to Chagan.

It made sense. What if the gang of the kidnappers was big and heavily armed? What if shots are fired during 'Operation Black Cat?'

"You could have raised all your doubts before we started?" Chagan asked with slight anger.

Finally, Chagan agreed. If they had a search warrant, nobody could stop them from entering the house. That meant they would have to go wake up the magistrate to get the search warrant. If they could not get one, they would go their homes to come back in civilian dress, except for Bhaskar who was not in the uniform.

"Okay, here is what we are doing. Popat and I will take the van with us and will go home. We will come back as soon as we can, with a search warrant, in civilian dress. Once we are back, we will not waste time, we will enter the home. Till then Bhaskar, you have to keep a watch and call us if you see any suspicious activity," Chagan said.

"Sure, I can keep an eye on them," Bhaskar said.

Chagan and Popat left in the car. Bhaskar stood there alone, staring at the building.

It wasn't long before Bhaskar could use his daily shot of whiskey. That would come handy. In his experience, whisky had always enhanced his ability to perform his job. 'Operation Black Cat' was about the kidnappers. They needed the courage to break in to their house. There was enough time before Chagan and Popat returned.

With this thought in his mind, Bhaskar started out in search of a nearby bar.

⸺•⸱⸺◈⸱⸱◈⸱⸱◈⸱⸱⸺•⸱⸺

The bachelor party was going well. Except for Amit, who enjoyed the pineapple juice, they all drank as they talked about Satvik's love life and things they had to do to see that day.

The party had just begun. Yet, they quickly ran out of the alcohol.

"We need to get some more booze before the shops close," Gopal said.

"Do we really need to?" Satvik asked.

"Yes, we agreed with you to celebrate at home. That's it. Don't tell us we don't need more booze. This is the last day and then everything will change. You will be married. You may never party with us again," Amit said.

"Nothing will change. And of all the people, you shouldn't be saying that, you don't even drink," Satvik said looking at Amit.

"Can you go get it?" Sindbad asked Amit.

"I am not getting it alone. Not today. Either we all go or no one goes," Amit said.

"I am not coming with you. You three go together. I have to call Shubhangi and check how thing are going at Sadan," Satvik said.

After a long argument, they all decided to go together leaving Satvik home. They started on Amit's green scooter. It hardly accommodated three riders. As Sindbad and Gopal were drunk, Amit drove the scooter.

They went to the railway station. It had many bars in an alley that were open until midnight. The location made it a favorite amongst the commuters.

Amit parked the scooter at the corner under a tree. The neon lights on the billboards dizzied them. It was around 9 PM, yet many men stood in groups, most of them drunk. A group of college going girls in modern trendy dresses stood on the road playing songs on the recorder.

As they crossed the road and walked towards the bar, they were stopped by a man standing in the middle of the alley. He was clearly drunk.

"Driving license and registration?" the man asked.

"Are you the traffic police?" Sindbad asked.

"I am police. Show me the documents," he said.

271

"Why are you not in the uniform?" Sindbad asked.

"None of your business. Show me the documents," he said.

"But we are not driving, we are just walking," Amit said.

"You were. I just saw you park that green scooter over there."

Amit pulled out his driving license and registration card and gave it to the man who claimed to be a police. He did not give more than a glance to his documents.

"Do you know riding triple-seat is a crime?" he asked.

"Do you know you should always wear the traffic police uniform and drinking on duty is punishable?" Sindbad said.

"What did you say? Are you trying to teach me how to do my job?"

"Why should we trust you are a police?" Sindbad asked.

"Here, that's my card," he flashed his card.

"Bhaskar," Sindbad read his first name on his identity card. He was a police constable indeed.

"Now, you were drunk driving and over-loading the vehicle. You need to pay the fine," Bhaskar said.

"First, he is not drunk and he drove the scooter. Second, you are drunk on duty too," Gopal said.

"How dare you talk to me like that? I will throw all of you behind bars for stopping me from performing my duty. All three of you will rot in jail," Bhaskar said with an obvious anger in his voice.

By now, few bystanders gathered around them. The gang of pretty girls came closer. They were intrigued by the discussion between three men and a drunken man who claimed to be a policeman. The onlookers formed a circle around them.

"I don't think you have a right to give us a challan. You are just a police, not a traffic police," Sindbad said.

"Don't teach me the law," Bhaskar said.

"Okay. What is the law we broke and what is the fine?" Sindbad asked.

"Three people riding a scooter, that's not allowed," Bhaskar said.

"He is lying," someone from the gang of girls shouted. It infuriated Bhaskar.

"Okay. We don't have time. How much money we've to pay for the challan?" Gopal asked.

"Five hundred," Bhaskar said.

"Five hundred?" Gopal asked in astonishment. He counted and handed him five hundred rupees.

"He is lying," the same voice from girls shouted.

"Who said that? Who?" Bhaskar shouted back.

"Give them a *challan*," the voice said.

"Yeah, give us a *challan*. We want the receipt," Sindbad said.

Bhaskar pocketed the money and pretended to find a *challan* book. He was not traffic police. He didn't have a challan book. But he was too drunk and too arrogant to judge the situation.

"I am not carrying a *challan* book. You will get the *challan* tomorrow," Bhaskar said.

"What do you mean tomorrow?" Sindbad asked.

"He is a liar," someone from the crowd shouted.

"Come to the police station, you will get the receipt," Bhaskar said.

"Then you will get the money when we come to the police station. Please return us our money," Sindbad said.

"How dare you? You are not getting any money," Bhaskar said and started walking towards the road. It was getting late for him. Chagan and Popat must have returned, he thought.

It angered Sindbad. Sindbad held his hand and pulled Bhaskar towards him. As they came face to face, Sindbad held his collar and said, "I am asking you one last time. And very nicely too. You are not stealing money from us."

"Return the money. Return the money," The people around them said in unison. By now the circle around them had grown bigger.

"I am not returning money. Do whatever you can," Bhaskar said.

It angered Sindbad and Gopal even further. Amit knew, both Sindbad and Gopal were drunk and they had started liking the attention of the crowd. He tried to stop both of them but they pushed him aside.

"Hold him," Sindbad said to Gopal while he tried Bhaskar's pockets to get the money back. Bhaskar swung his hand and slapped Sindbad hard.

The crowd went "Ohh!"

Everybody was shocked. There was a silence for a moment until Sindbad laughed. He laughed louder. Before the crowd could understand what was happening to him, Sindbad jumped in the air and swung his fist hitting Bhaskar's nose with a full force.

Bhaskar found himself on the ground with his nose bleeding. His brain was shaken and the effect of alcohol was reduced. He stood on his feet in anger.

As Bhaskar moved towards Sindbad, Amit and Gopal pulled him back holding his hands. But Bhaskar raised his leg and kicked Sindbad between the legs.

The crown went "Oh" again.

"Never ever attack a police," Bhaskar said.

It left Sindbad squirming for a minute. He sat on the road, shaking his head for a minute trying to control the pain. When he looked up, Bhaskar was still standing next to him with his hands held by Amit and Gopal.

The crowd had made a circle around the four of the men fighting. Everyone in and around the circle, except for Amit, was completely inebriated. The girls were excited by looking at what was happening there.

When Sindbad felt better, he stood up. His eyes met with Bhaskar and anger rose in his heart. He ran towards him, jumped in the air and hit his right leg on Bhaskar's chest. Bhaskar flew in the air before hitting the ground hard.

Bhaskar got up but his back was hurt. He was limping. He was angry. But he knew he couldn't do much. He was outnumbered.

"You bunch of dogs. You can't get away with beating a police. This is not over. I will see you. I will throw you all in jail. I promise you," Bhaskar said.

Sindbad came closer. Bhaskar was terrified with his leg kicking abilities. Sindbad held him and pulled the money out of his pocket.

"You are a lucky man. I am drunk and I am happy today. Otherwise, you wouldn't be going home on your legs. Run before my mood changes," Sindbad said and pushed Bhaskar away.

Bhaskar turned and walked limping on the road. He was badly hurt. His nose was bleeding.

As Bhaskar left, the gang of girls clapped. The volume of the cassette player was on full blast and everybody danced on the road to the tunes of the latest Bollywood songs.

Sindbad bought a beer barrel and opened it for everybody on the road. People cheered and drank beer with them. Amit did not drink, so one of the girls offered him cola. They all danced and drank on the street outside the railway station.

It was a party on the street.

Satvik talked with Shubhangi at length while his friends were out. The *Sangeet* ceremony was in full swing at Chhaya Sadan.

While Satvik was on the phone, Chagan and Popat returned with a search warrant. They could not find Bhaskar. They waited for him for a long time. When he did not return, Popat suggested they go and raid the house.

Chagan and Popat were stopped by the guard at the entrance of the building. Chagan displayed his police card and his gun to him. The guard was scared. He requested them to enter in the visitor's registry before going in. Popat entered the details.

Satvik was done talking to Shubhangi. A smile still lingered on his face. Shubhangi told him how happy she was and how everyone at Chhaya Sadan was having fun.

With an unforeseen excitement, Chagan and Popat walked carefully towards the door. 'Operation black cat' was at its crucial moment. Chagan pointed the gun, at the closed door, holding it in both his hands while Popat knocked on the door and quickly sidelined himself.

Chapter 21

Satvik saw the dawn breaking in prison while waiting for his friends to come and bail him out. Not knowing his friends struggled to come together and to find his whereabouts. No one knew where Satvik was on the morning of the wedding day.

That morning, Nandi had a sumptuous breakfast with his wife, queen Devyani. Many a times, doctors had advised him to eat less and not anger his delicate diabetes. How would you know, Nandi asked his doctor, if you are not a king who is served with sumptuous food?

Although he ate breakfast to his heart's content, he was disinterested in the food. Nothing was interesting. Shubhangi had left an empty hole in his heart. If he wasn't a king, he would have brought her back and married her off to the orphan. But he couldn't betray the legacy of his forefathers. It was these thoughts of Shubhangi, which kept him restless through the night.

Nandi was alone in his chamber sipping on his morning Darjeeling tea when he glanced at a cheerful portrait of Shubhangi. Her smile bought back a flood of emotions and sadness filled his heart.

His breathing became heavy as his heart raced faster. He experienced the chest pain. Last time he had heart attack, he had experienced similar chest pain. It was the heartache he knew well. He tried to reach for the pills his doctors suggested to take every time he felt stressed at heart.

As he walked to get his medicine, he felt dizzy. Darkness spread in front of his eyes gradually. Soon everything was dark. He fell down on the floor. His huge barrel like body rolled couple of times before coming to halt.

Things were not normal, he understood.

"Devyani," He screamed.

Devyani was in the hall when she heard Nandi screaming her name. She knew something was wrong. He never screamed her name. She ran to his chamber.

Before Devyani reached, two of the servants were already there trying to help their king get on his feet. Nandi was senseless. Two other servants joined them.

"Call the ambulance and get the car ready," Devyani ordered them. They quickly ran outside.

Devyani sat next to the King Nandi. He was still unconscious. Mooni and the rest of the servants came running in the chamber.

"Your highness, don't you worry, ambulance is on its way. It will be here any moment," Mooni said.

Mooni called the family doctor and told him about the emergency at Pushkar Mahal. As doctor suggested, Mooni ordered the servants to massage Nandi's palms and feet. A few minutes later, an ambulance reached Pushkar Mahal. Nandi was taken to the hospital. Devyani and Mooni went along with Nandi.

→ ·→·•❦⋞3❦⋟❦·•·←··—

Sindbad could not believe how terribly wrong the bachelor party had gone. Before the day broke, all of them had scattered. The groom was missing from home. Amit and Gopal found themselves in *Hyderabad* and he woke up in a house full of cross-dressers.

After talking to Amit and Gopal, he was certain Satvik went to Chhaya Sadan forgetting his phone. That seemed a good possibility. He had a quick breakfast as he waited Satvik's return. When Satvik did not return for the next hour, he started getting worried. He knew he had to call Chhaya Sadan. He called his girlfriend Chahek.

"Finally you got time for me. How was the bachelor party? I am sure you just got up," Chahek said.

Sindbad had to be careful with her questions. He didn't want her to know how bachelor party had separated them all.

"It was great. We had fun. How are you and how was *Sangeet* last night?" he asked.

"I am good. *Sangeet* was amazing. You should have been here. Instead, you had to have a bachelor party," she said.

"Okay listen, I am in a hurry. Can you give the phone to Satvik? He forgot his phone at home," Sindbad said trying to hide the fact that groom was missing and none of the best men knew about it.

"Satvik is here?" she asked.

"I thought he is there. Can you check if he is there?" he asked.

"Let me check," she said.

"Don't let Shubhangi know I am looking for him," Sindbad said but Chahek had already asked Shubhangi if she knew where Satvik was.

"Nope. He is not here. Shubhangi has been trying his phone since morning but he is not picking up," Chahek said.

"Okay, just tell her he left his phone at home and had gone out. He will call her when he gets back. I have to go. Love you," Sindbad said.

"Wait. Shubhangi wants to talk to you," Chahek said. But Sindbad disconnected the phone. He didn't want to talk to her lest she would be suspicious.

Sindbad was worried. He knew Satvik wouldn't go anywhere other than Chhaya Sadan. Not without letting them know about it. He had to find Satvik but he didn't know how. He had to do something and he had to do it quick.

'Groom is still missing.' He sent a message to Amit and left home in search of Satvik. He left Satvik's phone at home along with a note to call him if he reached home.

He came out of the building and as he realized, he ran back inside. He had forgotten to check with the guard. The guard knew them well and they would definitely know if Satvik had gone out.

He went to the guard and asked if they had seen Satvik. The guard told Sindbad the entire story about what happened the previous night, leaving Sindbad dumbstruck.

"The police took him?" Sindbad asked still in disbelief.

"Yes. He was handcuffed," guard said.

"How do you know they were police for sure?"

"They were police. They showed their identity cards and also made an entry in the register," the guard said while pointing the entry in the visitor's register. Sindbad couldn't believe his luck. He looked in to the visitor's register.

Chaganrao Dhumdhere, 10:30 PM, the entry read.

"Do you know which police station?" Sindbad asked.

"No *Saab*, all I know is that they were police and they arrested Satvik *Saab*," the guard said.

Sindbad could not believe Satvik was arrested from his own bachelor party. He felt guilty for not being there with him. He tried calling Amit and Gopal to let them know about the new details. But they had boarded the plane and could not be reached.

Only few hours were left for the wedding and Satvik was in police custody. It was not going to be easy to find Satvik in one of many police stations in *Pune*. All he had was name of a police officer and that could very well be a fake name.

Sindbad pulled the car and started for the nearest police station. His confidence died down as he moved from one police station to another without finding Satvik. He searched many police stations without any luck.

After spending more than an hour, he was discouraged. He decided to call Jeejee and let him know what had happened. There wasn't much time left. Chhaya Sadan needed to know the truth.

Then it occurred to Sindbad. If the police had arrested Satvik, they could only do so if someone filed a complaint. And police register complaints only within their jurisdiction. He should not be searching Satvik in the police station near their home but he should be searching near Pushkar Mahal.

He drove his car as fast as he could and found the small police station near Pushkar Mahal. A smile spread on his face as he read the name 'Sub-inspector Chaganrao Dhumdhere' on the staff board, at the top, against 'Police Station Head.'

Sindbad dashed inside and ran directly into Chagan's cabin. Chagan was busy reading the newspapers. He looked at Sindbad with suspicion.

"Sir, good morning. My name is Sindbad," he said.

"Whatever it is, file your complaint at the front desk. Meet Mr. Popat," Chagan said and pulled the newspaper over his face.

"Sir it's urgent, please."

"What is it about?" Chagan asked with a curiosity as he kept newspaper down on the desk.

"There has been a huge misunderstanding."

"What misunderstanding?"

"It's about my friend Satvik."

That's when Satvik heard Sindbad's voice. He came close to the bars and saw him through the glass window of Chagan's cabin.

"Sindbad, is that you?" Satvik shouted.

As Sindbad heard Satvik's voice, he ran out of the cabin. He saw Satvik standing behind the bar.

"I found you," Sindbad said with a smile coming close to Satvik.

"I knew you would find me," Satvik said hugging him through the bars.

"Everything will be alright. Let me explain them," Sindbad said

By now, Chagan had come out. He had called the Popat. When Sindbad turned towards them, he was surprised to see Popat aiming a rifle at him.

"So you are the other gang member?" Chagan said.

"What gang members? What are you talking about?" Sindbad said.

"We know everything. You have kidnapped a girl," Chagan said.

"What girl? We haven't kidnapped anyone. There is some misunderstanding, sir," Sindbad said.

"This girl," Chagan said flashing Shubhangi's photo in front of his face.

"Shubhangi?" Sindbad asked.

"So you know her," Chagan said.

"Yes, because she is not kidnapped. She is safe. She has run away from her parents because she wants to marry him. Her parents jailed her against her will. If someone should be behind the bar, then it should be her parents," Sindbad said.

Chagan was confused. He didn't know what to believe.

"She is old enough to make her decision. Instead of protecting them from her parents, you have caught an innocent," Sindbad said.

"You think we are fools standing here and listening to your stories. Your friend told us the same story this morning. Why should I believe you?" Chagan asked.

"We can take you to her. Even better, I can call her right now. If she tells you we did not kidnap her and that she eloped with him, would you help us get them both married?" Sindbad asked.

It made Chagan think. If the man was telling the truth, then Chagan was making a big mistake. Instead of becoming a headline in the newspaper, he might end up being a subject of laughter. He decided to give them a chance to prove their innocence.

Just then, Bhaskar entered the station limping on one leg. He had spent his night in the hospital after getting in to a fight. His face was swollen. His broken nose was plastered. His left hand was wrapped in bandage and was supported by a strap around his stiff neck in the neck-collar. He walked in and wished a good morning to Chagan.

"What happened to you?" Chagan asked.

As Bhaskar raised his head, his eyes met Sindbad. He stood and kept looking at him for a moment. It was the man who had beaten him last night and made him spend the night in the hospital.

When he was certain it was him, Bhaskar ran limping towards Sindbad and punched him in the face. Sindbad was shocked when Bhaskar hit him. Bhaskar threw another punch at him but Sindbad stopped him.

"Bhaskar, what are you doing?" Chagan asked.

"Look at me. This was all done by him. This man and his two friends. They attacked me last night. They attacked a policeman, can you believe? He beat me until I blacked out," Bhaskar said and kicked Sindbad in his stomach.

There was no doubt in Sindbad's mind that it was him, the man whom he had beaten up previous night.

"He asked for a bribe," Sindbad said.

"Bribe? So you would beat the police? It is a big mistake. You shouldn't have done that," Chagan said shaking his head.

"He is the friend of the kidnapper we arrested last night," Popat said to Bhaskar.

"Great. Now you are going to die," Bhaskar said pushing Sindbad.

Sindbad looked at Satvik who was completely puzzled. He couldn't understand anything that was happening outside his cell. Minutes ago, he was happy with the possibilities of getting out of the police station.

"There are two more people in their gang. I know exactly how we can get to them. I want your permission," Bhaskar said.

"Permission? For what?" Chagan asked.

"To interrogate. I promise you I will get you the other two rascals and the girl they have kidnapped," Bhaskar said.

"But he says the girl ran away with him to save herself from her parents," Chagan said.

"Sir, look at me. If they can do this to a police officer, what would they do to a girl and her poor father? Do you trust these people over me?" Bhaskar asked Chagan.

Chagan thought for a moment. He knew Bhaskar had a point. If they beat the police, they were not innocent people. Sometimes one has to be stern. It was that time. The men kidnapped a girl, beat the policeman and lied to Chagan. They can't be trusted.

"Okay. We don't have much time. We have to get the girl as soon as possible. Do what you must do. Just make sure no one dies in my station," Chagan said as he walked towards his cabin.

"You are making a big mistake," Sindbad protested.

Bhaskar and Popat held him and took out his phone and accessories. They pushed him in the same cell with Satvik and locked the door.

Satvik helped him settle down.

"What did you do to him?" Satvik asked.

Sindbad looked at him and laughed.

"We beat him last night. All that you see on him, it was done by us."

"Really? I can't believe it. Is that why you guys couldn't return?"

"Yes. We tried but he wouldn't listen. He asked for it."

"And these people picked me up and put me in a jail when you were out. I thought you guys must have been searching for me through the night," Satvik said.

"Only if we had returned home in the night," Sindbad said.

"What do you mean? You never returned? Where were you guys?"

"Long story."

"I want to know everything." Satvik said.

Sindbad narrated the whole story to Satvik. He told him everything that happened after they left home for booze. He told him how he woke up among cross dressers and how Amit and Gopal reached *Hyderabad*.

Satvik told him how he was arrested and kept in jail overnight.

They were astonished at how things had gone out of hand. Yet they could not stop but laugh at what had happened. Satvik was pleased that Sindbad was with him. Although things had gone wrong, being with Sindbad made him feel good.

Doctors cleared Nandi within an hour of being brought to the hospital. It was just a case of bad gastric reflux and acidity. He had had a heavy breakfast loaded with sugars that led him into the hospital.

"What do you mean the breakfast did this?" Devyani asked the doctor.

"He is a diabetic and a heart patient. He can't eat everything he wants. This is what happens," doctor said.

"Can we talk to him?" she asked.

"He is still sedated. It will take some time before you could talk to him," Doctor said and walked off.

Devyani and Mooni sat in the waiting area outside Nandi's room.

Mooni had an unfinished business to take care. He had very less time. Now that Nandi was out of danger, he wanted to go and bring things in control.

"I should go now. I have few things I must attend to," he asked for permission to Devyani.

Devyani shook her head in agreement.

"You two stay here," Mooni ordered the two servants who accompanied them to the hospital. As Mooni walked out, he called the private detectives.

———⋅⋅✦⋅⋅❦⋅❧❦⋅❦⋅⋅✦⋅⋅———

Shubhangi called Satvik many times since the morning but he never answered her. But it was when Sindbad called Chahek to check if Satvik was at Chhaya Sadan, she was alarmed. As the day progressed, she was worried. She wanted to talk to him.

It was almost noon. She called Satvik once again, but he did not answer. Chahek called Sindbad but Sindbad did not answer either. They tried calling Amit and Gopal but they were not reachable. It wasn't long before they knew something was wrong.

Shubhangi and Chahek took the taxi to Satvik's home. As they expected, they could not find anyone at home. They found Sindbad's note to Satvik along with Satvik's phone. Shubhangi's heart sank. Her mind kept spiraling into negative thoughts. She was about to cry.

That's when Chahek ran downstairs to the guard. Shubhangi followed her. The guard knew Chahek well as she frequented with Sindbad.

"Have you Seen Satvik or Sindbad this morning?" Chahek asked the guard.

"Police came yesterday night and took Satvik *Saab* with them to the station. Sindbad *Saab* came in the morning asking for Satvik *Saab* and left in search of him," the guard answered.

He narrated them what he had told Sindbad.

"Do you know which police station?"

"I don't know madam. But here is the entry," he said as he showed the name of sub-inspector Chagan.

"Thank you. If Satvik or Sindbad comes here, ask them to call me," Chahek said.

Shubhangi wasn't shocked to know what had happened. She knew why the police arrested him.

"Let's go," Shubhangi said.

"Where?" Chahek asked.

"I am the only one who can get them out of the jail."

"Do you know which police station?"

"I think I know," Shubhangi said as she ran out.

This had never happened in Chagan's police station. But there is always a first time for everything. Big slabs of ice were brought to torture Satvik and Sindbad. Bhaskar was adamant on making them sleep on ice until they confess to the kidnapping. In the process, he wanted to take revenge for his insult.

"Nothing happens to them. Just scare them and get the information about the girl. It's already noon. You just have a couple of hours. We have to find the girl before evening, otherwise we will have to let them go," Chagan told Bhaskar and Popat.

"We can't let them go. What will happen to Operation Black Cat?" Bhaskar asked.

"If we don't have evidence, we can't keep them any longer. That's why I gave you permission. There must be no blood, no evidence of torture. You know the media these days, we could lose our jobs," Chagan said.

Bhaskar shook his head in agreement. He had no intentions to show any mercy to the man who beat him. The freshman constable brought Satvik and Sindbad out of their cell and tied their hands. They both knew it was not going to be pleasant.

"I will tell him where Shubhangi is," Satvik said to Sindbad.

"Don't be stupid. You have been through a lot. If you tell them now, there won't be any wedding today. Just don't give up yet. Hang in there for some more time," Sindbad said.

"They have plans to torture us. I don't want any of us getting hurt when we haven't done anything wrong."

"They can't do much. If they push it, I know how to stop them."

"He has got the ice slabs for us. I am not sure if I can lie on that for long," Satvik said.

"When you can't, just let me know. I will tell them about Shubhangi. I want to make sure they know we did not kidnap her and they pay the price for torturing us," Sindbad said.

"I never thought this is how my wedding day will turn out," Satvik said.

"There are few more hours for the wedding. Everything will be fine. If we had Amit and Gopal with us, everything would have been all right. It was my mistake to take them out yesterday night."

"It wasn't your mistake. You have already done so much. If Shubhangi and I were getting married today, it would be because of you. I had given up long ago," Satvik said.

That's when Bhaskar entered.

"What did I promise you? I will see you. You can't get away with it," Bhaskar said as he pointed to his limping leg and broken hand.

"It's time for payback," Bhaskar said as he paraded both of them in the interrogation room. Chagan could see them through the glass window of his cabin. He saw Popat and Bhaskar leading Satvik and Sindbad on to the ice slabs.

"It's cold," Satvik protested.

"What were you expecting, a bed for you. If you don't tell me where the girl is and your other two gang members are, you are going to die on this ice slab," Bhaskar said.

"You understand that this is illegal?" Sindbad asked.

"Ha ha ha. Illegal? You think hitting the police is legal? Only reason I am not killing you is because I want you to spend the rest of your life rotting behind the bars," Bhaskar said.

"We will see about that. Someone will be behind bars for sure," Sindbad said.

"You think you are smart? Ten minutes and you will shit all your smartness in your pants." Bhaskar said.

Satvik and Sindbad were forced on the slabs for more than five minutes. It was beginning to hurt. Their bodies were numb. Chagan looked at them through the glass window. If Bhaskar and Popat could get the details of where the girl was, he would call up the head office and let them know of this high profile case. Then he will rescue the girl.

293

'Operation Black Cat' would be reported in all newspapers in the city. He would earn the respect he rightfully deserved. All the kidnappers will talk of being scared of Chaganrao. Most importantly, his wife will be happy. She will have a reason to tell her friends and boast about the courage of her husband. He may well be able to fetch a promotion out of 'Operation Black Cat.' It would be an icing on the cake.

It was at that moment, Chagan's trance was broken when two women came running and dashed into his cabin. He stared at them with anger for the audacity they had shown towards the head of the police station.

As he stared at them, he realized he had seen one of the girls, but he wasn't certain where.

Chapter 22

"**W**hat do you think you are doing?" Shubhangi dashed inside the interrogation room shouting at Popat and Bhaskar. Chahek followed her. It scared Popat. He quickly disappeared behind Bhaskar avoiding the direct gaze of fiery girls. Bhaskar was taken aback by the angry intruders. Chagan come running after them.

"Shubhangi?" Satvik said hearing her voice.

"You are the girl these men kidnapped?" Chagan asked Shubhangi. He realized she was the same girl from the photograph Mr. Mooni had provided. He couldn't have forgotten that beautiful face. It explained why her face felt so familiar.

"Yes, she is," Popat said clearly remembering her face.

"I am not kidnapped. Leave them. Now! Or all of you will pay for it," Shubhangi said shouting in Chagan's face.

Chagan avoided looking at her face. She looked angry and authoritative. If she wasn't kidnapped, they clearly made a big mistake. He knew if things were not controlled, they may land in a trouble.

"Get them dressed and bring them to my desk," Chagan ordered.

"But sir, they beat me," Bhaskar said.

"I have more than ten witnesses who would testify against him. He asked for a bribe and attacked innocent citizens," Sindbad said.

"Bring them soon," Chagan said staring angrily at Bhaskar.

"Madam, please come with me," Chagan said to Shubhangi.

"I am not coming without them," Shubhangi said folding her hands and staring at Bhaskar.

It wasn't long before they all were seating next to Chagan. Popat and Bhaskar stood by Chagan.

"You are definitely the kidnapped girl," Chagan said looking at Shubhangi and her photograph.

"No, I am not kidnapped. I left my home. I want to know who complained that I was kidnapped," Shubhangi said in a stern voice.

"It was your father. We had no reason to believe he was lying," Chagan said.

"So you arrested them without any evidence?" Shubhangi asked. Chagan felt she was as intimidating as she was beautiful.

"I am twenty-one years old. I have a right to take my own decisions. I am marrying this man against my father's will and that's why my father is against us. But instead of protecting us, you are breaking the law by torturing them," Shubhangi said.

"You locked me up without any evidence. I told you many a times I've not kidnapped her," Satvik said.

"You tortured us. We are going to the press and let the entire world know about what you did to us," Sindbad said.

"Please. No. there is no necessity to do that. Listen to me. Whatever we did, we did to protect you. The complaint was false and we will take strict action against complainant. The police are there to offer any help you want," Chagan said. Chagan was worried he may have his photograph printed in newspaper for all the wrong reasons.

"But Sir, he and his friends beat me," Bhaskar said pointing his fingers to Sindbad.

"You had your revenge Bhaskar," Chagan said. Bhaskar squirmed. He was not happy with the way things were going.

"Why was your father against your wedding?" Chagan asked while he signaled Popat to take notes.

Shubhangi narrated to him their love story and her father's disapproval. She told them how she eloped with Satvik and that they were about to get married that day in the evening. It melted Popat's heart and left Chagan speechless. Popat was moved by the fact they were so deeply in love with each other that she ran away leaving behind her royalty.

"You are saying you are a princess? It makes your father a king," Chagan said.

"Yes, my father is a king, King Nandivardhan," She said.

"I don't know whom to trust now. I never believed the man anyway. I know King Nandi. I have seen him. The man who filed a complaint was a bald man, certainly not King Nandi," Chagan said.

"What? A bald man? That's not even my father. That must be Mooni uncle, my father's treasurer. He filed a complaint claiming he was my father?" Shubhangi said in astonishment.

"See. Now her father has changed. Can you believe these people?" Bhaskar asked Chagan.

Chagan signaled Bhaskar to keep quiet and listen to what they were saying. This, he communicated with gestures without a world. Bhaskar seemed to have understood what he really meant and kept quiet.

"We will help you. But first, we must meet your father. Don't worry, he will not be able to stop you two from getting married. If you are telling the truth, I will make sure of that," Chagan said.

"But that is possible when we meet with your father and confirm what you are saying is true. Then, we want to meet the person who filed a false complaint," Chagan said.

"Okay, but you must promise that you are not arresting my father. If he did it, then it was just because he loves me," Shubhangi said. She knew even if Mooni filed the complaint, it was possible only with her father's permission.

"We can't just let them go," Chagan said. Shubhangi kept looking at him with anger in her deep gray eyes.

"Fine, but I must warn them for false complaint and for wasting our time," Chagan said.

"We need to hurry up. We are running out of time," Sindbad Said.

"Let's go," Chagan signaled to Popat and Bhaskar.

A few minutes later, a police van set out to Pushkar Mahal. It was just minutes away. They reached Pushkar Mahal quicker than they had thought. As they entered the main gate, guards came running to them. When they saw Shubhangi, they were surprised.

"Her highness, everyone is at the hospital," one of the guards said.

"What happened?" Shubhangi asked.

"His highness had a heart attack this morning. Her highness the queen and Mooniji are with him," he said.

As Shubhangi heard those words, her heart sank. She couldn't believe she didn't know her father had a heart attack. She was about to get married without knowing that her father was in pain.

Satvik consoled her. He enquired from the guards about the hospital and made everyone including Shubhangi sit in the van. Soon, the police van started towards the hospital.

———◆◆◆———

Mooni and his two detectives entered Chhaya Sadan. When they couldn't find Shubhangi or Satvik, it only angered them. But he knew he had come to the right place.

Nobody at Chhaya Sadan knew Mooni. He pretended he was one of the relatives to Shubhangi. Jeejee noticed there was something suspicious about him and his two men. When Jeejee asked he does not remember they were invited for the wedding, Mooni couldn't hide it anymore.

He pulled out his gun and asked everyone to gather in the hall. Children, Jeejee, Gunjan, Amma and Sakhubai all came in the hall. Children were scared looking at the men holding guns.

"Is that a real gun?" Leela asked.

"Keep quiet. And listen," Mooni said.

"If you know where Shubhangi and Satvik are, tell me. No one is moving until I know where they are," Mooni said.

"They are not here. We really don't know where they are. Please don't scare these children. You don't have to do this. You could go to jail for taking children hostage," Jeejee said.

Mooni kept his gun inside.

"No one is a hostage. We just want to know where they are," Mooni said.

"Well, looks like you will have to find that on your own," Jeejee said.

"I will. You can do whatever you want. But you can't go out. You can't make a phone call. My two men will watch you until Shubhangi returns. Once she is here, you all are free," Mooni said.

Mooni was prepared. He knew both Shubhangi and Satvik would have to come to Chhaya Sadan, the wedding venue. He was determined to stop the wedding and take Shubhangi back to Pushkar Mahal with him.

Meanwhile, Amit and Gopal had reached *Pune*. After a disastrous bachelor party previous night and unforgettable ride to *Hyderabad*, they had made it to *Pune* for the wedding, well within time. They wanted to surprise Sindbad and Satvik by reaching *Pune* so quickly.

Instead of calling them, they started directly for Chhaya Sadan.

—·—•·◦❁❀❁◦·•—·—

Shubhangi ran in the front, followed by Satvik, followed by Sindbad and Chahek. They were followed by Chagan, Popat and Bhaskar. They all ran to the critical care room where Nandi was kept.

Shubhangi directly ran in to her mother's embrace. Devyani's face was lit looking at her daughter. A smile spread across her face.

"How is Dad?" Shubhangi asked.

"He is out of danger," Devyani said. It relieved everybody.

"It's all because of me," Shubhangi said with teary eyes.

"No, it's not your fault. You know him. He is diabetic. He ate too much. The doctor said it's nothing serious. Just heartburns, anxiety and hypertension," Devyani said.

Devyani looked at Satvik who stood by them listening to their conversation. Satvik stooped down and touched her feet. She kept her hand on his head and blessed him.

"Where is he?" Shubhangi asked as she walked in front of the glass window of Nandi's room.

"He is talking to Makhan Baba," Devyani Said.

"Makhan Baba? What is he doing here?" Shubhangi asked.

"He came to meet your father," Devyani said.

When Satvik saw Makhan Baba talking to Nandi, he knew things have started going in the right direction. He knew if Makhan Baba had come to talk to Nandi, it would not be long before Nandi would bless them for their wedding. They had few more hours before the wedding. Enough time to sort things out.

Satvik pulled Sindbad in the corner and asked, "You think Makhan Baba is doing what he is supposed to do?"

"I am sure about it. He doesn't have any other option. We will know soon."

"Well, I am prepared for everything," Satvik said as he walked towards Shubhangi.

Nandi and Makhan were talking animatedly. They were unaware of the crowd standing outside their room looking through the glass. Makhan Baba was clearly making Nandi upset. Shubhangi and Devyani kept looking and guessing what was happening inside the room.

"Why is the police here?" Devyani asked looking at Chagan.

"It's a long story Mother. Was he the one who filed complaint?" Shubhangi asked sub-inspector Chagan pointing at Nandi through the window.

"No, it was not him," Chagan said.

"I told you. Now, if it's clear, you may take leave. Thank you for your help," Shubhangi said.

"Not so fast. We want to meet him and talk to him. And we want to know who filed the false complaint," Chagan said.

"You will meet him but you must wait. We are family and we are yet to meet him. You will have your turn," Devyani said and walked away.

She must be the queen, Chagan thought. She walked with the grace of a queen, her hair very well done and even in that situation she had the composure only a queen could possess.

Just then, the conversation between Nandi and Makhan Baba ended. As Makhan was about to leave, Nandi folded his hands. Makhan raised his hand and blessed him.

As Makhan Baba came out, Shubhangi was eager to enter and meet his father. She rushed towards the door.

"Your highness, the king wants to see his queen first," Baba said stopping her and looking at Devyani.

Devyani drooped and touched Makhan Baba's feet.

"Long live the queen," Makhan said and left without looking at any of the men standing outside.

Satvik and Sindbad felt Makhan might have done his job. They sensed a victory in his eyes.

Devyani entered Nandi's room while Shubhangi and everyone waited outside.

Nandi was out of danger but that little accident made Shubhangi realize how much she loved her father. For the first time she was not sure if eloping with Satvik was a good idea. She loved Satvik and she loved her parents. She wasn't sure if she must choose between them. She wasn't sure if she was being selfish and not thinking about her parents.

It surprised Chagan how quickly things changed. Sindbad had apologized to Bhaskar for beating him and Bhaskar felt obligated to reciprocate by apologizing for the previous night. They started talking and quickly bonded like old friends.

All the men sat together while Shubhangi still stood by the window. That's when Satvik received a call from Amit.

"Where are you?" Amit asked.

"We are in the hospital. How about you guys?" Satvik asked.

"You will not believe it but we are at Chhaya Sadan. What are you doing in hospital? Is everything okay?"

"Everything is fine. You reached *Pune* faster than expected."

"We did but I guess not soon enough. Is Shubhangi there with you?"

"Yes, we all are in the hospital. Sindbad and Chahek are here too."

"Oh good. We have a bit of a situation here at Chhaya Sadan."

"What Situation?"

"We all at Chhaya Sadan including kids are taken hostage by Mooni uncle."

"What do you mean taken hostage?"

Sindbad got up from his seat and walked towards Satvik. Hearing the word 'Hostage', the three policemen were alert too.

"Mooni uncle is here with his two men. We came directly here to surprise you but found everybody here at his gunpoint. He wants Shubhangi. He allowed me to call you," Amit said.

"You stay there and make sure nothing happens to the kids. I will be there soon. The police are looking for Mooni and I am going to bring them with me," Satvik said.

"What happened?" Sindbad asked.

"We gotta go. Mooni had taken the children hostage. They have guns. Amit, Gopal, Jeejee, everyone is there. He wants Shubhi," Satvik said

"You don't have to go and neither does Shubhangi. Let me handle this," Sindbad said.

"No, I can't take chances with the kids. You know that," Satvik said.

"I know that. I also know Mooni can't touch them. You need to be here with Shubhangi. I will go. I will take the police with me," Sindbad said.

Satvik and Sindbad explained the situation to Chagan and his team.

"Don't worry. We got it," Chagan said.

"Bhaskar, Popat, get additional help on your way and go with the team. We have a new objective for 'Operation Black Cat.' The man there not only filed a false complaint but he himself is a kidnapper. He has taken children hostage. Be careful, he is dangerous and armed. Once I finish talking to the king, I will join you there," Chagan said ordering his constables.

"Yes sir," Popat and Bhaskar said at once.

Sindbad, Bhaskar and Popat left for Chhaya Sadan.

Satvik felt alone. Shubhangi maintained a distance from him. She was distraught. He didn't know what was going on in her mind. He was ready to accept her decision.

⟶ ⋯ ✦ ⋯ ❖❂❖❂❖ ⋯ ✦ ⋯ ⟵

Nandi and Devyani talked for a long time. It was evident from their faces that they were discussing something important. Shubhangi stood outside the glass window looking at her father without blinking. The wait was agonizing.

Nandi glanced at Shubhangi through the glass window a few times. Something in her had changed. Satvik sat aside with Chagan. He was not willing to meet Nandi. He knew the feeling was mutual and Nandi never wanted to see his face again.

After a long discussion, finally Devyani got up and walked towards the door. Shubhangi ran towards the door to meet her father.

Devyani stopped her.

"He wants to talk to Satvik first," Devyani said.

"But, I want to talk to him," Shubhangi said.

"He will talk to you. But first he wants to talk to him," Devyani said.

"It's not his fault. I eloped from home."

"We know. Just let your father talk to him."

Shubhangi went to Satvik and explained him. Satvik was reluctant to meet her father.

"I don't know if this is a good idea," Satvik said.

"Please, I will be there with you inside. Everything will be alright," Devyani said.

Satvik looked at Shubhangi. She shook her head in agreement and signaled him to go.

Satvik followed Devyani as they went inside Nandi's room.

Shubhangi was worried. Her father did not want to talk to her. She understood his anger. She knew what she had to do. She would talk to him. Ask him for the forgiveness. She would promise him that she would do what he wanted. She would forget Satvik and marry the prince he wanted.

Satvik entered the room and bowed his head in respect. He did not say a word. He just stood at a distance without looking at Nandi.

"Come here. Sit next to me," Nandi said to Satvik with a mellowed voice.

Satvik walked hesitantly towards his bed and sat next to Nandi. He was scared. He wished Shubhangi was there with him.

"Do you really love my daughter?" Nandi asked.

"More than anything in this world," he said.

"What can you do for her?"

"If it comes to that, I can die for her," he said with utmost sincerity looking at Nandi.

"Can you leave her alone?" Nandi asked.

"I can't. But she can and she will. If she asked me to do so, I will never see her again," he said.

"I thought she loved me more than anyone else in the world. You should know she loves you more than me. She ran away from her home, from her parents. Just to be with you. Do you understand what it means? She has sacrificed so much to be with you. But what would you do to have her in your life?" Nandi asked stressing every word.

"I can give up everything I have in my life for her," Satvik said.

"Can you become one of the Chakrapani? Can you name your children after Chakrapani? Can your son take forward the name of the Chakrapani dynasty? Can you stay with us at Pushkar Mahal?"

Satvik didn't reply. He was clueless. He was not sure if Nandi had just agreed for the wedding. Everything Nandi had asked in exchange, he would have done anyway.

"That is nothing to ask for. I would have done everything you asked for." Satvik said.

"Alright then, my daughter loves you and wants to marry you. So be it. You will be one of the Chakrapani after her coronation. Your son will be the son of the Chakrapani.

With Makhan Baba's blessing everything has come to a good end," Nandi said and raised his hand folding towards the sky in appreciation to Makhan Baba.

Satvik understood what was happening. Makhan Baba had convinced Nandi. His heart was filled with extreme joy. He was unsure what he heard was right.

"I shall tell you this," Satvik said.

"What is it?" Nandi asked.

"That I also have twelve children. They are not of my own. But they are no less than my own children. They stay at our home at Chhaya Sadan. Shubhangi knows them all. I love them. And I will be their guardian and they will be my children," Satvik said.

"I know about it. I've nothing but respect for you. You are a fine young man. You will make a good king. Now, ask my daughter's hand in marriage," Nandi said.

Satvik was confused. He was still in disbelief what he had heard.

He looked outside the window. He was surprised to see all his children standing outside the window with Shubhangi. Sindbad, Amit, Gopal and Jeejee stood there looking at them while Mooni accompanied by the police stood squirmed.

Satvik got up from his seat and sat on one knee on the floor next to Nandi. He bowed his head.

"Your highness, I love your daughter, princess Shubhangi. I want to marry her, that is, if you allow," Satvik said not knowing the royal protocol.

"Well that's not how it's done, but that would work," Devyani said laughing at him.

"Yes, you can marry my daughter," Nandi said and smiled at Satvik.

Satvik could not believe his ears. He touched Nandi's feet. Nandi put his hand on his head and blessed him.

That's when Shubhangi dashed in and came running towards Nandi and Satvik.

"What's happening here? Why are you not talking to me?" She said staring at her father.

No one spoke a word. They all looked at her. She was confused. She ran to Nandi and hugged him.

"I am sorry, dad. I am sorry that you had to be here because of me. It's not his fault. I made a mistake. But now I would do everything that you want me to do," she said.

"Can you forget this man?" Nandi said pointing his finger at Satvik.

"If that is what you want, I will," she said.

"It's too late," Nandi said and looked at Devyani with a smile on his face.

Shubhangi looked at her mother. She was smiling too. She looked at Satvik. He kept mum. Shubhangi was confused. She was not able to understand why everyone was acting weird.

"Will you do anything for me?" Nandi asked.

Shubhangi hesitated for a moment.

"Anything you want," Shubhangi said.

"Then you will have to marry this man," Nandi said pointing at Satvik.

For a moment, she did not understand what Nandi said. When she realized, her face was flushed with embarrassment. Tears rolled on her chicks.

"I love you, dad," Shubhangi said and hugged him.

"Come here," Nandi signaled Satvik.

Nandi held their hands together and said, "God bless you two!"

Everyone waiting outside clapped and cheered as Shubhangi embraced Satvik in a tight hug.

"I love you!" Satvik whispered holding her in his arms.

Made in the USA
San Bernardino, CA
30 December 2016